D0441940

Praise for *Requiem*

"*Requiem* is that rare joy, the perfect book that you didn't expect....Characters are masterfully drawn, full of surprises but always believable, just like people. I had despaired of ever reading a book this good again."

—*Interzone*

"Graham Joyce is one of the finest writers of supernatural thrillers in the world. He combines intelligence and style, a relish for a good story, and a strong sense of humanity to produce books of unique quality....Modern Jerusalem, a city almost collapsing under the weight of its history and reference, comes to vivid life in *Requiem,* as do Joyce's many outstanding and engaging characters. Books like this, which have the courage to look hard at the roots and meaning of our myths and make them relate powerfully, sometimes painfully, to our modern world, are enormously welcome to readers like me who are sick and tired of cheap sensations and recycled terrors, who demand real substance from their fiction, real engagement from their writers."

—Michael Moorcock

"Impressive....Joyce takes full advantage of the ready-to-hand exoticism of modern Jerusalem, using the city's density as a catalyst for an absorbing fantasy that's grounded in strong characterization....This is high-quality fantasy that at last puts Joyce on the American map."

—*Publishers Weekly*

Tor Books by Graham Joyce

Requiem
The Tooth Fairy

GRAHAM JOYCE

REQUIEM

A TOM DOHERTY ASSOCIATES BOOK
NEW YORK

This is a work of fiction. All the characters and events portrayed in this novel are either fictitious or are used fictitiously.

REQUIEM

First published by Michael Joseph in 1995.

A Tor Book
Published by Tom Doherty Associates, Inc.
175 Fifth Avenue
New York, NY 10010

Tor Books on the World Wide Web:
http://www.tor.com

Tor® is a registered trademark of Tom Doherty Associates, Inc.

Library of Congress Cataloging-in-Publication Data

Joyce, Graham.
    Requiem / Graham Joyce..
        p.   cm.
    "A Tom Doherty Associates book."
    ISBN 0-312-86452-3 (pbk. : alk. paper)
    1. Jerusalem—Fiction.   2. Dead Sea scrolls—Fiction.
  3. Miracles—Fiction.   I. Title.
[PR6060.093R4   1998]
823'.914—dc21   97-38516
                                                                 CIP

First Tor hardcover edition: October 1996
First Tor trade paperback edition: February 1998

Printed in the United States of America

0   9   8   7   6   5   4   3   2   1

To Sue, who said "Let's see what's up there!"
The Akrotiri at Corinth, 11 October 1988. About 4 A.M.

Acknowledgments

More than thanks are due to those who encourage and those who warn: Dave Bell, my editor, Luigi Bonomi, Ramsey Campbell, Catie Carey, Pete Coleborn, Christopher Fowler, David Grossman for creative lunches, Dave Holmes, David Howe, Sue Johnsen for her immense contribution of ideas and vital moderation, Chris Lloydal, the Rev. Peter McKenzie (for not minding the use to which I wanted to put his great wisdom and insight and for the use of his library), Rod Milner and Rog Peyton, Phil Rickman, Martin Tudor, Helen and Quentin Wilson. And still to the hidden ones.

REQUIEM

I

They were helping a party get out of hand, an end-of-term blowout thrown by a teaching colleague during Tom's probationary year. Noticing the dwindling supply of booze in the kitchen, Tom stowed his beer under a hard chair before stumbling out to the back-yard toilet. Fighting his way in again, he found the room crowded with energetic dancers and had to resort to crawling on the floor to grope for his hidden beer. Instead of glass, his outstretched hand fastened on a fated and shapely ankle.

The ankle was joined to an astonishing calf muscle. Meshed in sheer nylon, it discharged static to his fingers and climbed remorselessly to the most stunning thigh he'd ever seen in his life. Ten minutes later he was still holding on to that ankle, trying to speak coherently to its owner, who was meanwhile coolly intent on ignoring him.

"If you're not going to let go of my foot," Katie had said at last, "I'd better introduce myself."

Even though he was drunk—and he was not drunk often—Tom knew from the moment his eyes swept from ankle to thigh, and then to the plaited, honey-blond head of hair beyond, *this is It.* Tom in those days was a great believer in this is It.

Katie did not think *this is It.* All she thought at the time was that a drunk was holding her leg. For the first few minutes, she tried to ignore the scuffling at her feet in the hope it might pass. It didn't. With one eyebrow cocked high she listened as Tom gamely struggled to make conversation. Mysteriously he seemed to sober up. At some point in the evening he persuaded her to part with her phone number, and over the course of the next few months Katie began to think, *Yes, well, this may be It.* Within a year of meeting, they'd married.

Thirteen years ago.

For the first two years at least, Tom never—metaphorically—let go of her foot. He couldn't believe that this elegant, incandescent female had tumbled into his life; he would occasionally glance upwards for the hole in the ceiling through which she might have fallen. Around this time he also behaved extremely possessively, suspecting every other male in the vicinity of secretly plotting to take her away from him.

To Tom's possessiveness Katie responded with her own needs. She had an endless capacity to absorb his devotions, and where some people might tire of obsessive attention, Katie's thirst was infinite. She thrived on the kind of intimacy which excludes all other things and all other people. She grew more beautiful, more confident and more radiant on the ambrosia of his love.

Katie was a marketing consultant for a small business company. Compared with Tom's world, hers seemed grown-up and hard-edged. Of course, she was no more tough-minded than he was. He soon began to realize there were things in her life which determined her condition: dark things, slippery things, things growing in the deep, damp wells of her childhood which fed hungrily but noiselessly and which demanded greater and greater portions of the love he was able to bestow.

His greatest mistake in their relationship was that he did not help her to explore these secrets. He tried once, but her resistance was so strong he never tried to pull her that way again; but whatever those secrets were, they caused her to attach herself to him with such fervor he was afraid of what he might lose should they be disturbed. Anyway, he decided, the pair had settled into an acceptable equilibrium which demanded and reciprocated love in comparable measure, so why question it?

He neither foresaw nor suspected that those very demands would one day outstrip his own ability to meet them. But it didn't matter now because she was dead.

"If it's the matter," Stokes was saying, "if it's the mere matter of a few words being chalked on a blackboard—"

So he'd rumbled that, had he? "No, it's not about that," said Tom.

"Because, let me assure you, I've seen a lot of that in my time. And I'd root it out. Mark my words, I'd root it out."

Tom marked the Head's words by gazing out of the window. "No. I'm just ready for a change."

Flaming June was washed out. It was the last day of summer term at Dovelands school. The fifth-years had left weeks ago, and rain lashed the playground, dampening any holiday jinks planned by the rest of the kids. Tom Webster had crossed the yard to the Head's study after clearing out his desk. A solitary flour-bomb had burst on the wet playground, and he could see it as he gazed from the window of the study. It lay in a white puddle, an unexploded little sack of spoiled fun, bubbling slightly in the driving rain.

After the final assembly, with the school groaning through "Jerusalem" before the benediction, Tom had said his goodbyes and left the staff room quickly. He couldn't face the post-term exhaustion; the way colleagues became tender to each other in the face of the summer recess; the way they let the completed term slide from their backs like a heavy pack and took on a forgiving air. Parting was tinged with a surprising sadness for the forthcoming absence of colleagues who, day to day, were normally a source more of boredom than of comfort. Tom couldn't stand it.

"But what will you do?" they asked, the missionary look in their eyes revealing they all thought it had something to do with Katie's death, about which they couldn't bring themselves to speak. So he met the question with a shrug and a levitation of the eyebrows which did nothing to address their concern.

Before crossing over to Stokes's spartan study he'd unlocked his form room to collect a few personal possessions. He'd inspected the stock cupboard at the back of the classroom. There were some tapes and slides, and several books and magazines, all of which he'd bequeathed to his successor. His desk drawers contained little besides scrap paper and a wallet of photographs taken on school trips, but it all had to be cleared. He'd found a paperback science-fiction omnibus, one of the pages marked by a leaf of paper. He'd taken out the marker, on which was written: *This fleeting life. Get bread and milk and I will love thee.xxx*

Katie's handwriting. The book had been lying untouched for almost a year, with its shopping-list page-marker. Nearly a year now, and these tiny, inert phantoms kept turning up in drawers and cupboards and closets and boxes. When people die they leave behind tiny deposits, like dust or ash, littering the lives of those who have to carry on. Impossible to wipe a house clean. Memories dwelled in cobweb places behind wardrobes and between cupboards; they hid behind radiators; they lurked on shelves; like slivers of shattered glass, they waited for their moment to lodge deep in any vulnerable expanse of passing skin.

At first these were the only kinds of ghost he had to contend with, and with them, as always, came the thickening in the throat and the fluid gathering behind the retina. He'd been standing in his classroom, clutching the ghost-note, when he became aware of someone standing in the doorway.

It was Kelly McGovern from his English class. Mothers from the estate gave their kids American celebrity names; the boys were all Deans and Waynes, designated delinquents with gold-studded ears; the girls cutesy Kellys and Jodies, hard as nails. Kelly McGovern was fifteen. Just.

Go away, Tom thought viciously. Get out of here, you beautiful, diamond-bright little tart. "Hi, Kelly," he said with a smile.

Hesitating at the door, something gift-wrapped in her hand, she wore the regulation black school blazer, short black skirt and black tights. The school insignia stitched on to the blazer pocket over her immature breast was a bright red rose, the petals so embroidered that for Tom the rose would eternally spill a single drop of crimson blood. A classical scroll beneath the rose bore the motto *Nisi Dominus Frustra*. His inability to interpret that slogan meaningfully for the kids had hastened, though not caused, his resignation.

"It's Latin. It comes from one of the Psalms. 'Except the Lord keep the city, the Watchman waketh in vain.' It means: without God, all is in vain."

"What city?"

What city, indeed? They asked the questions, didn't they? The city of the human fucking heart, boy. You don't need to know what city. It's just your school motto. You don't need to know what it means.

"What can I do for you, Kelly?" he asked.

"I brought you a leaving present. Here."

She ventured inside the door, offering the package, unable to meet his eyes. Instead her gaze strayed to the open store-cupboard door. He closed it, turning the key in the lock. Then he took the package and unwrapped it.

It was a brand-new copy of a book of poems by the Liverpool poets, McGough, Henri, Patten. His own copy had been stolen by someone in the class. He'd kept the class behind after school, telling them he was delighted. He invited them to steal more poetry. Then he'd let them go.

"This is kind of you. I don't know what to say."

But she still wouldn't meet his eyes. She flicked her copper-colored hair and stood with her ankles crossed. He felt her tension. It was catching. She seemed reluctant to go.

"I've got to lock up here, Kelly."

"OK."

"I have to go and see the Head. Before I leave."

She looked up at him at last, light rinsing her pale eyes of chromium and blue. Then she turned and went out of the classroom, closing the door behind her. With an audible sigh of relief he collected up the few items he wanted to take away with him. Then he made his way over to Stokes's study.

"It's not too late for you to reconsider your resignation," Stokes was saying. "Even at this stage. I mean, you're a fine teacher. I'll be sorry to lose you. We all will."

Tom had never liked the Head, who was now leaning across his desk, large hands clasped almost in prayer before him, eyes bulging as if this was the most important conversation the two men would ever have together—which indeed it was. Stokes's bunker mentality rarely allowed him to stray from his office, and Tom despised his educational policies. The Dovelands Head was an ABC man: Assembly, Blazers and Curriculum, all designed to echo the ethos of the old grammar schools. He'd revived a Christian-based assembly even though a third of the kids were Hindus, Sikhs or Muslims; compulsory school uniform was rigorously enforced even under sweltering conditions; and a curriculum calculated to strait-jacket even the most creative teachers was guarded jealously.

Tom had committed himself to small acts of sabotage against this regime, though he wasn't above ingratiating himself with the Head by agreeing to teach Religious Education when no one else would. His cynical thought was that Stokes was now terrified that he wouldn't be able to get anyone else to touch it.

"Tom, you haven't got over your bereavement, have you?"

There. He'd said it when none of the other staff would. Tom couldn't deny Stokes had been kind, tolerant, even indulgent, in the months after Katie died. "No. Honestly. That has nothing to do with it."

"And you're certain it's not the matter of things scribbled on a—"

"No. As I said before, I'm just ready for a change."

"Really?"

"Yes. Really."

Stokes stood up, and his chair scraped behind him. He came

around his desk and offered a large hand that wanted shaking. "If you need a good reference . . ."

"I'll remember that."

And then he was out.

Thirteen years of teaching behind him. He was thirty-five and going on sixty-five, and it felt like retirement. The last twelve months had bequeathed him his first gray hairs. With the labored verses of the assembly hymn still echoing in his ears he climbed into his rusting Ford Escort. A few pupils were still hanging around as he passed between the school gates. Kelly was one of them. He nodded at her before steering through the driveway. Then he put his foot down and accelerated out of the educational system.

2

Tom climbed, shivering, into
bed before falling asleep. When he woke it was after six, and he was
relieved that this time his sleep hadn't been disturbed. He tried to
telephone Sharon. The call hooked up with the single ringing tone
of an international line, but no one answered. He'd not spoken to
Sharon in some months.

He put his hand in his pocket, feeling for the scrap of paper he'd
discovered in his desk at school: *This fleeting life...* Upstairs in the
spare bedroom was an ottoman, a chest for storing blankets that had
become a shrine to his dead wife. It contained all the things that he
didn't want hanging around the house but couldn't bear to throw
away. Photographs, letters, theater programs, ornaments with special resonance, even an answerphone tape with her voice on it. Each
object cold and remote, as useless and beautiful as moon rock.

He slipped the note into a wallet full of other papers. Opening
this chest was a dangerous business; when the lid was lifted, the
evening could be swallowed up with the contents spread across the
floor as he emptied a bottle of Scotch.

Here's one piece of moon rock, one that holds him in a trance-
like gaze for some minutes: a photograph, taken on a bracing east-

coast beach. As Tom holds it before him the slender white border
of the photograph extends outwards, dissolves and the two subjects
break their pose. One of the figures is Katie, a pretty woman but
with her mouth set hard against some bitterness. The other person
is Tom. It is a recent photograph. The hulk of a wreck lies in the
background of the shot. They have taken a long weekend—Tom's
idea—at an east-coast resort to see if they can repair the damage.

Tom collects his camera from, and thanks, the passing stranger
who agreed to take a photograph of the pair. They turn away and
walk up the beach toward the wreck, crunching pebbles underfoot
as they go. Both the sea and the sky have turned the color of cold
steel. It is well out of season, and a squall at sea has churned up the
waves, sending a stiff wind at right angles to the beach. They have
to turn their collars up to stop the wind from whipping sand in their
faces.

"I just hope it's not too late," she says.

He rounds on her, scattering shingle, holding on to the lapels of
her coat. "It was a mistake. We both know it. It can be put right."

"I hope you're right, Tom," she says, the wind lashing her blond
fringe across her eyes. "Because I think the time has gone." Then
she turns and walks up the beach, saying something about getting
her things ready to go, but he doesn't hear her properly because the
wind blows the words from her lips like flecks of foam from the
waves.

He walks on up the beach a little further, to where the wreck
lies beached and on its side, doomed a century ago on a spit of sand.
Tom sits down on the rotting hulk. A solitary gray-backed gull bobbing on the gray ocean under the gray sky cries, "Hark!" before flying off. A wave pounds at the shingle beach.

The scene dissolves, reconstituting itself in its original deception,
a holidaying twosome, fixed forever by celluloid and photochemi-
cals, the picture in Tom's hand.

Moon rock.

The ottoman was full of it.

If the circumstances of Katie's death had been different, he might
have been able to bury her properly. But the freak nature of the accident had left him nursing a terrible sense of injustice. A storm had

uprooted a tree, which had collapsed on, and crushed, her car. Katie was killed instantly. If she'd died in an ordinary road accident, Tom would at least have been able to attribute the tragedy to human or mechanical error—similarly if she'd died in a plane crash or a fire. The rage and the blame would still have been there, of course, but what he couldn't tolerate was the utter randomness of the incident. No mistake. No error. Just one parcel of nature destroying another through the accident of proximity. Tom could have understood a disease in terms of its predatory function, or an environmental disaster like an earthquake or flood in terms of its scale. But one tree falling on one car?

No: it felt personal. It felt directed, against him. A finger of judgment.

He lowered the lid of the ottoman. Then he tried Sharon's number again. Still no answer. He wondered what the time difference was. Perhaps no more than an hour or two.

Katie had not at first approved of his enduring friendship with Sharon, whom he had known since college days. "Old flames should be snuffed out," she'd said. "Would you like it if I dredged up one of my old boyfriends every other month?"

"We shouldn't have to lose touch with someone we once loved just because we now love someone else."

"It just seems odd."

"Nothing odd about it."

"It still seems odd to me."

But Tom could be a difficult person to argue with, and even though he was sensitive to Katie's suspicions, he persisted in maintaining innocent, irregular contact with Sharon, and she with him. And when Katie grew more secure in the relationship, and had met Sharon a couple of times, she began to trust and accept this friendship and also discovered in Sharon a friend for herself. The two women had developed a closeness of their own, and although it was never something from which Tom was excluded, it was a distinct evolution of his former relations with Sharon.

Since Katie's death Sharon had telephoned twice, and had written two letters, but Tom hadn't felt able to reciprocate. Now he felt

ready to see her. She was one of the very few people he could con-
template speaking to.

He dug out a Sunday-newspaper supplement with advertise-
ments for bucket-shop air flights. He'd already ringed one with a
pen. They operated a round-the-clock service, so he gave them a call.

Five minutes later he'd booked a flight, paid for by credit card.
The flight was leaving the following afternoon. His hands trembled
slightly as he began to throw things into a bag. A photograph of
Katie smiled approvingly from the mantelpiece. He turned it face-
down. He didn't want her to watch him packing.

Travel fever had him tossing and turning in his bed that night.
Then at 3 A.M. he was awoken by the usual tapping on the door. He
didn't answer it. He lay awake, listening, knowing that it would be
repeated at regular intervals. He knew who it was. He had answered
the door before, and there was never anyone there. He knew the
hand would continue to knock on the door until exactly 4:15. Then
it would go away.

Tonight it seemed to him a little more urgent. But he wouldn't
answer it. He knew who it was.

3

The plane landed out of the astonishing blue heavens at Tel Aviv airport, seeding passengers on to the hot tarmac. Still unable to contact Sharon, he took a bus to Jerusalem. He disembarked at a bus station teeming with alien life and was awed by the number of young women wearing the olive drab of army combat gear. Good-looking Israeli girls toting Uzi automatics.

He was still gazing after one of them when a boy wearing dark glasses and a Walkman thrust a leaflet into his hand. It offered the incentive of one free beer to stay at a backpackers' hostel. He was still reading the handbill when an elderly Hasidic Jew with gray locks and a farouche beard smiled at him from under the broad brim of a black hat, sliding another note into his hand. This second leaflet was printed in Hebrew; on the reverse in English it said: "AMERIKANS = AMALEKITES. *The daughters of Zion are haughty, and walk with stretched necks and wanton eyes, walking and mincing as they go, and making a tinkling of their feet.* NO TO NEW AIRPORT."

Tom thought he'd recognized the quotation. "Isaiah?"

The old Hasid shrugged, gesturing that he had no English. Then he scurried away to press his leaflets into the hands of two baffled Australian backpackers.

Tom hailed a Mercedes taxi, giving the driver Sharon's address, and the cab whisked him under the medieval walls of Old Jerusalem. Banners waved in the wind. Flags and streamers fluttered in the breeze high above the battlements of the Old City wall. The Golden Dome of the Rock breasted blue skies. Glimpsed from the speeding taxi, honey-colored light flaked the clouds, licked ancient brick, discharged long shadows from the antique portals. It was like the picture on a gilt-edged stamp he'd collected at Sunday School as a child, the stamp completing the set.

It was his first sight of Jerusalem. *Thou art beautiful, O my love, comely as Jerusalem, terrible as an army with banners.*

It was a Jerusalem which didn't exist. A Jerusalem he would never see again. He wanted to order the driver to stop so that he could get out of the cab, climb across the perforated, gilded frame of his vision and walk into history. Instead he watched the vision recede through the rear window of the Mercedes. He heard voices from behind the city walls. *Thou art beautiful.* And gradually the old citadel sank behind the hill as the taxi coursed along the Shekhem, north-east of the city. *Terrible as an army with banners.* This was childhood and mythology crystallized in the view from the back of a cab. It was a day of innocent arrival.

When he saw his own reflection in the smoked-glass doors outside Sharon's apartment, he thought he looked like a *golem.* A man in an unfinished state. An Adam in creation, awaiting the final breath of God. There was something incomplete about himself, some vital spark gone astray.

He rang the bell again. Perspiration gathered around the leather hand-grip of his suitcase as he waited. Still no answer. He pressed a neighboring bell, and a sleepy voice crackled over the communication system.

Tom ducked toward the buzzing speaker. "You speak English?"

"Yes. Ummm."

"I'm looking for Sharon. In the next apartment."

"Gone away. Ummm."

"What? What did you say?"

"Gone away. Gone away on holiday. Ummm. Back in a few days."

The low buzz of the intercom clicked off. He imagined a sleepy Israeli upstairs going back to bed. It was noon.

He stared stupidly at the hot, dusty street. All he could do was shift his weight from one foot to the other, squeezing the moist handle of his suitcase. The word *golem* fired in his brain like gunshot across a desert. Fresh sweat bloomed on his brow as he made his way down the marble stairway of the apartment block. He left the cool shadows of the building and walked out into the brilliant sunlight of the street.

Where was Sharon? The spontaneous act of flying out here, which at one moment had seemed cavalier and daring, now seemed bloody silly. He knew no one else. He was a long way from home, and he felt lonely and not a little afraid. The taxi driver who'd brought him here had ripped him off, he was certain. He regretted his pale appearance. He felt like a target.

Another cab cruised by, looking for a fare. He hailed it and told the driver to head back into the center of modern Jerusalem. "The block where you picked me up," he asked the driver on the way, "would they be mainly Jewish or Arab people living there?"

The driver looked over his shoulder and showed a mouthful of gold teeth. He evidently found the question too ridiculous to answer. Tom produced the hostel leaflet he'd been handed at the bus station.

"Would this be a decent place for me to stay?"

The driver glanced at it. "Might not be too clean."

"Is there a hotel you could recommend?"

"Hotel's gonna cost you a lotta money. A lotta money."

"I don't have a lot of money."

Gamely blaring his horn at some pedestrians, the driver said, "I got an idea. Basic. But it'll keep you out of some Arab hovel."

The hotel was situated just north of the Me'a She'arim ultra-

Orthodox district of Jerusalem, not far from the Old City. A large
sign had been erected at the corner of the street.

DAUGHTERS OF JERUSALEM: DRESS MODESTLY AT ALL TIMES.

The taxi pulled up at a gray-brick building. It was basic, barely clean
and run on the lines of a youth hostel. A young man with curling
black locks, *kipah* skull cap and eyes permanently aghast behind
thick spectacle glass showed him to a room. It smelled of warm dust.
Tom flicked back the yellowing sheets doubtfully. The boy assured
him they'd been laundered, despite their appearance. He accepted
the room and got a discount by paying in sterling.

After the boy had gone Tom flung open the window shutters.
Long rays of afternoon sunlight pierced the room, illuminating
mote-clouds stirred by his movements. He didn't mind the dust.
This was ancient dust, mystical dust. The dust of Abraham and
Jesus and Mohammed. These were the sweepings of religion.

A clump of jasmine grew outside the window, its cooling scent
mingling with the humid smell of the dust. He was exhausted from
lack of sleep the previous night, from travel. He wanted to lie down
on the bed and drift, but he was afraid if he did, the knocking on
the door might start all over again. He prayed he'd left that behind
him in England.

In any event, he was massively stimulated by the thought of
Jerusalem. His excitement was almost erotic. He decided to go out
again. Right now he wanted to take a walk in the world's most holy
city.

4

"Greetings, *monsieur!* Welcome! *Enchanté!*" The excessive gallantry made Tom think perhaps he'd made a mistake. To get from his room he'd had to pass through a large shared kitchen, where a diminutive white-haired figure crouched over the sink, rinsing cup and saucer. The old man turned. "A communal kitchen, yes. Please use it. The coffee is undrinkable, the tea unspeakable. But it's free." He gestured at a steaming urn as if presenting the riches of Solomon. Then he thrust out a tiny hand. "David Feldberg. Are you Jewish?"

"No."

"Not everybody can be."

He was wearing sweltering layers of cardigans and carpet slippers two sizes too large. The waistband of his trousers reached almost to his armpits, secured by a slim leather belt, knotted rather than buckled. His jaw dropped easily into a smile. A few peg-like yellow teeth remained defiantly in a moist, pink mouth, like grizzled but loyal troops. He had the physique of a boy but a jaunty, professorial air.

Tom liked him instantly. "Can I walk to the Old City from here?"

"By foot is best. In the foyer we have some maps. Permit me."
He fetched a tourist map and spread it across a table, marking it with
a pencil stub conjured from the pocket of his trousers. "Here are
we, in our small lives." He licked his pencil stub. "Continue here
and you will surely arrive at Damascus Gate."

Damascus Gate! Every place name in Jerusalem was electrically
charged. The old man began marking other places of interest but
stopped when he sensed Tom's impatience. "It's been there for
thousands of years. It's not going to go away." He smiled as he
folded the map. Tom thanked him and was followed to the door.
"Were you thinking of walking the wall, *monsieur?*"

"Tom. My name is Tom. Why do you ask?"

"I don't want to alarm you, but at this time of day it's not a good
idea. There have been incidents. Attacks on tourists. The Arabs
have found a new way of disrupting the economy. Better to do it
in the morning, when there are more people around. Of course, if
I were younger, it would have been a grand pleasure to escort you.
But with this leg . . ."

Tom smiled at the idea of the old man as a minder. "I understand. Thanks for the advice."

David Feldberg escorted him as far as the hotel door.

As he reached the brow of the hill on his way in, the Old City
was unveiled. The bone-colored castellated walls. The Golden
Dome. The sky a spiritual blue. The city was a polished, faceted
stone, hovering in a pearly mist accreted by the centuries. History
was a nacreous substance still in the process of delivering the city.

Odd: the flags and banners and fluttering pennants had been
taken down. Though, now he came to think about it, perhaps there
were no banners. Perhaps he'd imagined them on glimpsing the Old
City from the back of the speeding taxi. Perhaps it was only his own
elation he'd seen on the battlements. He knew how easy it was to
see things which weren't there.

Damascus Gate was in everyday tumult, thronged with people,
a riot of motion and color and cries. The bridge spanning the ancient moat was lined with marketeers. Tea vendors bore huge, or-
nate silver urns on their backs. Spice dealers competed with flower
sellers and fruit stalls. Felafel stands belched small clouds of hot oil.

Rug traders and bead pedlars spread their wares. The scent of the warm dust of the street was displaced by the spices and the hot olive oil. Guttural Arabic phrases volleyed across the sky.

A pair of eyes was on him. He looked up to see the silhouette of an Israeli soldier high on the parapet of the wall overhead, automatic weapon trailing from his hip. The boiling sun was descending behind the soldier. His face and uniform were in shadow. The image was timeless; his automatic could have been a short Roman sword. Or he could have been a Crusader, or one of Saladin's guard. He was *the* soldier on the wall. He had always been there.

Someone pressed against him—there was a strong whiff of masculine body odor, a root smell. He switched his wallet from one pocket to another. Meanwhile a hand palmed his buttock. He looked for the groper, but everyone seemed to be absorbed in trading activity. A small Arab boy, blowing wildly on a penny whistle, stared at him. It was not until he'd passed through the archway of the gate that he realized he'd been holding his breath against this sensory onslaught.

Beyond the gate the street was cooler and a little quieter, giving way to labyrinthine alleyways. He bought himself a felafel from a vendor near the gate. It seemed ill-advised. But he wanted to cram himself with authentic spices and aromas.

In the teeming Arab *souk* knots of Arab women in purdah crept about the street, wraiths in black veils. Shutters were going up, and he sensed the crowd thinning. A hand brushed his thigh; he turned angrily but, as before, all possible candidates for blame were thoroughly busy.

He left the *souk,* threading through a few gloomy, dirty, narrow streets before finding himself on the Via Dolorosa, the processional route of Christ's Crucifixion. The sacred path! His eyes fell on a plaque describing the spot as one of the Stations of the Cross.

A handsome young Arab approached. "Beautiful, isn't it?"

He was still looking around him in astonishment. "It's sensational."

"English? I like English people. What you're looking at is noth-

ing. Come here. I'm going to show you something even more amazing."

He immediately became suspicious. "What?"

"Believe me. Just five meters away." The Arab stepped up the
incline of the Via Dolorosa and indicated something on the ground.
Tom followed cautiously. The Arab was pointing at striations in the
paving slabs. "That," he announced, smiling proudly, "is the spot
where the Roman soldiers cast dice for Jesus' clothes."

"You're joking!" cried Tom, squatting down to look more
closely. Sure enough, there were rough carvings, undoubtedly ancient, of squares and circles divided into segments.

"I don't joke," said the boy. "It's famous. It was a game they
played with dice."

Tom ran a finger along the striations in the warm stone. When
he stood up again, two other boys came to see what the fuss was
about. "Do you like it?" said the first.

"It's amazing."

"My pleasure. I enjoy showing it to friends from England."

"Thank you."

He smiled broadly. His friends smiled too, nodding approval.
"Do you want a guide?"

The light suddenly dawned on Tom. He stepped back. "No.
Sorry. I can't afford a guide."

The young man was still smiling. "Really? I'm a good guide. I
know everything in this city."

"Thanks, but no."

The Arab's features darkened. His friends' faces also darkened.
"Would you like," he said, "to give me something for this?"

"For what?"

"For showing you this." He held out a leathery hand for money.
Now he appeared less than handsome. Tom looked round. No one
else was near.

Tom was a tall man, and, though never violent, he liked to think
he could take care of himself. Yet it seemed senseless for a coin. He
handed over a couple of shekels and chalked the slate of experience.

"It's not enough," said the Arab, moving in.

Tom locked eyes with him. "Suppose I just smack your head against the wall instead?"

The Arab boy jumped aside as Tom made a half-hearted effort to snatch back his coin. Tom moved on, ignoring the mouthings from behind him.

He knew that if he followed the Via Dolorosa, he would come at last to the Holy Sepulcher, but the encounter with the Arab youth had unnerved him. He walked quickly along the Via, ignoring the plaques and the history and the antiquities accruing around him. Here there were more tourists. Another Arab made a hissing noise, beckoning. He played deaf.

At the Holy Sepulcher he was dismayed to see an enormous queue of pilgrims waiting to go into the tomb. It was possible to enter the church built over the sepulcher, a vast, domed structure owned by the Greek Orthodoxy, so long as he didn't want to go into the tomb itself. The air was heavy with incense; icons winked in the russet gloom. Some untoward scene was taking place at the front of the queue. Uniformed church guards were dragging away weeping elderly Greek women in widows' black who evidently didn't want to leave the tomb. The pilgrims at the front of the queue looked sheepish; the guards behaved as though this was a daily occurrence.

Tom felt slightly sickened by the brawl. He wandered behind the tomb, where, at the back of the rock, a small shrine was sunk into the floor. He peered in at a tiny altar resplendent with gold and silver icons. Candles flickered within, and the crevice was smoky with incense. By stooping he could just about squeeze into the darkened shrine.

"Welcome!" A fat black spider with a human head popped up from the shadowy recess. Tom stepped back and cracked his head on the rock. "Welcome!" It was a priest in Eastern Orthodox stovepipe hat, crouched in the far corner of the shrine, swathed in black robes. His gray beard reached to his waist and tucked into his belt. Eyes glittering, he nodded enthusiastically at Tom.

"Fuck!" said Tom, nursing his head. His harsh words to the Arab youth echoed back at him. "Fuck!" Then he remembered where he was, so he said, "Shit! Oh, Jesus!"

"Yes! Welcome!" This was obviously the limit of the holy man's English. The spider-priest reached up and touched Tom's brow. He removed his hand quickly, making a hissing sound and shaking his head. "Bad!" Then he pressed into Tom's palm a small plastic crucifix. "Donation!" he said, holding out his hand, smiling brightly.

Tom glared back before fumbling for a few shekels. The spider-priest accepted the shekels and gave him another plastic cross. I'm tired, Tom thought, as he left the Church of the Holy Sepulcher. This is all too much for a first day.

He studied his map, looking for the shortest route back to Damascus Gate. The sun had dipped behind the rooftops. Sharp-edged shadows crept from rancid walls. With streets and alleys almost empty now, he traced his route with a finger on the map, hesitating, sensing he'd made a mistake. He passed under a series of crumbling arches and then along a narrow, high-sided section of cobbled street, a passage smelling of piss and chlorine and rotting vegetables. His footsteps echoed hollowly. Emerging on to a deserted thoroughfare, he stopped to check the map. The street should have been straight like an arrow, but he'd just made two left-hand turns. He'd entered some gloomy zone of the Old City where, it seemed, the sun never penetrated.

He was distracted by a movement some yards away, where a truncated alley ended under a scrolled arch. A locked and rotting gate stood to one side of the arch. In the shadows beneath, a veiled Arab woman beckoned.

The gesture was feeble, yet compelling. His instincts told him not to be caught, but something held him, something mesmerizing in her gesture. He took a step forward and was assailed by an odor of spice, deep, pungent spice, like balsam.

The woman was dressed in rough clothes. Her black veil fell below her chin. She was an old woman, with hands like crumpled, tanned hide. He caught the luster of an eye through the veil.

But something was wrong. Tom's stomach turned. Something about the old woman frightened him.

She beckoned again. Then she raised her hand to her mouth, touching her dry finger to her tongue through the black material of the veil. She turned slowly and with her index finger wrote something on the wall at the back of the arch. The corroded stone crumbled to powder at her touch.

It was a D.

"I have to go," Tom tried. "I have to . . ."

The woman continued to write. More figures began to appear on the wall, as if chiselled there by a mason. But the letters were unfamiliar, maybe Hebrew or Arabic, indecipherable to Tom. The odor of spice became almost sickening. Tom dropped his map, retreating quickly, leaving the old woman scratching on the wall.

Within moments Tom had found his way back to Damascus Gate. He stopped to lean against a wall. He was breathing heavily. He felt ashamed of himself. Two small boys mounted on a donkey trotted by, staring.

At the recollection of the old woman, his stomach contracted. Feeling ridiculous, he made his way out of the gate. The crowds had gone. The sun was spilled across a low bank of cloud.

When he reached his hotel room, he locked the door behind him and closed the shutters. He took off his shoes, lay down on the bed and thought about Katie. He wept before falling asleep.

Then he heard the voice.

5

I'm trying to tell you what happened," said Katie . . .

6

It's simple. I quit."

"But, *monsieur.* To be a teacher is a state of mind. It is not a toga to be put on and taken off. One does not cease to be a teacher because this or that government stops paying you."

"Call me Tom."

"May one ask why you turned your back on prestigious and rewarding work?"

"Shall I make more coffee?" Tom got up. "It was never prestigious and only occasionally rewarding."

Conversation, Tom was learning, was what David Feldberg lived for. He lurked in the kitchen, waiting for subjects. He was skilled in leading quickly from innocuous remarks about the weather to matters of contention, until you realized you'd been recruited into a set-piece conversation. It was like finding yourself seated in front of a backgammon board, with your fingers being gently closed around a dice-shaker. There was a frame and certain rules to this type of conversation: no loose remarks permitted, words all carefully selected and any throw-away comment held up to the light for a bout of sporting criticism.

Tom had found David in the kitchen again that morning. To be more precise, by waiting there, pretending to rinse cups, David had found him. Within moments he'd offered Tom some decent coffee in place of the mud provided free by the hotel. Minutes later he insisted on their breakfasting together on fresh croissants and pastries from a nearby delicatessen. Tom suggested they go together, but David showed great reluctance to step outside the hotel.

When Tom got back, David had laid the table. Coffee had brewed. As they ate, the old man coaxed information from Tom with practiced skill: that his wife had died, that he was thirty-five, that he had traveled a little and that he'd quit teaching suddenly and for reasons he was not about to divulge.

Tom in turn learned that David was born in Greece, had lived in Paris, London and French Algeria and, in addition to the languages of those countries, spoke both Hebrew and Arabic. He made his living, he said, as a poorly paid translator of academic papers.

"So how was your first visit," David asked, steering the subject elsewhere, "to the Holy City?"

"Disappointing." Tom refilled his coffee cup.

"From which remark I take it that your visit to Jerusalem has special significance?"

"You're asking me if I'm a Christian? Yes, I am. But I keep forgetting."

"Why were you disappointed?"

"Everywhere I went I was being ripped off. Christians, Muslims, Jews. I was a target."

"Why are you surprised? Is this not the city where your Lord overturned the tables of the money changers? It hasn't improved."

David's manner made Tom smile. "But I hoped to feel something. Inside."

"And you didn't?"

"At first. I got a big rush when I approached the city. Then it was sullied by the people. I mean, it doesn't help your faith, does it? If you have any."

"Faith? Faith is the bridge, *monsieur*, between hope and a dirty world. If it is to be broken so easily, with what poor materials did you build it?"

"Do you have faith, as a Jew?"

He let a finger float toward the ceiling and sat back in his chair. "On a good day. On a day when I can get good coffee and fresh pastries and talk like this with intelligent company. What will you do today?" The conversational game board was being folded away.

Tom told him about Sharon, mentioning her address. "Would that be a Jewish area?"

"Of course. Arabs don't live up there."

"I'm sorry. Sometimes Jews and Arabs look the same to me. In the street I see blond-haired, blue-eyed Jews and dark-skinned, brown-eyed Jews. Yet the Jews are supposed to be a race. How can that be?"

David threw his hands in the air and closed his eyes. That question, clearly, was another game of backgammon. Tom changed the subject and told him about his encounter with the Arab woman. David listened carefully. "Was this in the Christian quarter?"

"I don't know. I might have strayed into the Arab quarter. The woman was, I think, an Arab. She spooked me, but in all probability she was just after a tip for showing me a bit of archaeology."

"In all probability," said David.

Tom was not about to be intimidated by Jerusalem. He'd hardly done justice to any of it, and the Old City was a dense catalog of spiritual and archaeological interest, a square mile of religious labyrinth. He wanted to swim in its secret pools and explore its caverns. He wanted to stand at its center.

Katie always wanted to come here and never had.

Did this city have a great secret? Was there a secret? The Crusaders considered Jerusalem the center of the world, spawning the great monotheistic faiths that conquered the world like tidal waves, fought over with the same religious blood-lust since time unrecorded as it was still being fought over today. Here it stood, still spinning from the collision of the European, African and Asian continents. The landmasses of Europe and Africa were like the straddling legs and Asia the head of a vast nutcracker, bearing in on Jerusalem, the bittersweet nut.

There *was* something here in this place, cracking, splintering, oozing. It seeped between the stone blocks of the venerable buildings and down the runnels of the ancient streets. It washed under the feet of the city's inhabitants with their brief lives. It glowed darkly in the excavations under the floors of their homes. You had to be dead not to feel it! The very dust was alive, like a radioactive substance. It stuck to your sandals, thought Tom; it got under your nails, ingrained your skin, dried your throat and made you thirsty.

It does all this. But it doesn't make you a better person. And it doesn't bring Katie back.

This time he approached the Old City via another entrance. Outside the wall young men and women of student age went about in olive army fatigues, Uzi machine-guns slung across their shoulders. To see so many young women militarized intrigued him. Beautiful girls, armed, strong, confident, somehow unassailable. He was both appalled by this emancipation-through-arms and strangely energized by the spectacle. The guns made the girls more desirable.

New Gate admitted directly on to the Christian quarter. He had nicked another map from the hotel and had bought a guide book. When he reached the Church of the Holy Sepulcher, a new queue of visitors had formed, alongside a sizable gathering of folk in wheelchairs.

He sat on a flight of stone steps and studied his guide book. Within ten seconds he was approached by two touts who wanted to guide him. "Get out of my face!" he yelled.

What was it about this city? You couldn't stay still for a moment. If you didn't keep moving, you became a target. Stillness was weakness. Keep circulating, or be bitten. You had to live like a small fish, darting away from bigger fish who moved in at you from all sides.

He returned to his guide book. He was dismayed to learn that there was doubt about the authenticity of the site of the Holy Sepulcher. An alternative site for the Crucifixion and the Resurrection was proposed just north of Damascus Gate. It had never occurred to him that the Holy Sepulcher might be bogus. He flipped the guide book over, checking the name of the author to see if it had been written by a Jew or an Arab, someone with an axe to grind.

This site, it claimed, had always been within the city wall, whereas tradition dictated that the Crucifixion had taken place outside the city. He looked over at the rows of wheelchairs, lined up as if for a race, and hoped they hadn't come to the wrong place. The present site, the book stated, was chosen by Helena, mother of Constantine, Emperor of Byzantium, three and a half centuries after the Crucifixion. Helena had made a pilgrimage to Jerusalem and was disappointed by the absence of shrines. So she built one here.

Tom snapped his book shut. He went inside the church again. Guards were still hurrying people in and out of the chapel inside the church. Around the back the spider-priest was busy palming plastic crosses to tourists. Tom left.

He visited the Dome of the Rock, having read that the Golden Dome, its gold melted down to pay the caliph's debts, was actually rendered in aluminum-bronze alloy. From there he drifted back through the Muslim quarter toward Damascus Gate, threading a narrow street of market stalls selling rush matting and spices and exotic fruits. If he paused to look, the traders plagued him. To escape he passed beneath a shady, arched passage, which pitched him into a quiet cul-de-sac. It was familiar.

It was the site of his encounter with the old Arab woman. He swallowed hard. Just a few yards away was the terminal arch and the stone on which the old woman had scratched letters. Today she was gone. Tom inched forward into the shadowy recess, curious to see what she'd been trying to show him.

There was no one around. A faint murmur came from the street of market sellers beyond the arches. He moved closer and at once recognized the cloyingly sweet and evocative balsam that had characterized the encounter. He could see no markings of any kind on the wall. Indeed, it was a concrete block, probably no older than twenty or thirty years. He'd expected to see something of note, perhaps a brick or stone pillaged from an earlier age. Whatever the woman had been scratching on the wall, it had left no traces.

Yet he'd clearly seen her writing on stone which crumbled like powder.

At the foot of the wall lay the map he'd dropped in his haste.

He picked it up. It was still folded for quick reference to the route back to the hotel. But now the location of his hotel had been marked by a dark, oval stain.

Tom held the map up to the available light. What he'd taken to be a stain was actually a small thumbprint on the page. At first he thought the thumbprint was simply an impression left by greasy fingers.

Someone cooed at him softly. He looked up and saw an Arab in headdress staring at him from the passage. The Arab clicked his tongue and cooed again. He was an aged, portly man, but his eyes were alert, suggestive. Tom leaped forward and shouldered his way out. Startled by this deft movement, the Arab shouted something incomprehensible after him.

Not until he was through Damascus Gate did he stop to examine the map again. Now, in the strong sunlight outside the city, he could see that the mark gave the extraordinary impression of having been branded on to the paper. It was clearly a thumbprint but scorched on the page as if by a charred hand.

He looked about him, wanting someone in the crowd at Damascus Gate to offer an explanation. The tourists and the traders ignored him. He looked at the ramparts of the city wall. The old stone battlements seemed unpleasantly moist, sweating under the relentless dry heat.

Tom put the stained map in his pocket and made his way back to the hotel.

7

I'm trying to tell you what happened, but you don't listen. You've stopped listening to me."

"No, I haven't."

"Yes, you have," Katie had said. "Do you know how hard it is? When something is slipping away as fast as this? How hard it is to stop it?" Her voice had fractured. Her blue eyes were splintered with ice, thawing, refreezing, thawing. "Don't you know that it requires work—real work? From the depths. This is from the depths. Do you know how difficult this is for me? I'm hurting just to speak to you. Every word is paid for. From the depths."

8

"Agoraphobia," said David. "I am cursed with a fear of the marketplace."

This literal translation of the term was offered with a genial smile and a hitching of trousers. In the course of his conversations the trousers would work their way down by degrees from the proximity of his armpits to somewhere below his hips.

"When did you last go out?" Tom wanted to know.

"Independence Day. 1978."

"You've been indoors for fifteen years? How do you manage?"

David made a gesture. "People are kind."

Tom had returned from his morning in the Old City looking to take a nap. The June sun outside was a furnace. The dust of Old Jerusalem and the traffic fumes of New Jerusalem hung in the heat. Yet the Hasids and the Arab women outside went garbed in stifling black clothes; clearly, it was more important to suffer in Jerusalem than to awaken unmanageable desires.

After sleeping he found David at his station in the kitchen, poring over a grizzled copy of *Reader's Digest*. Recounting his morning, Tom omitted all mention of the scorched map. He alluded to the signs in the neighborhood restricting women's dress.

David seemed to bridle slightly. "When in Rome . . ."

"Is every man in this city a seething cesspit of uncontrollable lust that women can't show their elbows?"

" 'I charge you, O ye daughters of Jerusalem, that ye stir not up, nor awake my love, till he please.' " David pushed his glasses further up the bridge of his nose.

"Yes, I know the Song of Songs. But it's the women who have to wander around at boiling point, swathed in blankets, because the glimpse of a funny-bone is too much to handle."

At which point David remarked that to go out at all must be a pleasant experience. "People are kind," he repeated, patting into place the loose pages of his *Digest.* Then he got up and shuffled out of the kitchen, making Tom think he'd either offended or saddened him.

Tom intended to walk up the Mount of Olives to Gethsemane, taking advantage of the cool of early evening. To complete his walk before dusk he knew he should leave immediately. But a sudden impulse propelled him outside, to return with sculptured ice creams for himself and David. He didn't know which was David's room.

With the ice cream melting over his fingers, he rang the bell to summon the young hotel superintendent. The boy with the locks and the bathysphere-glass spectacles squinted oddly at Tom when asked for David's room number. He seemed not to want to part with it.

"It's just an ice-cream, for heaven's sake!"

The invocation to heaven rendered the information. Tom knocked softly on the door. When David appeared, he looked at the pink-and-brown ice cream running along Tom's fingers, took off his spectacles and wept. He sat down in an old armchair, horsehair protruding from splits in the upholstery. Tom followed him inside without an invitation.

The room was shelved on all four sides, lined with books. A door on one wall gave way to a second room, offering a glimpse of an unmade bed. "I brought you this," Tom said, unnecessarily.

David recovered, patting his eyes with a grubby handkerchief. "I apologize, *monsieur.* Please sit down." He got up and moved a pile of papers from the seat of a hard-backed chair.

"Are you going to take this before it melts completely?"

"But of course." He accepted the ice cream as if it might at any moment metamorphose into a butterfly. Tom was relieved when he finally stuck a pink tongue into the melting wave. "When I saw you standing there you reminded me of someone. It was like a scene from a long time ago. Yet you don't even look like him. He was darker than you. His skin was of a sandier color. He was brown-eyed; your eyes are blue. But it was the ice cream, melting over your fingers. *C'est extraordinaire.* Something in your gesture. It was our last happy moment together."

"Who was he?"

"My father. I lost him a long time ago."

"How?"

"In a terrible place called Belsen."

Tom closed his eyes. History flickered across his retina like an old newsreel. He made a quick calculation from the end of the concentration camps to the present and figured David to be about seventy-five years old. Ghosts. All haunted, one way or another.

"It's an old story," David said, rescuing him. "This city is full of the details, should you ever want to hear them. Look, my ice cream, it is gone!"

Tom fumbled for a change of subject. "So many books. Have you something about Jerusalem I could borrow?"

David took a heavy volume down from a shelf. "I would gladly let you have free use of this library, if only that were possible. But there are some things you should not see. Come here."

He unlocked a cabinet, from which he withdrew a sheaf of plastic folders. Taking the folders to the table, he spread them out. Inside the heat-sealed transparent envelopes were gray parchment fragments speckled with faded Hebrew script. "You know what they are? Pieces of the Dead Sea Scrolls."

"Are they genuine?"

"Of course."

"What are you doing with them? I mean, aren't they priceless? I thought the scholars were sitting on them."

"*Monsieur*, you don't seem to realize just how many fragments were found."

Tom inspected the discolored parchments closely. No secrets jumped out of them. When he drew back, David gathered them up and locked them away.

"I keep them in this cabinet," he said. The remark struck an odd note, almost as if he were inviting Tom to steal them.

"I must go," said Tom. "I want to get up to Gethsemane before it gets dark."

"If you are walking, it will be dusk before you reach the Mount of Olives."

"I'll try anyway."

"Don't forget the book. And thank you for the ice cream."

He'd left late to begin the walk up to the garden of Jesus' betrayal. But it had been nighttime when the guards came to Gethsemane to arrest Jesus after Judas betrayed him; there he had sweated blood; and there swords had been drawn in a skirmish before Jesus was led away. Tom would have preferred to visit the place at night; he might have gone up to the garden and enjoyed the warm dusk and the sweet scents of the evening.

But this city disquieted him. The vibration of violence discouraged the idea of moving around alone at night. Tourists were easy prey, and though he could have made it up to the garden before sundown, he doubted if he could make it back again before dark.

He stood with the massive blocks of the eastern wall at his back. Behind him the false Golden Dome blazed in the setting sun. Across the valley, at the foot of the Mount of Olives, stood the singular edifices of Absalom's tomb and the dark portals of James's and Zachariah's tombs. Behind them, on the slopes of the Mount, was the scattering of headstones comprising the Jewish cemetery of souls waiting to greet the Messiah on Judgment Day.

Bones, dust.

Tom's gut trembled. His entire experience of Jerusalem had so far been mediated by an abdominal fluttering, as if the dry landscape, with him in it, was gripped at some corner by a vast and shivering hand. If he closed his eyes for a moment, the trembling continued.

Forgoing the walk up to Gethsemane, he turned back to look at the city wall. What he saw there made his stomach flip.

The sun was setting from across the other side of the city, flaking cloud-edges and discharging rays of light, a scene from a child's painting. Light lanced from the golden cupola peeping above the battlements. The walls took on the hue of rotting parchment. Suspended on the wall, halfway between the battlements and the ground, like a bat or bird pinning an insect, was the Arab woman in her black veil.

Twelve feet up on the wall.

There were no foot-holds. The wall was smooth and vertical. Yet the woman clung to the wall by her nails. She wore the same brown robe, the same black veil reaching below her chin. She was beckoning him.

His bowels compressed in a hideous squeeze. He felt a drop of urine hot on his thigh, and there was a roaring in his ears as the ground tilted. A crease appeared in the blue sky, as if it were buckling under a tremendous weight. A familiar smell of spice, of balsam, rolled over him.

The old woman was scratching something on the wall. In letters a foot high she began to write in Arabic script. Then she abandoned the effort, instead carefully scratching the Latin letters DE PR. . . .

The wall dissolved into powder at her touch. The letters were clearly branded into the brick, twelve or fifteen feet from the ground. The veiled woman continued to scratch at the soft stone with her crooked index finger.

"Tom! Tom!"

He heard someone calling his name. It could have been from another continent. The words came keening out of the sky, like the squeal of gulls.

"Tom!"

A hand was placed on his shoulder. The sky healed itself. His breathing came back to him.

"Tom, what is it? What's the matter with you?"

It was Sharon. Tom turned to her, tried to speak. Words failed to shape inside his mouth. The woman on the wall was gone. The letters engraved in the brick were already fading, like writing in windblown sand.

"I've been scouring the city for you. A neighbor told me an Englishman came to the house. Why didn't you leave an address or something?"

"I . . . I didn't know what to do." Tom was disoriented. He looked back again at the wall.

"What is it? Are you all right?"

"I thought I . . ."

"You're not all right, are you? Let me look at you."

"It's just my stomach. Really."

"Travel gut," smiled Sharon. "Had the squirts? I've got something for that. Come on, my car's over there."

Tom let himself be led to the road. Blisters of sweat dripped from his brow. The bunch of keys in Sharon's hands rippled light. Tom looked back again at the wall.

"Come on, old son. I'm taking you back to my place."

9

Remember? Remember that time I came home early and caught you?" said Katie. "I caught you reading the Song of Songs. I thought, my God, Tom's reading the Bible again. Remember me mocking you? How I used to take the piss? And you said it was the most beautiful work of literature ever written?"

"I don't recall saying that."

"Yes, you did. I asked you to read it to me. You wouldn't. That's when I knew. That's when I *really* knew."

"Knew what?" Tom said.

I O

Frist we get you out of that
fleapit," Sharon, constructing a pot of tea out of a clatter of spoons
and mugs, slammed cupboards, rattled drawers, music playing at
volume, "and into this fleapit."

Sharon was a loud person. It was the thing that had originally
attracted Tom. In their initial year at teacher-training college they'd
been mysteriously drawn together: fate could have chosen to yoke
together two more obviously kindred spirits, but it didn't. On the
first day, taking English class together, Sharon had arrived late to
sprawl in the seat next to Tom. He hardly caught a word of that first
lecture. He was too fascinated by this large-boned woman with a
yard of blond curls and a sweater of unraveling wool, the sleeves of
which reached the middle knuckles of her elegant fingers.

Halfway through the lecture she'd pinched him sharply on the
forearm saying, "Lend us a friggin' pencil, will ya?"

Tom was instantly seduced by the warm Mancunian tones. He
never got his pencil back, but he did embark on the most loyal
friendship he ever made at college.

There was nothing ostensibly sexual about this early mutual at-
traction. Later they were to give sex a sporting bash, yet the friend-

ship endured even when that failed. In those days Tom was a hesitant and inexperienced student with a late acne problem, and they
somehow managed to chum up without any of the normal boy–girl
tensions. When anyone inquired, they were very fond of invoking
the sterile protection of Plato. Except that Sharon would always say,
"Plutonic. It's plutonic." And no one knew what she meant, in-
cluding Tom.

Tom had hung a *Desiderata* over his bed. Sharon, invited in for
coffee, read the thing aloud in her unleavened Manchester accent,
and when she came to the line "Avoid loud and aggressive persons
for they are vexations to the spirit" she said, "Well, that just about
tells me to fuck off, doesn't it?" Whereupon Tom took down the
Desiderata and binned it.

"Actually, I don't like it," he'd said. "A girlfriend bought it for
me."

Sharon, interpreting this act of compliance as massive generos-
ity of spirit, was touched. From that moment forward an easy sympathy existed between the two. The bond thereafter hardened and,
since that day, had remained unbroken.

There were sizeable differences of background and temperament
across which they had to help each other in order to make this
friendship endure. "There's a Christian Union meeting," Tom had
said during that first week. "It would mean a lot if you came with
me." Shrugging, Sharon had gone along without demur. Afterwards
Tom asked, "What did you think of it?"

"You want me to be honest?"

"Of course."

"The singing was flat. The guitars ought to be smashed. The
songs were shit, and the baked potatoes were awful. Plus I felt stupid holding a candle all night. Honestly, Tom, if that's your idea of
a good time, I'm glad I'm Jewish."

Tom had blushed to his scalp. He'd unwittingly dragged a Jewess along to a Christian Union evening. No wonder the chaplain had
greeted her oddly.

"Tom, let's be serious. The bar is still open. It would mean a lot
if you came with me."

So the partnership survived. For Tom the Christian Union meetings eventually went the way of the *Desiderata*. He would "forget" to go to meetings. Not that he'd lost his faith as a Christian, he pointed out; he'd just lost his taste for baked potatoes. Meanwhile neither judged the other nor asked for anything in the way of compromise. And when people asked one of them, in the way people will, "Hey, why do you hang around with him/her?" each would answer, "Because he/she never talks dirty behind my back," in a way which immediately silenced the questioner.

At college Sharon had been from week to week a blond, a brunette, a brunette-and-blond, a redhead, a raven-head, a carrot-top and whatever the adjective is for someone with luminous green hair. Here in Israel, as she crashed down cups and saucers, her hair was blond streaked with silver-fox. Her face had seen too much direct sunlight over the years, but her Semitic brown eyes suggested a young temple prostitute.

"Thou art comely," said Tom.

"What?" Sharon laughed, brushing a stray silver-blond tress from her eyes.

"I said, thou art comely. You always were comely. That's why men can never leave you alone."

Tom had observed this from relatively close quarters. Truth was that Sharon couldn't leave men alone either. In her student days she constructed a heart that could shatter and reassemble in a matter of days. Tom often found her in a deluge of tears; worse still, he was sometimes put to comforting drunken young men, also oozing tears over Sharon. Meanwhile very little, in those days, was happening in his own love life.

"These affairs," Tom had said to her once, "they never seem to give anyone any *happiness.*"

"Happiness?" Sharon had broken off crying to blow her nose. "Happiness is never the object."

"Then what is?"

Pause. "Experience."

For a long while after that Tom thought he might be living life on the wrong note.

*   *   *

"So you've quit teaching?" Sharon asked. Tom had taught since qualifying. Sharon, by contrast, had never used her qualification. She had been a holiday courier in Spain, a timeshare-shark in the Canary Isles, a Butlin's Redcoat, an adventure-playground worker, a kibbutznik . . . Now here she was in Israel working as a counselor for alcoholic women. Along the way she'd picked up some kind of diploma in psychotherapy. "I couldn't believe it when I read your letter."

"Yep. I just quit."

"Going to tell me why?" Sharon saw an alphabet of *Angst* appear on his brow, so she jumped tracks. "Anyway, to practical things. There's a spare room here. Stay as long as you want."

"How about rent?"

"Nonsense! Put something in that fridge as a contribution. Finish your tea, and we'll go and fetch your stuff. How did you like living near the Me'a She'arim?"

"Everyone looks like Moses in a frock-coat."

"Hasids." Sharon said the word as if it was something nasty on the tip of her tongue. "Don't judge the Jews by those bastards. Most Israelis are secular and can't stand 'em. You know that some of those Hasidic sects don't even recognize the state of Israel? They won't pay taxes; they won't let their sons go into the army; yet they want protection from the Arabs, sure enough."

"So why are they here?"

"They're waiting for the Messiah—not your Messiah: Jesus wasn't Messiah enough—and not until the Messiah comes will the state of Israel be declared."

"But how will they know when the Messiah comes?"

"They won't. They'll argue about it, like the last time."

"Seriously. If someone declares himself to be the Messiah, how would they know?"

"Signs. There will be signs. You know my views on the lot of 'em, my lot, your lot, the Arabs too. This is Jerusalem. City of signs."

I know it, thought Tom.

✻   ✻   ✻

At the hotel, with Sharon waiting outside in the car, Tom settled his debts. Wanting to say goodbye to David and not finding him in the kitchen, he went to his room and tapped softly on the door. There was no answer, but he heard a stir inside, so he knocked again. After a few moments David appeared, swathed in an over-sized tartan dressing gown. He looked ghastly.

"*Monsieur,*" he said, biting on the words, "as you see, I am indisposed."

"What is it, David? You look terrible."

"Your ice cream has undone me. You win. Take your spoils." He seemed slightly delirious.

"Can I get you something? Is there anyone I can tell?"

"No one and nothing. Do your worst, and please go." With that David dragged himself through to the adjoining room and climbed into a bed piled high with blankets. He curled into a fetus and lay shivering.

Tom thought of Sharon with her engine running. He found an empty wine glass, filled it with water from the sink and placed it on the bedside table. Then he went out, closing the door softly behind him.

He rang the bell for the superintendent, but no one came. No one else was around.

"Shit," he said, back in the car.

"What is it?"

"There's an old man. I wanted to say goodbye. He's sick, and I feel bad about leaving him."

"It's not your fault he's sick, is it?"

"No."

"Right," said Sharon, booting the accelerator. "Jerusalem by night."

11

Tom dredged himself up from a hangover, mouth furred with sour Maccabee beer. Sharon had dragged him around Jerusalem's bars, and Katie's name hadn't been mentioned. Back at the apartment he'd spent an uncomfortable night. In his dreams someone had been trying to speak to him, whispering in his ear throughout the dark hours in a language which he was unable to understand but which he thought he should know.

At least there had been no hand knocking on the door in the dead of night.

As he sprawled naked on the bed, his eyes rested on the tiny tattoo etched just above his ankle. Whenever he had a hangover, Tom looked at his tattoo. Two years into marriage and Tom, a decent mid-fielder for a Sunday League outfit, had gone to Dublin for a week's jaunt with his football team. One night, when the Guinness had gone down too well, he lost some kind of bet. The forfeit was to have a tattoo.

Tom chose a point just above his ankle as the least visible place to be marked. Befuddled as he was, to the disgust of his peanut-crunching, cheering-and-jeering team-mates, he determined the nature of his tattoo without their help. By the time he got back from Dublin the image had scabbed over.

"What the hell is that?" Katie had said, throwing back the bed-sheets on his return home.

"It's a tattoo."

"What?"

"A tattoo."

"Tom! It looks more like a scab."

"That's what it is. After a while the scab falls away, leaving a nice bright tattoo."

"You asshole! You absolute asshole!"

"Maybe."

"What does it say?"

"Wait and see."

"You went to Dublin and came back with a tattoo!"

Over the next few days Katie couldn't help picking at the dried scab. Her long, manicured fingernails scratched delicately at it until the dried skin and blood flaked away.

"It's the sacred colors," Katie breathed.

Tom knew nothing about sacred colors. The tattoo was a red heart, glistening against a purple-and-gray background, with a scrolled inscription of yellow-gold. It said: KATIE. UNDYING. LOVE.

Katie was simultaneously appalled and delighted. She shook her head in disbelief and continued to do so every time she looked at it for the next ten years.

Tom got dressed. Sharon had gone to work. He pottered around the flat for an hour before deciding to visit David. He felt sorry for the scruffy, neglected little scholar with baggy pants and knotted belt. An old person like David could easily rot unnoticed in such a place. Beyond that, in this city of cities, it seemed the decent thing to do.

"Remember tomorrow is Friday," Sharon had said the night be-fore.

"What of it?"

"The Muslims don't work on Fridays. No Arab buses, shops or taxis. The Jews don't work on Saturdays. And your lot don't work on Sundays."

"It's only half a city."

"Yep."

He found David at his station in the kitchen, rinsing cups. "Tom! I heard you checked out." He seemed to have recovered his heartiness, even if he looked a little lethargic.

"Yes. It's what I came to tell you yesterday. Are you better?"

"*Monsieur*, can you forgive me? It seems I owe you an apology."

Tom, baffled, was urged to fetch *baklava* from the bakery while David made fresh coffee. He was then ushered into David's room.

"What's this about an apology?"

"First eat!"

Tom made himself sticky with *baklava* before David announced, quite formally, "I thought, Tom, that perhaps you had deliberately poisoned me with your ice cream."

Tom laughed, licking his fingers. Then he saw the blots of David's eyes magnified behind spectacle glass. He was perfectly serious. "You're crazy."

"A little paranoid, but crazy, no."

"But I don't go around poisoning people."

"This I understand now. But, as I said to you, I made a mistake."

"But who would do that to you?"

"Believe me, there are people."

"Why?"

David got up and opened his cabinet. "The scrolls, *monsieur*. The scrolls." He took out the plastic folders. "And yet they are worth nothing."

"You're losing me."

David rested the folders on the table and stood with his hands on his hips, looking out of the window. "In 1947 some little bedouin boys found the first scrolls in a number of jars in a cave near the Dead Sea. Fortunately, they thought they might be worth something, so they took them to an antiquities dealer in Bethlehem. Over the next few years those caves were scoured by bedouin and archaeologists alike. Hundreds were found in fragmentary form. Hundreds.

"Some were biblical, like the copy of the Book of Isaiah, a thousand years older than any previously extant copy. These established that the Old Testament was fixed a long time before the scrolls were made and contain few variations. Some scrolls, however, were not biblical. They contain new works; they have been given titles such as 'The War of the Sons of Light with the Sons of Darkness' and 'The Manual of Discipline.' There were thousands of these fragments.

"One such scroll, called the 'Temple Scroll,' was kept illegally by whoever found it, and it came into the hands of an Arab dealer. A Professor Yadin spent years trying to negotiate for the return of this scroll. Vast sums of money were demanded. Then in June 1967 the Six-day War broke out.

"Professor Yadin was also a senior military adviser. On the Wednesday of the war he heard that East Jerusalem was in Israeli hands. The Arab dealer's shop was within that territory. Yadin sent in two intelligence officers, who broke into the shop and confiscated the scroll. It was kept in a Bata shoe box, wrapped in a towel and Cellophane—can you imagine?

"There were also three Karel cigar boxes with other fragments inside them, nothing to do with the Temple Scroll. Some coffee had been spilled on the outside of the cigar box."

"How do you know so much about the details?"

When David turned from the window, Tom already had his answer. "I kept one of the cigar boxes. My colleague kept another. We delivered the shoe box and the third cigar box faithfully to Yadin."

Tom got up and went over to the folders on the table. The earth-colored fragments seemed to take on a more sinister quality. "Are you saying that people would kill you to get their hands on these?"

"They don't want me dead because then I couldn't tell them how many fragments they should be looking for. But somehow they have found out, and they want them. And in case you think of me as nothing but a paranoid old man, let me tell you that I have been visited."

"Visited?"

"Franciscan scholars. University professors, both Zionist and secular. Vatican representatives. And intelligence officers of the Israeli government. All very friendly visits. All civilized, polite inquiries, and all over the past two years. And, in case you were wondering about my colleague with the other cigar box, he died twelve months ago. A heart attack. Why not? He was an old man, as I am. But before he died he gave me his fragments of the scrolls. Because he said he was afraid."

"But if these things are so valuable, why on earth did you show them to me? Why deliberately show me where you keep them? Even now I could steal the things."

"Steal them. Go ahead. They are forgeries."

"Forgeries! This gets more absurd!"

"I suspected you. I let my paranoia run away with me, and I was testing you. When I fell ill I genuinely thought you had poisoned me with ice cream. I thought you were going to steal these forgeries. By the way, they are very good forgeries. If you had been after them, you would not have known. But you did not take them: your motives were clean."

"Are they copies of the real thing?"

"No. They contain information on exact measurements for constructing a temple in the time of Herod. The real things are far more interesting."

"So where are the real ones?"

David deliberately made a gesture, a stage Jew. *"Monsieur!"*

"Stupid question. But why are you making me party to all this information?"

The old man took off his glasses and swung them in his hand. "Because I want you to take these scrolls out of Jerusalem."

Tom sucked traces of *baklava* honey from his fingers.

12

Why me? Why should I be of any use to you?"

"Not everybody can be." It was what David had said the day he'd asked Tom if he was Jewish. "But somebody must be. You have no vested interest. I don't care where you take the damned things. Take them to a university in one of those gray places in the heart of England, some quiet place where a professor of theology will make sense of them. Only get them out of Jerusalem."

"Why can't you just hand them over to the École Biblique?"

David's face reddened. Veins sprang into prominence on his forehead. "Those bastards! Over forty years they sat on the scrolls and refused to let other scholars even get close to them, allowing through only a trickle of insignificant stuff. Less than a hundred of the five hundred manuscripts have seen the light of day."

"But they have to protect them from handling."

"Don't be an idiot! Have you never heard of photography? They won't even let *copies* of the scrolls out of their paws. Only recently, by complete accident, have photographs of the scrolls leaked out to scholars in the United States. They've begun publishing, and yet their work is condemned as theft. For forty years this . . . committee has sat on the treasures of civilization like a dragon in a dark cave. When I think of the scholars, friends of mine, learned men who have died in the interim, deprived by selfishness and jealousy—and who knows what other motives?—of access to the secrets of our culture, our civilization, our humanity, I could weep."

He was trembling with rage. Exhausted by his own fury, he collapsed into a chair.

"There's something you must understand," he said, recovering a little. "It was King Hussein's government, in what was then Jordanian East Jerusalem, who gave control of the manuscripts to the scholars at the École Biblique. Of course, even though these were all Jewish scrolls, they were given to Christian scholars. The team commissioned to publish the scrolls was exclusively Christian and led by a Dominican monk."

"Are you suggesting they found things . . . ?"

"Of course they found things! A few of the scrolls were even written just before, or during the time of, Jesus Christ. The information would probably undermine the basis of the Christian Church."

"That's a big statement."

"It may be that the Christian Church is founded on a big lie."

"I'm a Christian," Tom said sourly. "What makes you think I might want to help undermine my own Church."

David shrugged. "I think nothing. I see only what I see. And I take you to be a person who is not afraid of the truth."

Not afraid of the truth. Tom's thoughts zoomed back to his last day at school: the Head trying to persuade him to stay on as he gazed out of the rain-lashed window across green playing fields, hardly listening to what Stokes had to say. *"If it's the mere matter of a few words being chalked on the blackboard . . . let me assure you—"*

Tom shook his head. David saw he'd lost him somewhere and softened. "In any event, the scrolls are leaking out, despite the best efforts of the cartel now squatting on them. Look, the fragments in my possession are no more than pieces in a jigsaw. I won't press the matter with you."

Irritated, dissatisfied, Tom walked back to the Old City. He doubted the old man's fantasies and dismissed his fears. Granted, certain fragments of scrolls might have fallen into David's possession. There were thousands of scraps of hundreds of manuscripts, he knew that much, and he couldn't argue with what had been said about the scholars squatting on the hoard. That was an international scandal.

But now David was trying to recruit him into some paranoid network, all because he'd poured him a glass of water one day. And what was he offering? The chance to make a tiny contribution to confusing further the impossible arguments over the origins of Christianity? He had sympathy with scholars who felt the documents were Jewish, but if they were contemporaneous with Jesus, were they not also Christian documents?

And did he really care? When enough scholars had pored for long enough over the Dead Sea Scrolls and made their pronouncements, would life change very much for anyone? Passing under Damascus Gate on his way to meet Sharon, he resolved not to see David again.

Sharon had promised to collect him after work, outside Dung Gate. Heading for the Wailing Wall, he walked directly past the Temple Mount. The sound emanating from the El Aqsa mosque made him stop and listen.

It was the *adhan,* the Muslim afternoon call to worship. Since the *adhan* was dedicated five times a day, Tom was growing accustomed to the exotic broadcast. But today he could tell that the call was offered up by a live voice, not by the usual tape-recording via a minaret. The voice was different in quality, in timbre, from any he'd heard previously.

The song of the unseen *muezzin* was sweet; it soared on the air, as if riding thermals. It made him look up. A fiery red ball hung over the west of the city.

Allahu akhbar. La ilaha il' Allah Muhammadun rasal Allah.

He knew the litany. These were the first words whispered in the ears of Muslim babies, and the last words spoken to the dying. They began and ended each day. *God is great. There is no God but God, and Mohammed is his prophet.* Today's sound of the *adhan* chased a disquieting ripple along the hairs of his arms. Something stooped to breathe on his neck. The words were unleashed into the sky above the Holy City and went winging like brown birds into the sun.

Tom prided himself on a knowledge of religions other than his own, but the moment had entered him, and he realized with what smugness he pretended sympathy for the world's other great belief-systems. But for the very brief interval of the Crusader period, this city had been Muslim for 1,500 years. Now it was as if the voice of Islam had suddenly uncoiled and flicked at him the tongue of a beautiful serpent.

For a moment he was beguiled by both sensations of pleasure and feelings of invasion. He hurried toward the Wailing Wall, anxious to reach the gate and the New City beyond, where the mundane sounds of traffic and the engines of technology might restore a proper sense of order. But his way was blocked by trouble up ahead.

To get from the El Wad road to the Wailing Wall it was necessary to pass through a tunnel and a turnstile checkpoint guarded by armed Israeli troops. Tom heard the clamor of voices and sensed tension in the small crowd blocking the passage ahead. A man's voice was raised in an incomprehensible cry. Screams echoed from the brickwork, and there followed the muffled report of two rifle shots.

The crowd ahead reared like a wave on the sea, and the people began running toward him. One man tripped and went sprawling full-length in the dust. Tom couldn't tell what was happening as the runners bore down on him. A smoking canister landed in their midst, and he stood watching. Someone bellowed at him in Hebrew or Arabic, he couldn't tell. Then a young Arab yanked his arm.

"Gas! Don't stand watching! It's tear gas!"

Tom, open-mouthed, watched the young man abandon him. Then he decided to run with the crowd. People were screaming. He heard the dull thud as another tear-gas canister dropped somewhere at his heels. The crowd ran back up the El Wad. His legs began to seize with fear. When a small group of youths peeled off from the main group of runners into the narrow streets between the El Wad and the walls of the Temple Mount, he followed them. They quickly outstripped him. He heard footsteps coming up behind. An Israeli soldier was running at his back. Tom stopped dead. The soldier bundled him aside and chased the youths further toward the Temple Mount.

Someone waved to him from an alley, beckoning him. He couldn't make out who was in the shadows. Whoever it was gestured urgently at him with a tanned, outstretched arm, calling him to safety. He ran toward the alley.

He pulled up short. It was the black-veiled woman. In the dark of the alley, she clutched her old robes at her neck. Her exposed hands and wrists were as dry and cracked as old scrolls, but he saw the bright glitter of eyes from behind the veil. With a trembling, outstretched hand she pointed at something engraved on the wall. Written on the stone, in smoky yellow lettering a foot high, were the words: DE PROFUNDIS CLAMAVI.

Tom had only a moment to take in the scene. Behind him he heard a loud, metallic click. He turned to face an Israeli soldier with an automatic levelled at his head. The soldier's face was distorted, rubberized, red and ugly with rage and fear. He bellowed something. Tom didn't need a translator to know he was screaming at him to get out of the area. The soldier roared at him again, and Tom ran back on to the El Wad.

Soldiers were everywhere. Thin wisps of dirty white smoke hung around the El Wad. He tried to head back to Damascus Gate, but he was brusquely marshaled into the Christian quarter, where he joined tourists being pressed down toward the Holy Sepulcher. From there he was able to get out of the Old City by Jaffa Gate.

Soldiers on the battlements had switched from routine sleepiness to a state of high alert. They were stepping around the ramparts with their weapons trained on the ground below.

Whatever the incident was, the immediate danger seemed to have passed, but the street outside Jaffa Gate was incandescent with rumor. People huddled in tiny groups, strangers cemented in place by conjecture. Gossip generated a smell in the air, like ozone after thunder. The walls rippled with heat and tension, and the blue sky above Jerusalem, for a moment, seemed to buckle.

Tom leaned against a wall to recover his breath, to take in what had just happened. He let a curse pass his lips, side by side with a prayer.

13

They were at a party. It was thrown by the same teacher at whose soirée they'd first met. Twelve years had passed, and their host had since escaped teaching. Now he sold life policies and wore a toupée with a grain like varnished oak. After inviting himself around to Katie's and Tom's house one day with a leather briefcase and an impressive lap-top computer, he'd abandoned them to consider a printout and an invitation to the party. Katie enthused about the party but dismissed the insurance. Tom suggested the converse, but Katie had her way.

Tom watched Katie applying lipstick, popping her lips at the mirror. Under his cool gaze she wriggled into a tight black dress. The thighs that had once stopped his heart were on display again. He wondered where his sex drive had gone.

"Bit short," he remarked.

"Really? Is it too much?"

"No, it's fine." He regretted saying anything. It was so easy to knock her confidence these days.

At the party, where they'd hoped to see familiar faces from long ago, they knew hardly anyone. Only the music was the same, more than a decade out of date. Tom wondered if the bands playing that music also wore oak toupées now. The place was full. Katie was instantly monopolized by the host. Tom headed for the kitchen to find beer. It was guarded by a ferocious drunk with a huge foaming, nicotine-colored moustache. The drunk was holding forth to three or four sullen guests.

"It was a put-up job!" he roared. "A set-up. A stage show. They'd got it all stitched up, and it went wrong." His poached-egg eyes invited someone to argue with him. No one offered. "I mean, for Chrissakes, you'd do the fucking same!"

Tom helped himself and retreated to the lounge. Katie was surrounded by three suits. He winced. What sort of men went to parties dressed in suits? He escaped back to the kitchen, where everyone was avoiding eye-contact with the drunk, who immediately fastened on Tom. "You're the Messiah, right?" he said.

"Me?"

"Yes. And you've gotta prove it. So you know all the prophecies, right?"

"I do?"

"Yes, you do. Because you're a fucking rabbi. Which is what Jesus was, from a long line of fucking rabbis. So you know the Scriptures inside out, right?" He sucked happily at the beer foam on his moustache and nodded his head in vigorous concurrence with his own ramblings.

"I hate people who talk about religion at parties," Tom joked to the other men in the kitchen, drawing a chuckle.

"Me too," said the drunk, grabbing his arm. "Have another beer. Have two. So you know you've gotta fulfill everything in the prophecies. You hire an ass, right? Pay a claque to sing you into Jerusalem, all that. You get every detail carefully worked out." He had a delivery like a Victorian actor-manager. Tom wanted to get out, but he couldn't tear himself away. "You even know they are gonna nail you up, right, because Jerusalem is *awash* with would-be Messiahs, and this is what they do to them. But here's the bit of magic: you've found a way of staying alive on the Cross, right? Then—" The drunk looked beadily across Tom's shoulder. "Jesus,

Mother of God, look at that horny bitch in the black dress. Thassa hot, hot woman. That's what I call God speaking in tongues. That's—"

"That's my wife," said Tom.

"Hell. Sorry. No offense."

"Maybe I should break your teeth." Tom wasn't joking.

The drunk swayed and looked up at Tom, six foot four and an athletic fourteen stones. The other men eased back a few inches. The drunk offered up his right cheek. "Go on. I deserve it. Hit me here. I've got an abscess on the other side."

Tom pushed the drunk's face away with the palm of his big hand. He scooped up his beer and returned to the lounge.

A couple of hours later Tom spotted the drunk pawing at Katie. He knew she could look after herself, but then he recalled how drunk he himself had been on first meeting her in this very room. He joined them.

"I was just apologizing," said the drunk, bulging eyes leaking moisture, spittle spraying in Tom's direction, "for m'earlier gaff."

"It's true," Katie said. "He was."

"This woman would be the apotheosis of any man. She's one of the seraphim. Believe me. I've had firsthand 'sperience." He swayed dangerously.

"Well, we're just leaving."

"Look after her," bellowed the drunk. "She's a fuckin' seraph!"

The party host was at the door to help them on with their coats. "Hey, who's the yeti?" Tom asked.

"Sorry," said the host, planting a damp parting kiss on Katie's proffered cheek. "He's my brother. He's just left the priesthood."

14

In this country, when you hear someone shout, 'God is Great,' that's when you take cover." Sharon dispensed this advice lightly as they walked the wall of the Old City. They were able to cross the area from Zion Gate to a little before Damascus Gate. The rest had been sealed off as a result of yesterday's shooting incident. The number of soldiers on the walls had been doubled. They looked edgy.

"Did the newspaper say what happened?"

"There's never an explanation. A young Arab ran through the street wielding a knife and shouting exactly that, 'God is Great,' before stabbing two Jews. Then he was shot dead by a soldier. The soldiers then chased any Arabs in the vicinity and beat them half to death."

"But what made him do that? What made him explode?"

They stopped at David's Tower and leaned on the wall, looking in across the Armenian quarter. Sharon lit a small, wrinkled cigarette, and Tom identified the odor of hashish. "You can't explain it in the way you want. It's part of the *intifada*, the Palestinian uprising. They see it as an ongoing struggle to rid the land of the Jews. We see it as a holding operation; we're staying. That's it. The thing flares up from time to time in incidents like this."

"But why shout about God before doing such a thing? It doesn't make sense to me."

"No, not to you. But to these Palestinians—and to some of the ultra-Orthodox Jews here—religion and politics are indivisible. Exactly as it would have been when this city was founded, or in Jesus' time."

"How long will it go on?"

"Forever is my guess."

Walking the wall was Sharon's idea. From there, she'd told Tom, he could get a better picture of the layout of the city. He was glad of her company. The armed soldiers flicked glances of loneliness and longing at her, and she took away from him the whiff of the naïve tourist. He felt less of a target when he was with Sharon, and her strength and confidence temporarily insulated him from the city's phantoms. Now he'd had a taste of the political violence emanating from the city. He didn't know which scared him most. He was waiting to confide, to tell her what was happening to him. He was afraid that if he started talking now, it would snag or knot or, worse, his head would unspool entirely and he wouldn't be able to put it back together.

She bit on the smoke from her reefer. "What do you think of it from up here?"

"It's still beautiful."

She pointed out the ethnic divisions. "Four quarters. Each contributing twenty-five percent of stupidity and bullshit. See the Jews at their Wailing Wall? Half of them don't even know what it is. They think it was the wall of Solomon's temple. Have you seen them stuffing written prayers in between the cracks? They think God is a spider? It wasn't the temple wall—it was the foundation of the retaining wall of the platform on which the *Herodian* wall was built. Herod's, not Solomon's."

She ground the butt of her cigarette into the stone. "Imagine spending your afternoons whispering to the wrong stones.

"Then there's your mob. Marginally more stupid. All of this because some Byzantine emperor's mother was disappointed to find nothing here when she made the very first pilgrimage. So what have we got? The Way of Sorrows built on an imaginary path. Great chapels built over guesses. Churches stretched over vague holes in the ground. Have you seen the shrine of the Virgin's milk? That's the best. The Virgin spilled her mother's milk here. Please give three shekels—that's the best. They don't *know* where Jesus was cruci- fied. They don't *know* where he walked. They don't *know* where he was buried. It's all arbitrary. It's all a lie. A theme park. A fuck- ing Byzantine Disneyworld for dimwit pilgrims." She pointed across to the left. "Have you been through the Armenian quarter?"

"Yes."

"That's the saddest. Singing Armenian songs and teaching their children dances to hang on to a pocket of the past. A patch of Ar- menia preserved in amber. Then there's the Muslims, with their Dome, where Mohammed ascended into heaven, and their random stabbings because God is Great. Aw, what's the use?"

She'd burned out her exasperation before dealing effectively with the Muslims. Leaning her elbows against the wall, she squinted across the rooftops. "It's a hologram. Sometimes I despise this city."

"I know all that," Tom said, "and yet it's still astonishingly beautiful."

"That's the strangest thing about it. You're absolutely right. Are we going to talk about Katie?"

From his pocket he took a piece of paper on which he'd writ- ten three words. He gave it to her.

"*De profundis clamavi,*" she read. "What does it mean?"

"I was hoping you could tell me."

"Is it Latin?"

"Yes. I feel I should know it. It was a message someone gave to me."

"Who?"

"A woman."

He folded the note and put it back in his pocket. He too squinted into the sun to avoid her gaze. He couldn't allow his eyes to meet hers for too long.

"It's not easy, Sharon. It's not easy. It's been a bad year." He felt her hand squeezing his. "I've been hallucinating from the mo- ment I arrived in Jerusalem."

"Hallucinating? You're supposed to hallucinate in Jerusalem. That's why it's here. The entire city is an hallucination."

"I'm serious, Sharon."

"Sorry, babe. Did that sound like I was teasing you? Come on, I know a café in the Armenian quarter. We can go there, and you can tell me about your hallucinations."

15

The aromatic coils of rich roast coffee had hauled them in off the street. Shopping in town one Saturday afternoon, they'd stopped at a café. But they'd run out of words. Unspoken anger hung like a pall between them as they stared into *cappuccino* dregs. Suddenly there was another's presence looming over the table.

"Couldn't help seeing you. Had to come over." It was the drunk from the party. The absconded priest. He stroked his moustache nervously. "Wanted to apologize for my behavior at my brother's party the other night. I was being a bore by all accounts."

Tom shrugged. "It was a party."

"You were no trouble," said Katie.

"It was my first night of freedom, so to speak. The drink got the better of me, and I made a fool of myself."

"Forget it," said Tom.

"Anyway, my name's Michael. Michael Anthony." Rather formally, he shook hands with both of them. He hovered for a moment, perhaps waiting for an invitation to sit down. When he realized that an invitation wasn't about to present itself, he said goodbye decisively and hurried out of the coffee bar.

Katie glanced up at Tom. Tom looked away.

16

De *profundis clamavi.* The words held no significance for Sharon. This left one other person known to him in all of Jerusalem, so, despite his promise to himself, Tom paid another visit to David Feldberg. He hoped the old scholar might be able to divine meaning in the writing on the wall, or at least to identify the literal sense of the words. So far he'd told Sharon nothing of David's efforts to entangle him with the scroll fragments.

Sharon had listened patiently to his account of the hallucinations. He preferred to speak of "hallucinations" because it deflated the experiences, even though the woman had been as substantial as the city walls. There was nothing vague or smoky or translucent about her. Even his recollection of the experiences triggered an intensity, a brightness, and that mysteriously associated cloying perfume. Only the phantom's gravity-defying manifestation on the perpendicular walls cast doubt on her appalling physicality.

"Perhaps she's a real person," Sharon had suggested at the Armenian café.

"Suspended from the wall?"

"A trick of the light?"

"Some trick. She keeps trying to talk to me."

He told her about the voice in his head. "It's in those moments before I fall asleep. I hear this voice. Like she's telling me a story I can't understand. I don't know who or what it's about. As if it's in a language I almost know, but not quite. And every time I focus on it, I lose it, like a radio frequency drifting out. God, it's weird. Could it be too much sun, do you think? I've felt strange ever since I got here. Trembling. Quivering. Could it be the sun?"

"You're not suffering from sun-stroke, if that's what you mean."

Sharon's manner suggested she knew exactly what he was suffering from. If she did know, she fell short of telling him.

David was absent from his usual place in the communal kitchen. A dozen or so chipped mugs and cups, all ringed with moldering tea or coffee dregs, were clustered around the sink. When he tapped on David's door there was no answer, so he tried the handle. The door swung inwards. David was on his sick bed. Someone had cleaned and tidied the room. Pillows were propped under his gray head, and a grim cortège of colored pills was laid out on his bedside cabinet, beside a bottle of blackcurrant juice.

He was dozing, but he blinked open his eyes. Seeing Tom, he groped weakly for his spectacles.

"Someone been poisoning you again?" Tom settled uncomfortably on the edge of the bed.

David raised his limp arms. "You won't let me forget." His voice was feeble. The whites of his eyes were stained yellow.

"Have you seen a doctor?"

"I have. A most unpleasant old friend of mine."

"And? What are you suffering from?"

"From surfeit of life, *monsieur*. Surfeit of life. Are there many cups in the kitchen?"

"One or two."

"Can you tell me, please, when people are given a cup, why is it that they cannot rinse it out after using it? Why? I am forever rinsing out cups."

Uncertain whether a smile was required, Tom offered one. "I'll have a look at them on my way out."

"Humoring me, is that it? What brings this visit?"

"I wanted to ask you something. But you don't look well enough to be bothered."

"Ask."

Tom produced a scrap of paper from his pocket and unfolded it. Taking an age to hook his spectacles around each ear, David finally, carefully, adjusted them on the bridge of his nose. Though there were only three words inscribed there, he read the note over like a letter from home. Then he refolded the paper, taking off his glasses before handing it back.

"Well? What is it? What does it mean?"

"It is Latin. I know enough to tell you what it says. It says: *Out of the depths.* Or perhaps it could be rendered: *Up from the depths.*"

"*Up from the depths?* But what does that mean?"

"Mean? That's another question. You asked me what it *says.* I've told you. What it might mean is another matter entirely."

David closed his eyes and dozed again. He looked peaceful enough. He wasn't a man who'd been poisoned. Old age had him, and had sprinkled on him a layer of frost. His chest rose and fell under the blankets, a slight movement.

Tom decided to leave him alone. He got up to go, but as his fingers touched the door handle, he was summoned back to the bedside. "Tom. Could I ask a small favor in return?"

"Of course."

"Go to my wardrobe. There is a jacket I need altering. I want to wear it when I am well again. I've decided to step outside, for the first time in years."

"That's good, David. A fine idea. Is it this one?"

"No. The Harris tweed, at the back of the wardrobe. Yes, that's it. I bought it in England a long time ago. Quality. I will wear the Harris tweed. But you must take it to the tailor's and have it altered."

He insisted Tom should take it to a friend who'd been in the tailoring business and who would carry out the alterations for a very modest fee. Concerned that he should incur no extra expense, he made Tom write down the name of the tailor, who lived only a few streets away. He knew, David assured, all his measurements.

The jacket was old but barely worn. There was a Savile Row label. It smelled of something Tom associated with old men and more than a trace of naphthalene from the wardrobe. Folding it across his arm, Tom was about to ask when he should return with the altered jacket, but David had fallen asleep.

On his way out he rang the supervisor's bell. The boy appeared. "The hotel owner should be told about the old man in room seven."

The boy looked puzzled. "What is it?"

"He's very frail."

"I know. But he's seen a doctor. What else can we do?"

"I don't know," Tom said. "It's just that I don't think he's going to be alive much longer. He needs proper attention."

"He refuses to go to hospital."

"But shouldn't the hotel owner know about his condition?"

"You misunderstand," said the boy. "He *is* the owner of the hotel."

"What? David Feldberg owns this place?"

"That's right."

Tom was astonished. "But he's always complaining about the coffee!"

"Yes."

Tom went directly from the hotel to the tailor's shop that afternoon. He should have noticed before reaching the address that all was closed for *shabbat*. He'd forgotten it was Saturday.

He shrugged and headed toward the bus station, still carrying the jacket over his arm. Then he turned again, realizing there would be no bus service on *shabbat* and that he would have to take a shared *sherut* Arab taxi back to Sharon's apartment.

17

Returning to Sharon's apartment, Tom turned the key in the lock, swung into the living-room and caught Sharon in bed with a young Arab. The door to Sharon's room was half-open: the young man lay on his back with Sharon astride him. Both were naked. The moment failed to register, and with David Feldberg's jacket draped across one arm, Tom gazed dumbly at them, as if puzzling out what exactly it was they were doing.

They didn't hear him come in. Then the Arab man lifted up his head and, on spotting him, smiled stupidly. Tom backed out of sight, shutting the door, eyes closed, cheeks burning. Sharon would be furious.

After some minutes, the door opened and the man came out. Sharon, now wearing a silk dressing gown, held the door as the Arab nodded at Tom. She bade the man goodbye.

"I'm sorry," Tom burbled.

"Forget it."

"Really, I—"

"It's nothing. Want a coffee?" She scratched the back of her head. "I'm going to have a shower."

With Sharon in the bathroom, Tom stood in the doorway of her bedroom. The bedcovers had been hastily pulled back into place. The room reeked of coitus. He retreated from the bedroom, draping David's jacket over the back of a hard chair.

Sharon emerged in a bathrobe, her skin shell-pink from the shower, a white towel swathed around her head. She picked up the jacket from the chair and ran her hands across its silk lining. Standing behind him, she took off her wet bathrobe and slipped on the jacket. "Cold silk," she said, slumping on the sofa. "Love it." She pulled the hem of the jacket across her thigh to hide her cunt, a partial concession to modesty. "Didn't shock you, did it? When you came in like that?"

"Not at all."

"You lie."

"Well, it was a bit of a surprise."

"My boyfriend thought so. Actually, he's not my boyfriend anymore. We were just saying goodbye, so to speak."

"Goodbye? He didn't look like he was saying goodbye."

"He didn't know it."

Sharon reclined on the sofa, her crossed legs steaming slightly from the hot shower, her natural coloring poking from under the hem of the jacket.

"Why are you doing this, Sharon?"

"Doing what?"

"Sitting there, like that."

"Does it make you uncomfortable? I'm sorry, I never think of you in that way."

While she was dressing Tom thought about the time they'd fallen into bed together one evening at college. They were both drunk. Both were suffering from unrequited love, and they'd grabbed at each other for comfort. For two days they pretended to find True Love right under their noses. On the third day they admitted to each other it wasn't working. Ordinary friendship was resumed, apparently undamaged, and the episode was never referred to again.

Sharon reappeared, dressed, still rosy and perfumed from her shower. She sat down on the sofa beside him and took his hand.

"You must miss her like crazy. I didn't even want to mention it. But she was my friend too, Tom. She was my friend too."

"Waking up. That's the worst thing. Every morning you wake up, you remember what happened to her. Every morning."

"I know how hard it is, Tom. But it's been a year. Life has to go on. And I'm not sure it was a good idea to quit your job. I mean, it put structure into your life."

Tom said nothing.

"Did something else happen? Something that made you leave the school?"

And for a moment he was back there. First Monday of the summer term, with the emptiness of the Easter holidays and Katie's absence still very much in mind. He'd collected his form register and was on his way to the classroom. A drizzle of rain outside. Kids with a crumpled, whey-faced look as they filed into their respective classrooms. As he pushed open the door to his own room the children became unusually quiet. With an unfelt heartiness he expressed the hope that they'd all had a good break before their murmured replies made him wonder why they were so strangely subdued. He became aware that they were focused on something behind him. An instinct. *If it's the mere matter*, the Head had opined, *if it's the mere matter . . .* That instinct had made him turn, very slowly. The entire class stiffened as they waited for him to discover what they'd all seen the moment they'd entered the classroom.

"I don't know, Sharon. Maybe."

It was Monday before Tom took David's jacket to the tailor's. Jacob Sarano was a miraculously tiny figure, rescued by only centimeters from the condition of dwarfism. His white hair, white moustache and heavy black spectacles, coupled with his stature, suggested a mythological species of Jewish tailor. His workshop was piled high with bales of cotton. A nude tailor's manikin stuck with pins stood in the window. He smiled sadly as Tom entered his shop.

"David Feldberg sent me with this. He wants it altered."

The smile vanished from the tailor's lips. He came from behind his counter, bolted the door and pulled down the black window shades. A bare bulb hanging from scorched flex lit the room.

"I hear David is dying."

"Dying? Possibly. I didn't know how poorly he was. I'm just doing this as a favor."

"A favor?" He spread the jacket out on his counter.

"When can I collect it?"

"It will be two minutes. Here, it's almost done." He took a large pair of shears and carefully separated the lining at the vent, following the stitching very carefully around the jacket. "I haven't seen David in years," he said as he worked.

"Oh? I got the impression you were old friends."

"Old friends, yes. We were in Belsen together. That's when we met. I'll tell you how we became friends." He readjusted his glasses on the end of his nose and resumed his work, now skimming the blade very slowly and accurately around the lining to the front of the jacket. "There was a particularly cruel captain. Always trying to find ways of adding to our misery. Knowing I was a young tailor, he came to me one day with a copy of the Torah. It was all vellum, beautiful leather, understand? And he insisted that I make a jacket for him out of the pages. Can you imagine, a jacket from the Torah?" He paused for Tom to appreciate the blasphemy.

"What could I do? I wrung my hands. If I did, it was a desecration. If I didn't . . . perhaps I wouldn't be here now. Anyway it was David who told me what to do."

The tiny tailor busily separated the lining from the sleeves, anxious to ensure that the rest of the lining could be detached in a single piece. "Do it. Make him a jacket, David told me. Talk with the rabbi. Find every curse written on those pages and make it from that. Make it beautiful so that he will want to wear it all the time. Make the strongest curses on the inside, nearest to his heart and his liver and his lungs. Make it the most beautiful jacket he ever had.

"There was a rabbi there with us, and he helped me. I took the curses and woes from Deuteronomy and Isaiah and wherever I could find them. All the plagues and the diseases and the sore sicknesses and the rest of it. And I made the most beautiful jacket. And the captain wore it. He wore it! Here. We've finished."

Laying the jacket aside, he spread the lining on the counter, inside uppermost. Now Tom could see that something had been stitched to the inside of the lining itself. Carefully sewn, so as not to extrude, were three cloth rectangles. The largest rectangle was in the middle and had been stitched at the back of the jacket. The two side pieces had hung at either breast. Together they made a kind of triptych, still attached to the silk.

"Scrolls," said Tom.

"David had me make this up for him. He told me he would send for them one day."

"It's incredible." He examined the stitching. Fragments had been sewn together with almost invisible thread, to make up the three pieces. "The skill." The scrolls themselves had been written in the highly unusual form of a spiral, presumably to be read from the outer arm of the spiral toward the dense concentration of letters in the center.

The tailor folded the lining carefully, finally wrapping it in tissue paper. "Now you can take them to him. Tell him I'll repair the jacket, and you can come back for it in a few days."

The tailor moved to the windows and let up the blinds. Then he unbolted the door. Tom stepped outside into the sunlight.

"There's one thing," Tom said. "The German captain. At the concentration camp. What became of him?"

"I don't know, so I can't say." The tiny tailor had a murderous gleam in his eyes. "All I can tell you is that within two weeks he was sent to the Russian front."

The door was closed softly. Tom was left standing in the street clutching his bundle of silk scrolls wrapped in tissue paper.

His first thought was to get back to David and dump the scrolls. The hotel was only a few streets away, but it seemed every passing pair of eyes was fixed on the tissue-wrapped package under his arm. Every ultra-Orthodox brain mysteriously detected the contents: *See! He has the scrolls. The stolen scrolls. The legacy of Jewish culture. The literature of our people.*

He was sweating heavily when he reached the hotel. With some irritation he rapped on David's door, annoyed to have been used in this way. When no one replied he tried the handle. The door was locked.

He went to find the supervisor. The boy's dark eyes were swollen blots behind his glasses. "He died," the boy said simply.

"Died?"

"Yes."

Tom stood holding the package. The palm of his hand was sweating on to the tissue paper. "Has he got any family here? Anyone I could talk to?"

"He never had anyone. This hotel is all he had. Anything I can do?"

Tom shook his head. The boy shrugged and went back to his room. Then Tom looked in the communal kitchen. Dirty mugs and cups were piling up at the sink.

He considered having the room unlocked and simply dumping the scroll fragments there. Let them become someone else's problem. Then he realized what David had done by passing them on. He'd made an attempt to clean up things before he died; he'd tried by this gesture to rinse something from the bottom of his own cup of life. He'd known it was *shabbat,* and he'd known he was dying when he gave Tom the jacket. He could easily have removed the lining from the jacket himself. But the problem of what to do with the things had been successfully passed to Tom.

18

How's it going with this new boyfriend?"

"He's not my new boyfriend," Sharon protested. "He's an old friend from college days, that's all."

"I don't believe it. You come in, you're late, you look a state, you look like something's keeping you awake nights." Tobie was the founder-manager of the Bet Ha-Kerem rehabilitation center where Sharon worked as a counselor. She had a habit of treating her staff like clients. They were having coffee in her office.

"Stop fishing, Tobie. I look perfectly well, and I was here before you this morning."

"So if I was late, that makes you not late? Don't talk snot, darling." "Talking snot" was an expression she'd picked up from one of her alcoholic clients. Tobie picked up and discarded expressions on a fortnightly basis. "Anyway I'm the boss. I can't be late. It's a contradiction in terms."

"He's over from England for a while. That's it."

"Only I don't want you emotionally upset. You know what happens here: you get upset, all my women get upset, I get upset.

Everyone here is like a single mind. I despair of it. So if you're having a bad time with this English what'shisname—"

"Tom."

"Sharon, you're lying."

"No, I'm not."

"I know you." Tobie was a plump little gray-haired woman with
spectacles permanently resting on the tip of her nose. She came
over and held Sharon's face between her hands. "I worry. So? Are
you fucking him?"

"Tobie!" She was the only person Sharon knew who could
swear without emphasis.

"Because if you love him and you're not fucking him, that's bad
for all of us. We all gonna suffer."

"Listen, I've got to make a start. My group is waiting."

"Now you won't talk to me? It's worse than I thought."

"Look. I don't love him. I'm not fucking him. I do want to talk
to you about him, but about some problems he's having."

"To hell with his problems, *darlink*, it's you I'm concerned
for." When Tobie said "darling," it always came out "darlink." It
drove Sharon crazy.

"Another time, OK, Tobie?"

"Sure."

Sharon went to join the group of women waiting for her in the
meeting room. Tobie finished her coffee and pulled a face. Damn
it, she thought. Sharon's falling in love with this guy. Now we're
in for a shit time.

19

Get that," said Tom.

"Get it yourself."

The telephone rang unanswered. Katie sat on the sofa, her long, elegant legs drawn up under her. She'd brought work home with her. Tom was sitting at the table. He had a pillar of exercise books stacked on either side of him, and he was marking them with a red pen. The phone stopped ringing. Katie looked up at Tom, who carried on with his marking.

A few minutes later the phone rang again. Katie threw down her pen and got up. Tom attended to her side of the conversation.

"Hello? Oh, hello. No, that's quite all right. What can we do for you? Yes, he's here now. Marking schoolwork. Yes, he's a teacher. No, I'm not, and I wouldn't want to be. That's very flattering of you. I wouldn't worry about that. Yes, he's just here. I'll get him. Hang on."

Katie cupped the mouthpiece. "Tom, it's Michael Anthony."

"Who?"

"The man in the coffee bar. The drunk at the party. He wants to speak with you."

"What does he want?"

"How should I know?" She waved the phone at him and made a furious face.

Tom got up wearily and took the handset from Katie. "Yes?"

Katie saw Tom listening almost in silence, for perhaps fifteen minutes, occasionally punctuating with a grunt. Finally he wrote a number down on a pad, said goodbye and put down the phone.

"Well?"

"He asked my permission," said Tom, "to ask you if you would walk with him in the park on Sunday afternoon."

"What?"

"He was very correct. Very formal. Wanted it all to be above-board."

"Why does he want me?"

"He said he thinks you're beautiful. He also said he's dying. The doctors have given him between six months and a year. He made it sound like a condemned man's last request."

20

I see how it's been done. The fragments have been heat-pressed on to some very fine fabric, before being stitched into the silk lining, to stop them from falling apart."

"Can you tell if they're of importance?" Tom asked.

"I've no idea. It's Hebrew, but I can't read it," said Sharon. "If you want to know, you're going to have to take the thing to someone who can."

Sharon's tanned arms rested on the table either side of the scroll-cloth like two temple pillars. Tom eyed her supple muscles. He'd almost forgotten how easy was the confidence she exuded.

"Lots of these fragments are around," she told him authoritatively, "though I've never seen any, except in the museum. Chances are all these contain are measurements for building the temple. 'And it shall be forty cubits, and thereafter twenty cubits, and the wall shall be another ten cubits.' That's all a lot of them have to say."

"David seemed to think they were important."

"You also told me he thought the Vatican was trying to poison him. I think your David was a little bit soft in the head."

"He didn't say it was the Vatican. I don't know. Any ideas who might help us?"

"Decide whether you want to turn the thing in or not. If you give it to the Hebrew or Christian authorities, you won't see it again. That's certain. We could find a scholar to look at them privately. But if it says anything interesting, pretty soon everyone will know you've got it."

"Hell. What are we gonna do?"

"Look, there's this friend of mine. Ex-client, actually. I was trying to avoid suggesting him, but . . ."

"Ahmed el-Asmar," said Sharon, hammering on the door for the third time. "He's probably sleeping. And even if I've woken him, he won't answer until the fourth knock. The *djinn* only knocks three times, or so he told me."

"The *djinn?*"

They had returned to the Muslim quarter of the Old City. In the northeastern quadrant Sharon had steered him to a shuttered medieval building. The narrow street reeked of mildew and donkey. "Demons. Ahmed is not your ordinary Palestinian Arab. He also regards me as slightly insane."

"Why?"

Sharon didn't have time to answer. A shutter opened several feet above their heads, and a sleepy Arab blinked at them. Tom saw a tousled head of black hair and a thin moustache. The man regarded them blankly for some moments. "The mad Jewess," muttered the Arab. His head withdrew from the window. A few moments later he reappeared to toss down a key. Sharon caught it and let them in.

The interior of the house was cool and shady. Tom followed Sharon up a flight of bare stone steps and into a fragrant room, where the man struggled into a pair of jeans and a T-shirt. He blinked theatrically and tried to stroke sleep from his eyes. Tom guessed him to be about forty years old.

The other two kissed each other on the cheek before Sharon introduced Tom. "He's from England."

"England?" said Ahmed, as if Sharon had said he was from the lost city of Atlantis. "England?"

Tom extended a hand. The man stared at the outstretched hand for a long moment of horrified fascination before accepting it. "Tea. I would like to offer you some tea."

Unasked, Sharon had already lowered herself on to one of the large cushions scattered against the wall. Ahmed gestured that Tom should do likewise and then stumbled away to his kitchen.

"Don't worry," Sharon whispered. "He's still half asleep."

"I heard that," came the shout from the kitchen. "Are people so rude in England? I mean as rude as this mad Jewess?"

"Yes," said Tom, "they are."

"I know. I've been there. I just wanted to see if you were a liar."

Silence followed as Ahmed made the tea. The solid stones of the old apartment muted any sounds from outside, so that the interior was beautifully calm. The walls were decorated with hangings and fabrics of geometric design. A scent like incense hung in the air, along with another familiar but more acrid odor that Tom was unable to identify. Ahmed returned with tray and glasses. In each glass was a sprig of fresh mint and two cubes of sugar. Tom wanted to decline the sugar, but Ahmed was already pouring. "So how do you like Palestine?" He passed a glass.

"I'm still making up my mind. It's a violent place."

"Yes. It will be more peaceful when we get rid of the Jews."

Sharon was smiling. "We're like your demons, Ahmed. We're always going to be with you."

Ahmed addressed Tom as if Sharon wasn't in the room. "She is right. I don't know who is worse: the *djinn* or the Jew. I wouldn't mind if all of them were like her, but the others . . . *Allah!* How is the tea?"

"Delicious!"

He pressed his chest with the palm of his hand, as if the compliment was profound and personal. Then he turned suddenly to Sharon. "You haven't visited me for six months. Where have you been, you bitch?" Sharon shrugged and sipped her tea. "What kind of a friend is she, Tom, that doesn't come to visit me in six months? Are people so bastard-bitch rude to their friends in England?"

"You asked him that already."

"Yes, I did. Sorry, Tom."

"In any case," said Sharon, "you don't visit me. I told you to come and visit me."

"Sure! And get my head shot off by a teenage Jew, with his Uzi machine-gun, for being an Arab in my homeland! What do you think of that, Tom? An Arab is not safe in his own land."

"Ignore him. It's not the soldiers who keep him indoors. He's afraid of the *djinn.*"

"Now she's getting at me. If I didn't love her, I would kill her. Anyway, she's mad. Why? Because she doesn't believe in the *djinn.* Only mad people don't believe in the *djinn.* Do you believe in the *djinn?*"

"In demons?" Tom hesitated. "Well, I believe in God, so I also believe in the existence of Satan . . . so, I suppose, yes is the answer."

"There!" said Ahmed, as if an old argument had ultimately been settled. "More tea?"

At length Sharon said, "We've brought something for you to look at."

Tom produced the rolled cloth. Ahmed took it from him, spreading it on a low table. Before inspecting it he reached for, and lit, a handrolled cigarette. Tom identified the second smell of the apartment as that of hashish. Ahmed bit off a lungful of smoke and gazed at the scroll fragments.

"The spiral is unusual. How did you come by it?"

"It fell into my hands when someone died."

He stared at the fragments for a little while longer, then appeared to lose interest.

"Could you study it for us?" Sharon asked.

"Is there a fee?"

"No."

Ahmed breathed in another lungful of smoke and vented a deep sigh.

"Ahmed is a brilliant scholar," Sharon said to Tom. "He knows the ancient scripts of Hebrew, Aramaic and Arabic. He also knows Greek and Latin. Then there is English, French, German and . . . what else, Ahmed?"

"The mad Jewess thinks if she flatters me enough, I'll read this rag for her. She's wrong."

"Spanish. Berber. Thieves' argot. What else? Really, he's a true polyglot. It's his one shining talent. That's why we came to him."

"Not because I'm a nice guy? Tom, do you work for nothing?"

"We don't know what's written on the thing. But we've reason to think it might be important," said Sharon. "If it is, you can copy it and break the scholarship. It will help with your reputation."

"My reputation!" Ahmed laughed cynically. "My reputation."

"He'll do it," Sharon said to Tom. "He's already said yes."

"She's wrong," said Ahmed. They were still talking to each other through Tom.

Ahmed went away and returned with fruit on a silver tray. With a sharp knife he carved melon and oranges into equal segments. Tom marveled at the precision with which he executed the task. Talk changed to other things. They discussed the political situation, recent outrages, government policy. The question of the scrolls was not reopened. Ahmed, well informed about British politics, plied Tom with questions about British opinion concerning the Palestinian question. Tom did his best to answer. Ahmed smoked two or three of his home-rolled cigarettes during this time and was charming. Despite the banter, it was obvious that the other two were very comfortable with each other.

Sharon got up to leave, and the two kissed lightly. The scroll-cloth remained on the table. Tom took his cue from Sharon to leave it there. Ahmed shook his hand and expressed the hope he might see him again.

Sharon led the way down the steps, with Ahmed between her and Tom. When they reached the bottom Ahmed opened the door and Sharon stepped out into the light. But the Arab blocked Tom's progress for a moment. He leaned his head toward him, and for one ridiculous moment Tom thought the Arab was going to try to kiss him. But he whispered urgently, "You are carrying a *djinn.*"

"What?"

"The *djinn.* I see the *djinn* you carry. She is trying to speak to you, but you have closed your ears to her."

"I don't understand you."

"Don't be alarmed. I also carry a *djinn*. Many *djinn*. Listen to her. She wants to talk to you."

Sharon called to them, and in the next moment Tom was steered through the door already closing behind him. All thoughts of the scroll-cloth had been swept from his mind. He stood in the street feeling bewildered.

"He'll do it," said Sharon. "He'll find out if there's anything of interest. Tom, you look pale."

"I've known him for about ten years. He's always saying this or that person is carrying *djinn*. You should ignore it."

After visiting Ahmed, Sharon cooked dinner. Fastidious in her preparation of the food and yet careless in its presentation, she served up chunks of roast lamb wrapped in *pitta* bread with exotic salad. They wolfed it.

"But my hallucinations, the woman! I think he saw them. Somehow."

Sharon stopped eating. She wiped her mouth with a napkin. "Look. He may very well have his *djinn,* and you may very well have yours. But you can't see each other's."

"Why not?"

"Because yours exist only in your head, and his exist only in his—that's why not."

"What are his *djinn?*"

"Can't tell you. Professional etiquette. I first got to know him when he came to me for psychotherapy. He was in a bad way, guilt-ridden and deeply depressed. Tormented by all sorts of demons of his own making. He has a brilliant mind, that Ahmed, and it had turned itself to plaguing him."

"Did you help him?"

"I flatter myself that maybe I did. And he helped me. He refused to accept the normal doctor–patient roles and insisted that I reveal personal things to him as much as he confided in me. I went along with it. And he destroyed a lot of my own illusions about things— this is why he calls me the mad Jewess by the way. I was as ill as he was. It stopped me believing in the doctor–patient routine myself.

He made me realize all this role-acting was complicating the healing process rather than helping it."

"But he recovered?"

"He's functioning effectively; that's the important thing. I couldn't get him to change his mind about the *djinn*, however, which are still a source of torment to him. Tom, something has changed about you."

"Oh?"

"It's in your eyes. You look at me with deep critical judgment. Almost mistrust. Has Katie's death done this to you?"

Tom ignored the question. "So how do you explain his *djinn?*"

"Or your *djinn?*"

"Yes. Or mine."

"It's sexual."

"Ah-ha! Easy as that."

"Like most people," said Sharon, "you don't like being told what you are."

"But it's banal to say that everything comes down to sex."

"*Djinn.* Demons. Hauntings. Hallucinations. In fact, pretty much everything occult or religious is a displacement of sexual energy."

"I don't see it that way."

"That's because you're deliberately shying away from any kind of sexual interpretation of what's obviously simmering below the surface of things. You're desperate to deny it, just as you're desperate to deny your own—"

"My own what?" The mood suddenly tilted.

"What do you do for a cuddle now Katie is gone?"

"And I thought we were talking about *djinn.*"

"And I told you what I thought about *djinn.* It's you I'm interested in. I care about you, Tom." Her head was resting on the back of the couch, her cinnamon eyes opaque with pity. He couldn't take her intensity. She'd assumed too early the old intimacy. Now she'd decided to counsel him, like one of her woman alcoholics. Tom felt a sudden flash of hatred for her.

"What happened to Katie?" said Sharon. "And what happened at the school?"

21

Gethsemane was a garden of cool respite from the heat of midday Jerusalem. Botanists claimed to have dated some of the ancient olive trees to the time of Jesus. None of the trees, however, could have belonged to the original garden, since it had been cleared in A.D. 70, but Tom was beginning to weary of his own skepticism. He stepped up to the oldest-looking tree in the garden and leaned his back against it.

The sun in the blue heavens was like a lion's eye. He'd bought a straw hat in the Arab *souk* to protect himself from its unblinking stare, making his way up to the garden alone after discouraging Sharon's offer of company. He was still hiding from her questions. The sun powered through the shimmering green leaves of the olive tree. He closed his eyes and wondered what he was running from most.

If it's the mere matter, the Head had suggested, *the mere matter . . .*

He'd pushed open the door that day to find the children unusually quiet. The smell of rain, of dampness steaming from black blazers. They shuffled uncomfortably, strangely subdued, wouldn't meet his eyes. Slowly becoming aware of something chalked on the board behind him, he turned to look at it. It was busy with angry, three-foot-high letters. The class became silent, watching him take it in.

Thou shalt not fuck another man's wife was written there. *Thou shalt not commit adultery. Mister Webster fucks schoolgirls. Cunt, shit* and *bastard* and *cocksucker* and *bollocks* and *fuck fuck fuck.* A crudely chalked erect penis ejaculated into an equally crude mouth.

The silence of the class pressed behind him like a flat wave. It foamed at his back, threatening to swamp him, a tidal force approaching and retreating from the blackboard obscenities. He read the words again. Then he picked up the eraser and quietly rubbed out the words and in their stead he wrote, with a trembling hand, the words *Today's R E. What Do We Mean by the "Old Testament"?*

"Take out your study books," he said, struggling to disguise the fracture in his voice. "Turn to chapter twelve."

In the Garden of Gethsemane a bead of sweat trickled inside his trouser leg. He saw a Franciscan monk enter the cave of sand-colored rock. Tom stroked the trunk of the olive tree before deciding to follow the monk inside.

The cave was cool, spacious and airy. The calm interior was half-lit by lamps placed in alcoves, reflecting an amber glow from the walls. The monk, in brown Franciscan robe and leather sandals, was sitting on a stool at a desk. He was writing. There was something reassuringly authentic in the spectacle of his writing. At least Tom didn't feel he was in a theme park. The monk looked up and smiled. He was a large-framed man with thinning dark hair and velvet eyes.

"Excuse me."

The monk wasn't writing at all; rather, he was using a ruler to draw lines on a blank sheet of paper. He ruled a new line before laying down an expensive-looking ballpoint pen. "Sorry," he whispered, looking up. "My English . . . not good."

Tom had in his hand a piece of paper, and now he wasn't sure whether to show it. "It's just this. I mean, it's Latin. I wondered if you recognized it."

The monk took the paper.

"De profundis clamavi," Tom said impatiently. "Up from the depths."

"De profundis clamavi," the monk cooed encouragingly. He put down the scrap of paper and got down off his stool. He let an index finger float heavenward as he struggled to remember some English words. *"De profundis,* eet ees Psalm, yes, Psalm one-hoondred and tirty." His eyes were bright with the little task he'd been set, his voice a soft and reassuring whisper. Tom thought he was perhaps Spanish. "Up from ze depths have I cried unto zee, O Lord. My soul wait for ze Lord more zan zey zat watch for ze morning. Eet ees psalm of mercy. Forgiveness. Redemption, yes."

Tom turned to squint out of the cave entrance into the bright light beyond. When he looked back at the monk, his eyes were moist. The monk saw it, smiled and put a hand on his shoulder.

This poor man thinks I'm moved by the beauty of the psalm, thought Tom. He felt ridiculous, childish. How was the monk to know his eyes were filling up because of his own personal tragedies? Because of his own betrayals? Because, above all, he couldn't remember which he'd lost first, his wife or his faith?

He thanked the man and turned away. He sensed the monk watch him walk from the mouth of the cave. As he stepped from the cool, the heat of the sun rolled over him like a lion's breath. He felt unsteady, dizzy. He approached an ancient olive, taking off his hat and leaning against the tree. Heat ripples distorted his vision of the garden. White light bleached the foliage. A stab of migraine made him close his eyes.

If it's the mere matter of a few words being chalked on a blackboard, Stokes had said, *well, that's happened to most teachers. Anyone offended by it is as sad as those who take pleasure in chalking it.* But Stokes was wrong. It wasn't the mere matter of the words.

The problem didn't go away. The writing came back several times. He'd had his suspicions but no proof. He even began to suspect some of the pupils of shielding him, of wiping the board clean before he reached the classroom. Then the culprit was finally revealed, not through any detective work on his part. Two boy pupils spoke to him after class one day and gave him the name of a third, whom Tom had suspected.

The boy was a reasonable student, a slightly surly but bright fourteen-year-old who had mysteriously hardened his attitude toward Tom some time ago. Tom detained the boy and confronted him. Initially the boy denied everything, but eventually he broke down and admitted some responsibility, though he remained oddly defiant that he'd chalked the vile messages on only one occasion, even though Tom had himself wiped the board six or seven times. It was only when Tom promised not to take the matter to his parents that the boy was prepared to offer any kind of explanation. He had a violent attachment to Kelly McGovern, one of Tom's fourth-form English group, and Kelly in turn, Tom was surprised to learn, had a passionate crush on Tom. The youth was pathologically jealous of Kelly's feelings for her teacher.

Tom had done the kind thing and had let the youth go away with a warning, under sanction for what would happen if there was any repetition of the events. He'd also reassured the boy that crushes for teachers were not uncommon and, even if they weren't, he was a happily married man with no interest in schoolgirls.

No, it was not the matter of "mere words" which had caused Tom to abandon teaching.

When he opened his eyes to the garden, he saw the veiled woman.

She stood under another olive tree, shaded from the dazzling light. She was poised only a few feet away, the same Arab woman who'd dogged his movements through Jerusalem. But she was transfigured. Her rough brown robes had gone. In their place was a robe of bleached white. She wore a new veil, of fine gray material, semiopaque. The sun striking from her white robe almost blinded him. The familiar spiced scent trailed like a ribbon in the still air. Tom blinked. She waited under the tree, not a phantom but flesh and blood, and beckoned to Tom to follow her.

She stepped from under the tree, walking deeper into the garden. Tom went after her.

He followed her through the ancient olives, the air tingling with the scent of opal balsam. There was a sudden quickening in the leaves, a shimmering as she stepped between the trees. Balsam streamed across the garden, rising from cracks in the arid soil. The woman unexpectedly turned and waited for him, and he experienced a folding sensation; the universe creased and spilled itself. The woman moved toward him, hands outstretched, and her perfume, her balsam, was overwhelming. She lifted her veil, but her face was in shadow as she kissed Tom fully on the mouth. Her felt her tongue probe his lips, and in an instant there was no woman, only the brief awareness of a large bee as it entered his open mouth and the pain of the sting as it penetrated the soft tissue inside his lower lip.

A moment of panic followed in which he felt himself falling and he knew he'd swallowed the insect. Hacking, coughing, he stumbled blindly back through the olive trees, toward the cave and the Franciscan monk.

22

Ice is what we need now. Ice for you to suck." Sharon, in charge, conjuring the Jewish mother from deep within herself. She'd applied a weak solution of soda to the inside of Tom's hugely swollen lip and was now clattering a tray of ice-cubes into a glass. She became worried when Tom complained that his throat was swelling. "Suck the ice on the other side of your mouth so's not to wash away the soda."

"The shoda ish awful," Tom said. He was finding it difficult to pronounce certain words. His face, still inflating, was beginning to take the shape of a Hallowe'en pumpkin.

"Just leave it there!" Sharon threw up her hands. "A bee sting in the mouth, imagine!" Any minute, Tom thought, and she's going to say *oy vey*.

The moment Tom had returned from the Garden of Gethsemane Sharon had swung into action. She pressed another large ice-cube into his mouth. "Imagine if that monk hadn't been there! How did the thing get into your mouth? I mean, did you encourage it? I don't mean that: I mean I never heard of it before. You say the monk hooked the sting out of your mouth? With his fingernail? God, I hope his hands were clean! Think of the infections! What kind of monk was he?"

"Franshishcan."

"Franciscan? Are they hygienic people? Here, suck another piece of ice."

Tom had sought help from the monk immediately after the bee stung. The monk had tugged at Tom's lip, looking for the sting remnant, a sensible policy, to try to remove the poison sac before it released more acid. But he had difficulty finding the thing. When he finally claimed to have removed it, Tom was certain he was only exercising a little psychology.

Because Tom knew that what had stung him was a bee, and yet it was not a bee.

"What happened to the creature?" Sharon wanted to know, feeling his brow for a high temperature.

"I think I shwallowed it."

"Swallowed it! You mean it's inside you? Oh, God, I hope it's dead."

"Of course it'sh dead. Anyway I'm not sure."

On trying to spit it out, he'd felt himself swallow the bee. He'd felt a vibration in his throat. It seemed absurd, yet there it was.

"Do you want to lie down?"

"No. I jusht want to shit here and feel misherable."

He couldn't tell Sharon what had really happened. How could he? How could he tell her he'd encountered his phantom again in the Garden of Gethsemane, and that she'd kissed him before metamorphosing into a bee?

Tom spent the night in extreme discomfort. He dozed fitfully, dreaming feverishly. His dreams swung wildly from school to Jerusalem. He heard the voices of schoolchildren and his former headteacher saying, *If it's the mere matter;* and he heard the voice of the phantom woman talking in dead languages and snatches of English, drifting in and out like a frequency signal on a short-wave radio. The voice went on relentlessly, just out of range, urgent, trying to recount to him some fantastic story, confused and broken. The name of Jesus was invoked and muddled details of a bungled crucifixion; the name Magdalene was repeated over and over, the tongue trilling and ululating on exotic verbs and phrases which themselves fluttered from her vibrating tongue like insects and chimeras and mutant birds which didn't want to die . . .

In the dead of night, as he lay awake and staring into the dark, an unknown hand knocked on the door of the apartment. His blood froze. His mouth dried. His tongue stuck to the roof of his mouth. There was a ringing in his ears.

So you're back. You followed me here. As I knew you would.

He strained to hear if Sharon in the next room was disturbed by the knocking, but she slept on. His clock told him that it was 3 A.M. For over an hour he lay like a corpse, waiting for the soft, intermittent knock on the door. He repeated the words of the psalm the monk had told him: *My soul waiteth for the Lord more than they that watch for the morning: I say, more than they that watch for the morning.*

When his clock indicated 4:15, he knew he would be left alone. His eyes were sore, stinging with repressed tears. Finally he fell asleep.

By morning the swelling of his mouth was beginning to subside, but the voices in his head carried over from his dreams. The dream voices somehow persisted, but they were muffled, as if trying to communicate from behind steel doors.

Sharon fixed him a fruit breakfast through a liquidizer. He drank with a straw. Breakfast was conducted in silence. Sharon hadn't resurrected the issue of Katie, of his resignation, but the matter was always there between them, like unwanted concert tickets pinned to a wall.

She fed bananas into the liquidizer and flicked a switch. "I had an affair," Tom said suddenly, above the gargle of the liquidizer. "Before Katie died. That's all, really."

Sharon switched the machine off and sat down. Her eyes were like new coins. She waited for more, but when nothing came she got up and switched the liquidizer on again.

"That's all," said Tom. "There's nothing more to it."

Sharon switched the appliance off. "Shall we have this on or off?" she asked pointedly.

"Off. It was someone from school."

"Another teacher? A colleague? And you feel guilty about it. You feel bad because Katie died while you were being unfaithful."

"Worse than that. I feel bad because I didn't feel guilty. Because with this other person it felt so good."

"You feel bad because it felt so good?"

"The sex. I went crazy for a while. I got hooked on the illicitness of it. I mean the sin."

"That, eh? I'm afraid you're out of my domain when you talk about sin. I've never been able to associate sex with sin."

"Sin has a special taste and smell."

"How does it taste and smell?"

"Honey and fire while you're fucking."

"Careful, Tom. Make sex precious and you make it dangerous."

"Isn't that how it should be?"

"No, I don't think so."

"I know how all of this must sound to you."

"No, you don't."

"Yes, I do. You see it all cynically. You think: *Stupid Tom, lost his head over an ordinary affair, then his wife died and he couldn't deal with it.* But how can I tell you anything about how much it hurt? And how stupid and ugly it made me feel . . . ? And, oh, God, my mouth still hurts!"

"Want some more ice?"

"No. My teeth are tingling from the fucking ice-cubes. It's women, Sharon. They're different from men."

"You finally figured that out."

Tom wasn't in a mood to be mocked. The candor of Sharon's sexuality confused his notions of where exactly that difference lay. Concerning male sexuality, he knew it to be only poorly hidden and permanently breaking the surface. Female sexuality was more recessed, in the shadows, better camouflaged, even if the difference was only slight, and even if women like Sharon occasionally contradicted that perception. But he knew from his own somewhat limited experience that women, once their ardor had been awoken, were the more demanding of the sexes. Men, accustomed to living just under the surface of the lake, broke water only to dip back happily under the waves until the next time. Women, however, brought to the mouth of the sea cave, stood there and roared.

Tom sucked air through his straw, making bubbling noises at the bottom of his empty glass. "You wouldn't understand," he said.

Sharon gave him a look as old as time.

23

The sun settled on the pavilion in the park, dropping slowly, already half-obscured, like a burnished dome in some fabled and exotic city. Shadows of late summer spilled across lush grass. The smell of autumn was already in the air, a whiff of damp, green leaves hankering after gold. Katie and Michael Anthony strolled through the avenue of ornamental trees. They stopped at some rose bushes by the children's playground.

"Blown roses," said Michael. "Omar Khayyám. You see it everywhere when your time is up."

"Can I link arms with you?" asked Katie. She did, and they moved on.

"Now that's a thing I didn't dare ask. Linking arms. My God. You know, I don't want to bungee jump, or drive a fast car round a race track, or parachute from an aeroplane. It's not those things. It's the small things. I want to sit with the sun on my face; take a beer with a friend; link arms with a woman on a beautiful afternoon in the park. I'm grateful. And I thank your husband."

"He's a good man."

"Where is he now?"

"He had to meet someone."

"Who?"

"He didn't say who or where. We've not been communicating well lately."

"Oh, you must! I should have married. I made a terrible mistake becoming a priest. I feel like all this time I've worked against my preference, and maybe that's what caused these cells to riot inside me. Who knows? But I know I should have married."

"It's not all beer and skittles, Michael. Shall we sit here?" They sat on a bench, with the sun on their faces, Katie's arm still linked in his. "Is that why you left the priesthood? To give marriage a late try?"

"No, no. It's too late for me. I've blown it. It was the fairy tales I couldn't stand anymore. Fucking virgin births—excuse me, I've just learned to enjoy swearing—and other sodding fucking children's stories."

"You don't believe those things then?"

"Believe? Look, Jesus was married. He was a rabbi, and they married. But the early Churchmen cut it all out when they edited the Bible. Jesus loved women, but we're not allowed to."

"What?"

"Oh, he loved women! In the Apocrypha there are accounts of him angering his followers by kissing his wife in public. Snogging, yes—they don't want that, do they? Not with that Magdalene tart, God love her. And why do you think he waited until his disciples were away before approaching the Samaritan prostitute at the well? See for yourself. Every time there's a woman at a well in the Bible, it means procreation. Fertility. Sex. It's a pattern. But it's all denied."

"Radical ideas," said Katie.

"Radical?" He laughed bitterly. "It's old hat. But as a priest you have to work hard to keep scholarship from coming into it."

"So whom did he marry? Jesus, I mean."

"Are you humoring me?"

"No."

"Mary Magdalene is my best guess. She was a temple-priestess out of the Canaanite tradition, regarded as a prostitute by the Jews. Jesus converted her, and he married her. It's in John, chapter two, but you've got to fill in the edited bits. Mary Magdalene was with him all the time. Remember the scene where she's outside the tomb, after he's resurrected, and she fails to recognize him? That's because it wasn't him. The Church wanted her to 'recognize' his brother James in order that he could lead the Church, and she refused. Puzzled? It gets better. Jesus' Church was hijacked by that psychopath Paul. But you'd be best to ignore it. Stick with the fairy tales."

"No wonder you stopped believing in God."

"Oh, no!" He touched her arm. "I never lost my belief. Never for a second, in Jesus or in God. I just stopped believing in all the fucking silly stories that go with it. Did I tell you how I love swearing?"

24

Sharon had promised to drive
Tom to the archaeological sites of Qumran and Masada by the Dead
Sea. Six bottles of mineral water lay on the back seat of the car. "Hot
up there," she said.

They drove through the desert with windows open to the hot,
humid air. Smells of warm dust and roadside sage wafted into the
car. Tom blinked at the soft-shouldered mountains, mauve and
hazy in the distance beneath the blue sky.

At Masada they got out of the car and Sharon pointed to the
summit. A serpentine path climbed to the top of the sphinx-like
rock, or there was a cable car. He surveyed the astonishing spiral
path. Two backpackers were making slow progress along an edge,
like two beetles, carapaces winking in the sun. It was already hot
and getting hotter. Behind them the arid desert plain, wind-
sculpted into weird pyramids and cones of sand, shimmered like
lime. A bubble of sweat formed on his brow. "I hope we're going
by cable car," he said.

"The more difficult route offers the best experience," she said,
sibyl-like. "We'll need the water."

She put three bottles in the rucksack, and they began to climb.

She set a steady pace. After they'd gone a little way, he decided to
tell her how he'd come to be stung. She stopped and took off her
sunglasses. She was breathing hard.

"You're still hallucinating? Is that what you're saying?"

"She's as real as you are. When she comes." He'd decided he
wasn't going to pretend or disguise or apologize for the truth. They
started to walk again. "Ever since I arrived in Jerusalem, I've had
this buzzing in the back of my mind. Like a bee, now I come to
think about it. Then at some point it changed into a murmuring.
And now it's become a monologue building up in my head. Always
just before I fall asleep."

"What does it say?"

"It changes. It's trying to tell me the Crucifixion story. But it's
all different. Mixed up. All the events are jumbled."

They'd been walking for about twenty minutes and were a third
of the way up the path. He took out a bottle of water and handed
it to her. They both drank greedily.

"I know what you're thinking."

"I wish you wouldn't keep saying that."

"Yes, I do. You're fitting it all into your psychologist's textbook. Your counseling program. I want to hear it."

"I won't insult you with it."

"Just *tell me* what you're thinking!" he said, his anger startling
her. "Just tell me straight! And take off your sunglasses. I want to
look you in the eye."

"All right. Ever heard of Jerusalem Syndrome?"

"Never."

She sat down on a rock. "Seems to me," she said, "that when
Katie died it caused a crisis for you. There's this affair, and a lot of
guilt around it, enough to make you give up your job and come here.
Why here? Well, I'm here, and that's convenient. But also because
at the center of your difficulty over this terrible loss is your faith,
your Christianity, which is connected with your guilt. The things
that happened back in England jolted your faith, and in a way you
came here to find it again. But it's not that easy. You don't find it
in old bricks and stones: it runs much deeper than that."

"Go on."

"You start having visions: a woman appears, trying to give you messages. Not so unusual in Jerusalem, believe me. Tourists of all faiths come here and sometimes, when their expectations aren't met, they start projecting visions. Or burning down mosques. Or shooting at people. The Tourist Police and the psychiatric units call this Jerusalem Syndrome. I've encountered at least three cases in my current work.

"This hallucination, this voice: she's actually a part of yourself, projected on to the big silver screen of Jerusalem. Oh, she wants to give you messages all right. You've got that bit right. Important messages, too. But they are messages from yourself to yourself. From the dark of your unconscious mind. *Up from the depths.* These messages are dangerous and have to be taken very seriously. They concern a part of yourself which you block and repress; and unless you integrate these two competing parts of yourself, your personality is in danger of fragmenting.

"When I say fragmenting, I mean that the classic symptoms of this kind of neurosis, which can even lead to schizophrenia, are the delusional systems you've described to me: hallucinating people and hearing voices." She put her sunglasses back on. "You asked me, so that's it, in a nutshell."

"I suppose I should be grateful for your honesty," Tom said quietly.

"Well, it was a bit clinical, but I've never been other than honest with you, have I? And, anyway, I should add that this is not necessarily what I believe anymore. Only what I've been trained to see. Maybe it's all rationalizing. Maybe Ahmed is just as right with his *djinn.*"

Tom took a grim swig from a bottle of water. Sharon offered a hand to pull him to his feet. "Ready to go higher?"

He was quiet for a while as they pressed on, pondering over Sharon's textbook analysis. At the flat top of the sphinx-like rock they stood at the fortress site of the mass suicide, looking back, breathing hard. A haze had settled over the sulfurous, sterile waters of the Dead Sea. The arid landscape crouched upon the water like a scorpion on its prey.

"Here's why I brought the third bottle," said Sharon, emptying it over her head.

Tom laughed, snatching the bottle and drenching himself. They went inside the ruins of the fortress. He'd expected resonances, ghosts of the mass suicide, screams against the Romans, the shadow of the end of militant Judaism, but there was only a vacuum.

They made their descent by cable car.

Sharon photographed Tom's Dead Sea Experience. He'd brought along a newspaper for the obligatory floating-read shot. The dead water was slimy; vapors from the minerals irritated his eyes. He drifted on his back, eyes closed.

As he relaxed a vision of the veiled woman in the garden rushed at him, like a shark in the null water. He scrambled to his feet.

"What is it?" Sharon laughed.

"Nothing. I'm getting out."

Sharon led him to the mud pools. She slapped curative mud on his face and body, and within moments she had him slaked in black mud. Under the pulsing yellow sun it quickly dried to a hard, gray crust. He wasn't Tom anymore. He was a twilight man, something primal, the *golem*.

He slapped a return pile of oozing mud on her belly, smearing it across her stomach. She went very quiet. He felt her calming in his hands. He massaged it into her face and neck and then he smeared her legs.

"Turn over," he said quietly and heaped piles of chocolate mud on her back, smoothing it across the backs of her thighs. He felt like a potter.

"Let me do your back," she said.

The pressure of her fingertips radiated to his bones, and he flushed hot beneath the layer of silky mud. She smiled through her mud face, the whites of her eyes and her white teeth flashing. When she swung a leg across him, gently lowering herself on to his bottom, he stiffened slightly, then relaxed. He was becoming erect behind the mud. He wanted to hide it.

They sat on the beach; the drying mud changing from choco-late to an ash-gray hue. It contracted as it dried, tightening across their skins. For Tom it was like the feeling of a penis engorging with blood. He wished he'd taken off his swimming trunks. He wanted to get closer to the mud.

There were showers on the beach. Each watched the other wash, carefully and in silence. It was a mysterious, primitive ritual. He felt clean and renewed and revitalized, as if he'd pulled on a new skin. Some used, shadowy version of himself had been discarded on that beach, like an empty wet suit, to be drawn back down under the mud pool.

In the afternoon they visited the archaeology at Qumran, but lassitude had taken them over. He felt vague, floating.

"For years they thought this place was a scriptorium for the Es-senes, somewhere to write all those Dead Sea Scrolls. All because they found one inkwell. They thought all these cisterns were for rit-ual washing. Now they've discovered this was a site for the perfume industry, with the money going to arm the Zealots who died up there. It was a factory for making expensive balsam."

When she said the word "balsam," Tom got a rich and heady whiff of that scent. It was a momentary but intense sensation. Then it was gone. He looked over the archaeological remains. Heat rip-pled from the ground. There was only the aridity of the excavated stones, and a scorching silence, and the smell of warm dust.

"What is it?" Sharon asked.

"She was here."

Sharon touched his arm. "Come on. Let's go."

They arrived back in Jerusalem, exhausted. Sharon made coffee, but they didn't drink it. She kicked off her shoes and started to fall asleep on the sofa. He joined her. When he awoke, the room was in darkness, and she was gone. She returned swathed in a towel robe, having showered, climbed back on the sofa and took his face in her hands. She kissed him.

"Don't, unless you mean it," he said.

"I mean it."

He opened her bathrobe and slipped it from her shoulders. Her nipples were dark buds. He pressed his lips to them. She put her hand inside his shorts. His erection grew to her touch. She weighed it in her long, slim fingers. Her breath was as hot as the desert, and the musk of her was like a rare spice from the market streets.

He went to kiss her belly, but she stopped him and said, "It's my period. I'm bleeding."

"It's all right," he told her. "You don't have to take a ritual bath for me."

"It's not you, it's I who hold back."

"It's only healthy blood. Life blood. Those twisted old prophets want you to hate yourself because you're a woman." He leaned across her and put his tongue inside her mouth. Her eyes were like black lakes in the darkness of the room. He put a finger deep inside her, withdrew it and put it to his lips. The smell of her sex flowered in the room. He could smell her sex on his hand, saline, mineral, like the salts and the silts of the Dead Sea. "All day I've been falling in love with you."

"I know."

She copied him, inserting a finger into her vagina, and she anointed his penis with the blood, drawing a ring of blood around the glans with her fingernail. He kissed her again, and she lay back, opening to him. He slipped easily inside her, and her heat rolled over him like a ball of fire. His mind flashed across the heights of Masada; lightning forked over the dry plains and over the Dead Sea. She'd told him it was the deepest place on Earth. When he ejaculated inside her he felt he was falling into the deepest place on Earth.

Afterwards she switched on a lamp. His cock lay on his thigh like a helmeted soldier shot in the woods. Her blood was already drying on him, flaking, rust-colored. She leaned over to inspect it, as if the blood had deposited runes or readable prophecies.

"What are you doing?"

"Reading the future."

"I've had my tealeaves read, but this is new."

"What's this? Look, it's like a Hebrew letter."

He looked. It was a: ב.

"It's a *bet*," she said. "The Bible starts with this letter."

"Come here," he said. "Come here."

25

He's a really lovely man," Katie said, "a really lovely man. I'm so glad I agreed to meet him."

"What did you talk about?" said Tom.

"The Bible. He hates Paul and loves Mary. He spent the entire afternoon unpicking the Bible for me. He didn't particularly want to, but I encouraged him."

"He didn't need much encouragement. He was mouthing off about it when we first met him. Will you see him again?"

"No. I offered to, but he refused. He said if we met again, he'd fall in love with me, and that would be torture for him. He said he'd be eternally happy with his one afternoon in the park."

"What about you? Would you fall in love with him?"

"No. I made my choice a while ago. I mean to stick by it."

Tom sniffed. It enraged her. She leapt up and crashed a fist into his chest. "Do you know what it means to me, our marriage?" she cried. "Do you know what it represents to me? Do you know how I feel when I think we're losing it? Do you know how it makes me feel? Do you know that I can't breathe? I can't breathe, I can't breathe, I can't breathe!"

26

Well, you let it happen again. Sharon driving to work that morning wondering, as always, whether she'd done the right thing. Since Tom's arrival in Jerusalem she'd been imploring herself to avoid this extra complication. Her emotional life proceeded from one wreckage to another. She attached herself to the walking wounded. She was drawn to them. She worked with them. She fell in love with them. And even when she wasn't *exactly* in love with them, as in Tom's case, she still sometimes ended up sleeping with them.

"You're gonna have to stop sleeping with men just because you feel sorry for 'em," she announced to herself. Then she snapped on the car radio to blot out her own censure.

And he was a wreckage, old Tom. Tight as a drum and, as far as she could tell, hallucinating and suffering more delusions than some of the alcoholics and junkies she was paid to help. But they had a long friendship, she and he, a rare friendship of the type that common wisdom said couldn't exist between a man and a woman. Plus she felt she owed something to the memory of Katie; and Katie would have in the end approved of what happened last night.

Sharon knew, from her counseling experience, that she could help Tom. She wasn't entirely sure whether his problem was an inability to come to terms with Katie's death, or if it was some incident at school, or a combination of the two. Whatever it was, she could help him. She had two options, both effective in limited ways. Either she could spend hours and hours of careful, sensitive counseling, helping him face his difficulties, rebuilding his confidence, relighting the lamp for him, comforting him and showing life in a positive light. Or she could achieve the same results, short-circuiting all the talk, by fucking him.

So what if she'd chosen the latter? Life is short, hey?

That's what Katie always used to say: *This fleeting life. I love this fleeting life.* It was her motto, her slogan. And her epitaph. Almost as if she'd known.

Had she known? Or was Katie just guessing that night?

Before Sharon had left England for Israel, she'd been passing through town, so she paid Tom and Katie a surprise visit. She'd arrived at the door bearing a bottle of Frascati. At the exact moment she'd touched a finger to the doorbell, Tom had opened the door. He was carrying a long, slim leather case.

"What's that?"

"It's a snooker cue. Tuesday is snooker night," said Tom, "with the boys."

"He can cancel," Katie had said, coming up behind him, kissing Sharon and relieving her of the bottle.

"That's right. I can cancel."

"No, you boys go and stroke your green baize. I'll stay in with Katie. All right if I stay the night? See you later, Tom."

The two women had spent the night gossiping and cackling. Katie always made Sharon laugh. When they'd emptied the wine, they went out to get another bottle from an Asian corner shop and decided to choose a video on offer at the same store.

Katie had pointed at the soft-porn section. "Tom's taken to renting these," she said sadly. "Just occasionally. He thinks I don't know."

Sharon pulled out one called *Inexhaustible*. "We'll rent it. See what turns him on."

So they'd gone back, drunk some more wine and smoked some grass Sharon produced from a little plastic sachet. Tom generally frowned on but tolerated the dope, so Katie had only these rare opportunities to indulge an old student habit. After a while they'd set up the video and spent the next hour howling at the Martian script and Wendy-house acting. Eventually Sharon switched off.

"Perhaps that's what he needs," Katie had said. "Three in a bed."

"Are you inviting?" Sharon was joking, but she sensed a strange mood in Katie.

"No," said Katie. "I couldn't ever share him. Not even with you, lovely Sharon, not even with you."

"Will you think that when he's old and gray?"

"I won't be around."

"What do you mean, you won't be around?"

"I'll never make forty. It's just something I've always known. I'll never make it past forty."

"Come off it!" Sharon had said. But she looked at Katie sucking on the remnants of a joint and saw that her friend was serious.

"I've been told."

"Told? You mean a doctor told you?"

"No. Not a doctor. There was a man. He just stepped out from behind a car and tried to hold my hand. Then he was gone. Then I saw him again. Have you ever realized that some of the ordinary people you encounter on the streets are not people at all—that they're some kind of spirits?"

"You're spooking me, Katie."

"I'm sorry. Forget I said it. Please don't say anything to Tom."

Katie wouldn't be drawn any further on the matter, tried to laugh it off. Something, though, must have happened to make them laugh again, because when Tom arrived home, he walked in to find them cackling and incomprehensible. They were both high as astronauts, and, unable to get any sense out of them, he went off to bed, leaving them to it.

It was the last time she saw Katie.

* * *

Now she had shared Tom, in a way it hadn't then been possible to predict. And she felt certain that if Katie had seen Tom, and the condition he was in, she would have forgiven Sharon and even approved.

Sharon glanced up at the city wall as she drove up the Hativat from Mount Zion, seeing three soldiers silhouetted against the blue sky, Uzis slung low. Sometimes it seemed you were driving round the rim of a bubbling volcano, always expecting it to spit fire or spout molten rock. Vast boulders were blasted out of its deepest core until, cooling, they changed and smoked and hardened into religions; or they cracked and burst open prematurely, expressing themselves as random acts of violence. It was a heat. She experienced this nucleus of cities as a kind of heat. Jerusalem. I've been living in this city too long.

As she turned up Yafo Street under the elaborate Jaffa Gate, the cool jazz music playing on her car radio experienced some interference, the frequency drifting in and out. A charge of noisy static obliterated the channel. She reached for the dial to retune, finding nothing on the wavelength. As she glanced up through the windscreen, the sky before her suddenly creased and buckled as if under terrifying weight. The sky collapsed in on itself. She gasped and stepped on her brakes, the car's wheels locking, squealing on the hot, dry road. The car juddered to a halt at an angle to the causeway. The static on the radio discharged itself, and a clear female voice filled the airwaves; *I can't breathe, I can't breathe, I can't breathe, I can't breathe . . .*

The voice faded out, to be replaced by a static burst again, and then the cool saxophone came back. Sharon looked up. The sky had straightened out again. Angry car horns sounded behind her.

"You look like shit," said Tobie as Sharon swung into the Bet Ha-Kerem reception. Tobie had a pad of cleaning cloth in one hand and a plastic bottle with spray-nozzle in the other. Even though Tobie ran the rehabilitation center, she cleaned the windows, changed the light bulbs and carried a set of screwdrivers in her handbag. She was the seventy-year-old founder of the center, a Freudian psychologist and a friend when she wasn't being either manager or janitor. "And you should have been here half an hour ago."

"Had a crisis," Sharon said, logging in.

Tobie lifted her bottle of detergent in the air. "It's not for me, darling. Have your crisis. Have your half-hour. Only there was your old friend Christina came back in this morning, and she's on a White Cloud and calling your name, so it never stops. Can I speak with her? Some chance."

When Tobie said White Cloud, she meant seriously fucked up. Christina was a former client—patients were referred to as clients at the Bet Ha-Kerem center—who had formed a particular attachment to Sharon. "What time did she come in? How was she?"

"How was she? She just walked up to the door when the sun was rising, and she was naked, darling, naked." Tobie pronounced the word *nekked.*

"I'll go straight through."

"Go easy: White Cloud. Don't forget staff council in an hour."

Sharon stepped into what they called the White Cloud Room. You had to take your shoes off at the door. It was a room reserved for serious counseling, carpeted, sound-proofed, all furniture padded. It was a room for shouting, screaming and weeping. They didn't need to use it very often, since rehabilitation for most of the alcoholic and addicted women was a long, undramatic slog in the exercise of ordinary living. But occasionally one of the clients went White Cloud.

Christina was on the floor, huddled in a white bathrobe supplied by the center. Her long, dark hair fell across her face. Sharon could see the swollen pink pouches around her eyes through the strands of her hair. She crossed the room and quietly sat down next to her.

"Hi, sister," she said softly.

No answer. She stroked the woman's hair from her eyes.

"What are you doing, coming here naked?" she said evenly. "What's the idea of that?"

"I'm not your fucking sister," said Christina, looking away.

"Please yourself."

"Where were you? Where were you when I came here?"

"I don't live here, Christina. I'm not here all the time. I have a life of my own, you know."

Christina had first come to the center after a drugs conviction. A one-time heroin addict, she'd been weaned on to methadone but hadn't been able to make progress from the methadone. At the center she'd become fond of Sharon, and a breakthrough was made, only for her to return to the center hooked on barbiturates. Another breakthrough after careful nurturing from Sharon only saw her return, this time with an alcohol problem. Each "cure" was only a displacement from one dependency to another. There was a hole in Christina raging to be filled. Finally, after scrupulous counseling and painstaking attention to routines and a disciplined timetable, Christina had declared herself clean, whole and fulfilled. She'd found religion.

On the day Christina had told them all the good news, Sharon remembered looking at Tobie, whose face reflected her own sense of dismay contorted by the need to seem positive.

"That's wonderful, darling. What kind of religion?"

"Adventist," Christina had said.

Sharon had bit her lip. Tobie, wiser and more resilient, had summoned a kiss for her. They had helped her pack and watched her leave the center after a small party for staff and the other resident women.

"Three months," Sharon had whispered as Christina lugged her bag through the door.

"Less," Tobie had added. "Less."

And Tobie had been right, by two weeks. Here they were, ready to start all over again. "Christina, are you going to tell me what made you come back here?"

'Sha-na-na-na-na, sha-na-na-na." It was Christina's trick, to hum pop tunes. A lightweight shield, often impossible to penetrate. Sharon sighed. She'd been here before more than once, right back at the beginning.

"I haven't got time for this. Sorry. It's boring me these days."

"Sha-na-na-na, SHA-NA-NA, na-na-na."

"Get stuffed, Christina."

"Sha-na-na-na. Wanna know how they did it? How they did it? Did it? Didit-didit. Dit-dit-dit-didit."

"Did what? Who did what? Look, I've got to go to a meeting."

Christina smiled, eyes closed, shaking her head to her own tune. "Didit-didit. Did it. Did-did-did-didit." Her expression changed suddenly to a snarl. "Broke his fucking legs! They BROKE HIS FUCKING LEGS!" Then she was smiling again, humming her beaty tune. "Didit, did-did-did-did-didit."

"Who broke whose legs?"

"That's how they did it. Where were you? I came here and you weren't here. I was looking for you, Sharon. You let me fall. You said jump and I'll catch you. But you let me fall."

Sharon vented an enormous sigh. She'd experienced this many times before, and not just with Christina, but each time the knot seemed just impossible to unpick. Sometimes she was exhausted with it. Sometimes she wanted to say to the Christinas, *Hey, go and rot. I do my best for you and every time back you come, sometimes worse than before. There are some I can help and some like you I can't help; why should I waste my time on the hopeless cases?*

Then she softened and stroked Christina's hair from her eyes again. "I don't know where you are, baby. But you're a long way away."

Then Christina blew her nose and shuffled closer to Sharon, laying her head on her shoulder. Sharon put a protective arm around the woman, as Christina began to weep softly.

27

I can't breathe, I can't breathe, I can't breathe. I can't breathe because HE can't breathe."

28

Why do it? Why do this work for no money? Oh, let's have a look. A lucky, lucky look. Damned scrolls. All the scribes were liars. Scribes and writers and editors and copyists and pen-pushing, quill-dipping scriptorium scrotum-scribblers. Let's have a look.

Ahmed was a tidy scholar. He pinned out the scroll-cloth on his spotless work desk, placing spectacles case, pens, pin-sharp pencils and writing implements around it like cutlery laid for a banquet. His work desk was an island in the *djinn*-and-hashish inspired vortex of his life. It was an altar, a place of sacrament, a refuge.

He picked up a large magnifying glass and peered first at the back of his hand to see if it had stopped shaking after another bad night wrestling with the *djinn*. There was a discernible tremor. The magnified image of his left hand revolted him. His nails were cracked and bitten, with a possible greenish tint, and the tips of his fingers were stained the color of polished oak from the nicotine. His knuckles were swollen and red, as if he'd been in a fist-fight, and the dark hairs on the back of his hand quivered in indignation at this examination. Was it possible, he considered, to become a *djinn* one-self in the process of a lifetime? He let his hand drop at the thought, and his attention turned back to the scroll fragments pinned out before him.

Stinking scroll, and for no money. Why am I doing this, if not because I dream about a night spent wandering the desert thighs of that glorious Jewish slut, for whom I would gladly die, for whom I would cheerfully fling myself from the heights of Masada in the hope of a perfumed kiss on the way down? Slut! Bitch! Whore! God, I would love you for eternity, and instead you bring me Englishmen with fragments of rotting scroll to translate! Pieces in spiral form disappearing into a dark shaft like a woman's hole, a cervix with no meaning. Sharon, do you realize, do you understand, that if only I had you in my bed, then, then, the *djinn* might *leave me alone!* This is hopeless. I need something to smoke before I can look at this.

Ahmed got up from his desk and with miraculous speed crafted two elegant reefers, one of which he lit. The other he laid alongside his writing implements, like a specialist tool. Exhaling a great plume of blue smoke through his nostrils, he sat once again at his desk.

Fumbling with his tortoiseshell-framed spectacles, he began to make a cursory study of the outer tail of the spiral. After two minutes, his heart sank.

"Genealogies! Fuck! Fuck! Why do I do this, if not for some futile dream of spreading your legs across the magic carpet? Hateful and consummately beautiful mother of all sluts!"

Ahmed had some experience of scrolls, both copies and original fragments: enough to know that most of them yielded nothing of interest. Many contained obsessively detailed instructions on how the temple should be rebuilt, or tiresome family trees beginning and ending with historical nonentities. The spiral scroll before him appeared to be of the latter type.

The Arab scholar also had some knowledge of paleography and the system of dating manuscripts by the shapes of the letters they contain. Hebrew script changed somewhat between the earliest scrolls and the latest, and the one before him was clearly a later scroll, written, or at least copied, around the Herodian period. It could have been one of the last documents that came out of Qumran before the siege of Masada, or it could simply have been a copy of a much older document.

Ahmed picked up his magnifying glass and squinted at the collision of Hebrew letters at the very center of the spiral. Here the writing was almost indecipherable and the lettering impossibly small. Ahmed put down his magnifying glass in disgust.

"Sharon," he said. "Oh, Rose of Sharon. I am sick of love."

29

Stopped. The voice in his head had stopped. The unruly narrative. It had suddenly stopped with the words *I can't breathe*. What had happened to make it stop?

He'd been dreaming. A nightmare in which he couldn't breathe. Some terrible weight had settled on his chest in the night. As he struggled to surface from his sleep, he realized it was not he who was unable to breathe. It was the voice.

The voice, the tongue, the presence, the haunting; the thing that had spread its wings about him since his arrival in Jerusalem. Every day, a whispering at the back of his mind. Not constant, but always waiting, always ready to pick up where it had left off, speaking to him out of nowhere. Now, as mysteriously as it had appeared, it had gone. One minute it had been there, like a subaudial humming from a defective hi-fi, and then it had been switched off.

He hadn't meant this thing to happen with Sharon. That wasn't why he'd come to Jerusalem. It couldn't go anywhere. He felt vaguely guilty, unable to guess at Sharon's expectations. He hoped he wasn't going to have to disappoint her. And there was Katie. Ridiculous as it seemed, he had in his head a picture of Katie observing them from a high place, watching them make love, coldly

scrutinizing his performance. Had he been the one who'd died, he
wondered, would he have preferred Katie to take comfort in the
arms of a close friend or a stranger? The answer, of course, would
have been: whichever one was sincere.

Sharon had gone to work, but the sharp odor of her was all over
him. The smell of her sex had drenched him. The intoxicating scent
of her cunt was on his fingers.

What was it people were after with sex? The answer wasn't as
obvious as it seemed. There were things beyond what the professional could offer: a prostitute can only take care of the need to
sneeze. Then comes the yearning, the voracious hunger for the in-
timate moment of transcendence in another's arms. That was exclusively, and would always remain exclusively, in the gift of one
person to another. It could be given or withheld; it might even be
simulated, but it could never be bought.

It was natural magic, a human miracle. It was the thing religion
had always tried to replicate and sustain, and the point at which religion had always failed. All religions. Everywhere.

The great Semitic religions had tried to replace it by defining the
thing it could never imitate as sinful and corrupting; they had sought
to regulate it by moral censure; they had tried to suppress it by
spelling out the destructive energies of its frightening magic.

It was simple: sex was diabolic in its origins, and, since men were
defining the terms, women made an easy shape for demons to
squat in.

Tom knew all about those demons and how they worked. He
sniffed at his hands, tingling at Sharon's marine odors still on his
fingers. Memories winged in on that smell, like angels, like demons.

At the school, after reprimanding the youth who'd scrawled obscenities on the blackboard, Tom began to notice the girl who'd
been the cause of the boy's jealousies. He saw how she watched his
every move, absorbed his every word, blushed when spoken to,
cringed at even the tiniest reproach.

At fifteen she was as pretty as a silk flower, down to the last eye-
lash. Her copper hair winked under the classroom lights, and her
complexion had a delicate undershine, like the gloss on an apple. He
could see how the boy might be crazy for her; why shouldn't he

be? She always sat at the front, under Tom's nose, wearing a starched white blouse through which he could see the outline of her young breasts. Over her left breast, the bleeding rose of her school-blazer badge. He remembered being momentarily distracted by the breast badge; whatever it was he was saying to the class, he missed a beat.

She noticed. She smiled at him; a minor triumph for her. He didn't return the smile.

Girls at this age had mysterious allure. No wonder mature women hated men who preyed on young girls, and there were plenty of men who did. But even after the first eighteen years that extraordinary bloom, that gloss, began to dry. Society, projecting a woman's sexually active years into psychological maturity, was at odds with nature, which scheduled her prime reproductive years in her schoolgirl period. How it must shadow women, Tom thought, much more than men. He knew it concerned Katie, with her jars of cosmetics and creams and her regimes; yet he'd always tried to convince her that it really didn't matter, that they'd gone beyond all that. He was sure he wasn't lying. He was positive he wasn't lying.

He eyed the young girl's legs as she tripped out of the classroom with the other students. Some of these girls attired in dull school uniforms were sirens. Provocative, short skirts. Black tights hissing in the corridors. Shoes shined to a wink. Flattering heels, high as they could get away with. Painted fingernails. Stretched necks. Bud-like breasts. Hearts beating beneath the starched white cotton and the bleeding rose. And under all of it was the fragrance of probable virginity, filling the air with wild pheromones, like poppy seed.

Mysterious allure? There was nothing mysterious about it.

Stop it, Tom had said to himself after the classroom had emptied. *Just stop it.* Every male teacher was torched by schoolgirl fantasies, and you either indulged them or you checked them. It was as simple as that. You checked them. These girls were only fourteen or fifteen years old. Fantasies of that order were distasteful, corrupt and predatory.

And impossible to stop.

30

The tape-recorded second call to prayer of the day vibrated across the baked rooftops as Tom walked through the narrow streets of the Muslim quarter. The streets smelled of rotting fruit, spices, warm dust. Early shadows were like moist ectoplasm leaking from walls and doorways. He had no difficulty remembering the place. He'd not told Sharon he was coming here.

He rang the bell and waited. Remembering, he rang a second, third and fourth time, whereupon a face and a tousled black head of hair appeared above him. A pair of blood-shot eyes peered down without recognition. Then a bunch of keys hit the dust at his feet, and the head retreated.

Inside the building the door at the top of the stone stairway stood open. He hesitated on the threshold.

"Welcome," Ahmed said, somewhat vaguely. The Arab scratched his head uncertainly. He wore a white cotton robe, and his feet were bare. "Sit, while I make some tea."

Tom squatted on a floor cushion and spent twenty minutes looking at wall-hangings. Ahmed seemed to have forgotten him. Finally he reappeared with a tray of mint tea and small pastries.

"You must forgive my appearance and my lack of orientation," he said, "but last night I had one of my worst fights with the *djinn*. The city is disturbed. They were in an appalling mood, and I was unable to conciliate them at all. I got barely a moment's sleep."

Tom felt less than equipped to deal with these remarks, offered as they were with yawns and dismissive gestures. Ahmed alluded to his demons as one might refer to the oppressiveness of the weather; yet he did indeed look like a man who had spent the night grappling—physically wrestling—with muscular enemies.

"Are there . . . more than one to contend with?" Tom felt slightly stupid in asking.

Ahmed regarded him steadily, surprised perhaps that someone might be interested in the subject of his tormentors. Tom took a sip of the delicious mint tea, if only to deflect his gaze. "Oh, yes. That is, there is, of course, the one which divides into seven, and these in turn into seven, and so on unless I can stop them." He got up, fetched a small carved wooden box and sat down again. Tom thought Ahmed was about to show him something in the box, but he merely withdrew cigarette papers and a packet of hashish. He rolled expertly and offered the reefer to the Englishman, lighting it only after Tom declined. "I mean, that is the thing, to stop the *djinn* from multiplying, isn't it?"

"Yes. I'm sure."

"Last night, Tom, they came with the faces of baboons to trick me."

"You remembered my name!"

"I don't forget intelligent company. Also I think it is beautiful how you blush and sip your tea. So I spoke sharply to them. *Don't think you can torment me as a pack of monkeys. Either we fight as men or not at all.* They understand that."

"They do?"

"Oh, yes. What's in it for them if you give up? They need you to fight them, otherwise they die."

Tom was baffled. "Isn't that what you want?"

Ahmed took a luxurious draw on his reefer and blew out a long, thin plume of blue smoke. He looked at Tom as if he felt slightly sorry for him. "The scroll. You've come to find out about the scroll. You want to know what I've found."

"Yes. I wondered whether you'd made any progress. I'm quite curious about what it says." It was a lie; or at least, partially untrue. Tom was mildly curious about the content of the scroll he'd placed in Ahmed's hands, but that was only a pretext for coming here.

Ahmed nodded. "The scroll. Yes. The scroll. It is proving to be very interesting."

"Oh? In what way?"

Ahmed thought deeply before answering. "In that it is unusual. And quite difficult to translate. Quite a headache, I can assure you. So progress is slow. But any day now I will have it all sorted for you." He smiled thinly. His smile was like a split in a fruit, and Tom knew he was lying through his teeth. He'd hardly looked at the thing.

"Good," he said. "I'm glad it is going well."

"Yes. It's going well. But slowly."

"Sharon says you have a first-class brain."

He made an ironic salaam. "I'm pretty sexy too."

"I didn't flatter you to try to get you to work faster on the scroll. I know that's what you were thinking."

Ahmed seemed impressed. "You are very intuitive. You think like an Arab. Hey, I've just realized something."

"What?"

Ahmed was staring intently at a point just over Tom's shoulder. "Your *djinn*. It has gone."

"Really?"

"Yes. Gone. I'd forgotten about it. But last time you were here it was clinging to your neck. How did you get rid of it?"

"I'm sure I don't know."

He sighed. "If you don't know, then for sure it will come back."

It was to talk about the *djinn* that Tom had come to Ahmed's apartment. He'd hoped the pretext of the scroll would be enough to justify a visit, but he was pleasantly surprised to find Ahmed so ready to talk about his *djinn*. He wondered what more Ahmed could tell. He asked the Arab to describe what he had seen.

"It's not a good idea," he said, "to describe your *djinn.*"

"Why not?"

He shrugged. "Because when you put words to them, you add to their strength. They like to wear words like feathers. Are you Sharon's lover?"

"No. Why does talking about them add to their strength?"

"Have you visited one of our mosques? It's forbidden to draw pictures of animals or prophets or even people. Only Allah, they tell me, can do this thing. Also it is written in the Koran that we should not speak of the *djinn* or of spirits and demons lest we awake them, and summon them, and they plague us. Why do you lie to me about Sharon?"

"I don't know. I just did. What difference does it make, if the *djinn* is already there?"

"So you are her lover."

"I want you to tell me what you saw."

"I saw it clinging to you. Hanging around your neck, like a corpse you couldn't shake off."

"How does a *djinn* come to a person?"

"It waits in a tree. And then, as you pass beneath the tree, it drops on you."

"Where was this tree? In England or here in Jerusalem?"

"Don't be a fool. It drops from a Tree of Life."

"Was it young or old? Man or woman?"

"I can't tell you how much I desire that woman. No, I think you lie. Come on, it's true, isn't it? You and she are lovers?"

"Perhaps. Yes."

Ahmed let out a wail and buried his head in his hands. When he emerged there were genuine tears on his cheek. Then he laughed. "Always someone is stealing her away from me!"

"You were Sharon's lover?"

"No, but I would have been if you hadn't stolen her away."

Tom couldn't tell if he was teasing, clowning for him. "Tell me more about my *djinn.*"

"OK, I'll tell you this. It was a woman hanging from your neck. A very old woman pretending to be young. Or maybe the other way round. Who knows? Maybe she's an Arab. I can't say. But she speaks many languages. Aramaic. Ancient Hebrew. Greek. Latin. She claims to have known Jesus Christ."

Tom felt his skin go cold. Bile swelled in his throat.

"Yes," said Ahmed, suddenly become grave. "I saw her. Now you see that Ahmed is not a crazy dope-fiend. Believe me: the *djinn* are real."

"I just had to know. I'm sorry I doubted you."

Ahmed's mood had changed. Tom realized he may have been play-acting before, but now his looks had soured. Clouds gathered in his eyes. "You're not the first. Not everything is explained by Sharon's damned donkey-psychology."

"She would admit that. But what else can you tell me about this woman? Do you know who she is?"

"I don't. But you do. I can tell you nothing more than I've just told you. I have given you the full extent of my knowledge."

"Then tell me about your own *djinn.*"

"Why should I? You come here—you have nothing to pay me with. Like most tourists, you come to Jerusalem just to take. Why should I disclose to a cold Englishman the secrets of my heart? Why the hell should I?"

"Because you're a kind man. And because when you see someone suffering you want to help them."

"Yes, it's true you are suffering. But why should I extend my hand? Do you extend yours?" Tom didn't know what he meant. Was he suggesting he should pay him? The cloud that had passed over Ahmed made him look older now; not the joking, boyish Arab, but something menacing, unpredictable, even dangerous. "No, I see what you're thinking. That's not what I mean by extending your hand."

"What can I give you?"

"I give you a confidence. You give me a confidence. I will tell you my secret. You tell me yours."

"I don't have any."

"Then drink your tea and let us shake hands, goodbye."

"Wait. I do have a secret."

"As I knew you must." Ahmed rolled another slim hashish cigarette and lit up. He waited for Tom to begin.

"It will mean nothing to you. It will sound foolish. But I'm going to tell you why I gave up my teaching job in England. I haven't told anyone else. I haven't even told Sharon."

Ahmed listened attentively and without interruption as Tom told him the full circumstances regarding his resignation from the school. When he'd finished speaking, Tom let out a huge sigh. The Arab nodded thoughtfully before offering his observations. "This is the tree, Tom, from which the *djinn* dropped upon you. A very shadowy Tree of Life. A very old *djinn*. Yes, she is gone for the moment, but who knows if she will come back? Now I have your secret."

"Yes."

"I could see it was hard for you to tell me these things. And I'm going to repay you with the story of my own secret."

Before doing so, Ahmed replenished the mint tea and rolled himself yet another hashish cigarette. He lit his reefer and looked hard at Tom. "Only truth will cross my lips. Lies are the enemies. Listen to me as I tell you this. Now I will give you something which will help you know the truth from a lie."

He inhaled a lungful of smoke and crossed the room. He put his mouth close to Tom's lips. "Open your mouth," he croaked through his crowded lungs. He steadied Tom's chin with his hand and gently blew a thin stream of smoke into the back of his throat. "Take it back into your lungs."

Tom breathed in the smoke. It was cooler than he expected, though the act of inhalation forced a slight convulsion in him and squeezed a tear from his eye. But he held it for a moment before exhaling. His heart knocked and he felt slightly dizzy.

Ahmed returned to his cushion and assumed a cross-legged position before beginning his tale.

31

Bismillah al-Rahmani al-Rahim.
In the name of God the merciful and the compassionate, let me tell
the tale without diversion or distortion. Let not the demons of un-
truth nor the spirits of false witness pull at my tongue. Though none
but God can look into a man's darkest heart and know what he sees
there, let me light the lamp of right speaking that we may pass from
shadow to illumination.

I first heard of the existence of the Masters, or the "Near Ones"
as they should more properly be known, when I was a student at
one of your English universities, in the city of Leicester. While I was
there I wasted my time on the normal undergraduate activities,
which is to say I flouted the Islamic taboo on alcohol and spent three
years getting horribly drunk and spending all my days—with occasional success—in trying to bed English girls. I stayed on for
postgraduate studies. I was a member of the Islamic Students' Society and a militant student activist, passionate about many causes—
I no longer remember which ones. Most of all I enjoyed being a dis-
grace to the Islamic Students' Society.

But I got my come-uppance when I fell in love with an unin-
telligent middle-class English girl called Victoria. She let me make

love to her once only and then refused to have anything to do with me. I cried openly. I wrung my hands on the public stage. I drank copious amounts of supermarket whiskey. I remember mornings when I woke up with my head feeling like a split cantaloup. Have you had that feeling?

A friend called Rashid, president of the Islamic Students' Society, told me to pull myself together, that I was making a grand fool of myself all over the university. He helped me. I stopped drinking and struggled through my final dissertation. Rashid took me away one weekend to stay with some friends in Bradford. I was talking with someone, and when I mentioned I was from Leicester, he told me of a man living there whom I should visit. The words Masters and Near Ones were used in my presence for the first time.

When I returned to Leicester I was curious, and I visited the address I'd been given. It was an unassuming terraced house in an Asian quarter of the town. I'd told no one of my intention to visit, but it was as if I was expected. I rang the bell and an Arab woman answered the door, beckoning me inside without a word. She led me to a room at the rear of the house, where there were low lights. In the middle of the room a man was sitting on the floor. A cushion rested opposite him, as if intended for me. I made to enter the room, when the man held up an admonitory hand.

"Stop!" he said. "Wait at the door. You are too full of alcohol." I was astonished. I hadn't had a drink in perhaps three weeks, and I told him so. "Three years," he said. "It will take you three years before these *djinn* will quit you, so long as you don't drink in that time. And so long as you stop blubbing over women you can't have."

My first reaction was to think someone must have set me up for this encounter, but it wasn't possible. My encounter in Bradford had been a chance meeting, which I'd initiated. I peered at the man sitting on the floor. In the shadows it was impossible to determine his age. His spectacles reflected lamplight, so that I couldn't see his eyes, but I could see his gray hair and the wrinkles of his skin. I thought perhaps he was Indian, or Iranian, but his Western dress gave away nothing.

He said, "I can't do anything for you with all this alcohol con-
fusion. Come back in a year."

"I won't be here in a year. I'm returning to Palestine." I was still
poised in the doorway.

His glasses flashed in the light. "If you stay in Palestine, you
won't be around for long," he said. Then he called the woman, who
all of this time had been standing behind me, and whispered something to her. She drew me into the corridor, closing the door behind her.

"You are lucky," she said, "a lucky young man." Then she
wrote, in Arabic, a name and address on a piece of paper. "Go to
see this man."

It was some place in Baghdad. "Baghdad!" I almost shouted.
"Why should I go to Baghdad?" I'd never been there in my life and
had no desire to go to Iraq, that oppressive, militaristic country.

"Then perhaps you shouldn't," she said, already ushering me to
the front door. Then I was out on the street, shaking my head.

I had no intention of going to Iraq, but I found myself pocket-
ing the scrap of paper. Within two weeks I had returned to Palestine, to Jerusalem, wondering about my future. I kicked my heels
for a while, tried this and that. I even tied a scarf to my face and
threw stones at Israeli soldiers. The fun went out of it when one of
their bullets passed clean through my thigh muscle. One inch higher
and you would now be listening to a eunuch.

There was nothing for me to do here. I thought of going back
to England. Then I remembered the scrap of paper, and I took myself off to Baghdad.

It was 1976, just a couple of years before the Islamic revolution
in neighboring Iran, and three years before Saddam Hussein became
Iraqi president. I made a terrible journey across Iraq by bus, and
arrived in Baghdad feeling depressed and ill. When I stepped off the
bus into a cloud of flies I felt like going home immediately.

But I didn't. I went directly to the address I'd been given in England. I was told the man I wanted to see had gone away. I would
find him in a small village near the oil town of Kirkūk. After two
days of weeping and cursing my stupidity I got on a bus and went

back across the desert. I had no intention of getting off the bus until it was back in Palestine. Imagine how I felt when the bus broke down in a village fifteen miles from Kirkūk.

I asked around for information about this man. No one knew him. Then a passing goat-herd pointed to a house. I went there. It was quite a wealthy residence. An oily servant told me I should wait on the porch, and there I met another young man, an Iraqi called Mehemet.

"Are you waiting for Abd Al-Qadir Al-Karim?" I asked the young man.

"The Tongue of the Unseen?"

"Yes, yes. Whatever you say." I was at the end of my patience.

"Yes, I am."

"And is he a Master? One of the Near Ones?"

"If he is, it's not for us to say."

"To hell with that. Is he or isn't he?"

The young man shrugged.

Well, I'd had enough. I trudged back through the sleepy village to the bus. Only to find that it was gone.

I returned to the house. The servant was busy packing two heavy bags with blankets and supplies. He gave one bag to Mehemet and one to me and told us to follow him out into the desert, where we would meet Abd Al-Qadir Al-Karim. He marched us for seven miles. Mehemet had turned very quiet and sullen. As for me, I was cursing this man's foreskin for the games he seemed to be playing. His servant would answer no question whatsoever. Finally, worn down by my persistence, the servant (who always marched three steps ahead) turned and said, "If he is your teacher, he will make you benefit from his luminescence, whether you know it at the time or not. He may discomfit you. That will be intended and necessary. He is modest and allows you to find out what you have to find out slowly. When you meet him, he will act upon you whether you know it or not."

Riddles. That was all we could get out of the obdurate servant. I abused him for his dullness. I called him all the names I could think of, and, believe me, I know a few.

Before nightfall we reached a cave in the desert. No one was there. We were instructed to spread our blankets and prepare to spend the night. Perhaps you already suspect, but for Mehemet and me it was almost three days before we realized the grubby servant was, of course, Abd Al-Qadir Al-Karim.

Mehemet and I spent three years with him, much of the time, but not all, in that very place. There was water nearby, and for food Mehemet or I would walk back to the village to collect provisions. Our needs were minimal.

And we learned things. Wondrous things. We meditated, and we prayed. Through discipline the mind can be purified of the sins and weaknesses of the soul, leading onwards and upwards to the divine. I learned the art of poetry. Our teacher taught us that Allah placed the moon in the sky to inspire love poetry. Mehemet learned the arts of forging sound and rhyme to manipulate the emotions of men. I mastered the skills of hypnotism. We learned how to raise the *djinn* and how to control them. We also learned that angels are powers hidden in the faculties of man and how we should awaken them.

Then after three years, in the middle of these teachings, our teacher disappeared quite suddenly. We awoke one morning, with the sun breaking over the lilac mountains and the moon still in the morning sky, and Abd Al-Qadir Al-Karim was gone. We waited for two weeks for him to return, but he never came. Finally Mehemet and I went back to the house in the village to look for him.

When we reached the house, we found a family living there. They denied all knowledge of Abd Al-Qadir Al-Karim. They claimed their own family had lived in that house for three generations. They looked at our rags and told us we'd spent too long in the desert.

We were stunned. Without our teacher we were directionless. What's more, we were reduced to begging for food; before now all our modest needs had been met by him. We hung around for a month or two, waiting for him to return. We were thoroughly miserable. We drifted back toward Baghdad, eking out a living by performing conjuring tricks and reciting poetry along the way.

But the political mood had changed. There was revolution in Iran. Saddam Hussein, the new president of Iraq, was afraid that his own country might go the same way, so he deliberately provoked the Iran–Iraq conflict. There was little tolerance for two vagabonds from the desert. I knew if we didn't get out soon, we would be drafted into the war.

"Our Master," Mehemet said to me one day, "he wasn't a man. He was a spirit, wasn't he? Was he a *djinn*? An angel? Or a demon?"

I grabbed him roughly by the collar. "Don't ever talk that way again!" I snarled in his face. "Don't ever!"

We begged a ride in a truck to Syria, where there were plenty of dispossessed Palestinians. We scratched a living. One day I found Mehemet weeping. After all this time he'd become like a little brother to me, so much did I love him. He wept for the days when we lived with our teacher, when everything was as clear as the course of the sun and the moon over the desert, and when scholarship was our all.

"We've lost our way," he said. "We are lost."

"No," I said to him. "Our teacher is still with us. The Near Ones haven't deserted us. This is a test. Do you remember how frequently the Master would discomfit us, and the meaning of his actions was never clear until later? So with this, little Mehemet. And until today we have been failing the test, living like dogs, forgetting everything we learned. We must go back to our old ways."

"But we can't go back to Iraq!" he cried.

"Not to Iraq. To Palestine."

By God's will, I successfully smuggled Mehemet into my homeland. Mehemet was amazed at what he saw here in Jerusalem, and across the West Bank we had the support and comfort of my family and friends. Then we found a place between Qumran and Jericho which suited our needs: a small cave with a spring nearby, so that we could live as before.

The living was frugal. My family brought us things. Other people were kind. We set ourselves to a life of meditation and prayer under the sun and stars. How far away this was from my dissolute years at Leicester University, Tom! The students of the Islamic Society would not have believed it.

After a while we began to get a reputation as holy men, and one day a peasant woman brought us her son, who was a cretin, and asked us to pray for him. What could we do? We prayed for him.

We asked Allah for compassion. I tried to place some suggestions in the boy's mind. What do you know? The woman brought him back every week for three months. She said he was much improved. I don't say it was true or not true, only that she believed it. Occasionally others would come, and sometimes we helped them. If they were possessed or demonic, we did our best for them. We said to the people, we can only knock on Allah's door, and he must decide if he opens it. They accepted this, and, whatever the result, they always left gifts of food.

But this new contact with people, and the new admiration of women—it started to make things difficult for us. A beautiful young mother came to us. Her child had dreadful asthma. She had nothing to offer us but herself, she said, and she laid the baby on the floor and, unbidden, went into the cave and undressed. Shall I lie, when I have sworn to Allah? First I went in, and then Mehemet. Afterwards we did what we could for the child. She never came back. Mehemet and I were ashamed.

You must understand, there is no monkery in Islam. There is no order for celibacy. I could see, after that experience, that Mehemet's mind, like mine, was turning toward thoughts of a legitimate marriage. To live without a woman is a curse greater than the trials of living with a woman, forgive me.

There was one nubile daughter of a goat-herd, living across the valley. She would come with her family to bring her brother, a boy with a withered hand. She was not yet fifteen years old and utterly radiant. In my eyes, the Evening Star. I put it to the father outright. If we'd been rich, he would have given us his wife too; but, as it was, he was appalled and bundled his family away. They never came again.

Then I made the greatest mistake of my life, Tom. I summoned the *djinn*, so that I might have this girl.

I never told Mehemet what I was about to do. I sent him on a journey to my cousin's house, knowing that he would be gone for at least three days. Then I set about the invocation.

It was a fine, clear morning when I awoke. The moon was still in the sky. The sun had spilled itself across the ochre rocks.

For two hours I performed the ritual purification. Then I spread

out my red prayer mat, faced the direction of Mecca and prayed two
rak'as, before smearing my face with red ochre. At this point I
began to repeat the mighty names of God. For this *djinn* it must be
the *jalali*, the terrible names of Allah, as opposed to the *jamali* or
amiable names. When I had finished, I began to pronounce the
names of the *djinn*, which I may not even now repeat to you. The
name must be repeated 137,613 times. Normally this is done over
the course of forty days, but I did not have the time, so I needed to
accelerate the ritual, omitting some special incantations and rituals
of purification, for which I was later to pay dearly.

At noon, with the sun glaring directly on to my bare head, I
paused. I had been at it for seven hours. I drank some water and ate
some seeds according to a strictly controlled diet. Then I began
again, repeating the name.

I broke off only to drink some water at sundown and to perform the grave exercise. In this it is necessary to imagine that you
are dead, that you have been washed and wrapped in a winding-
sheet and laid in a tomb and that all the mourners have departed.
Then I repeated the name of the *djinn* until the early hours of the
morning, when sleep overtook me.

In my dreams the *djinn* came to me as a shadow. When I awoke
it was to the sound of soft dust falling across the desert floor. The
moon was almost full, hatching rich shadows from behind every
rock. The soft ticking, as of dust falling, was of the desert coming
alive. But there was no dust: I swept my hand across my sleeping
bag, and it was clean. Yet still the white dust came down like snow,
being transmuted to invisibility the moment it touched the desert
floor.

In the morning I repeated the purifications and began again to
invoke the name of the *djinn*. I could feel its closeness.

At noon the heat of the sun made me afraid, and I invoked the
particular titles of Allah from among his ninety-nine names. First,
Al-Hefiz, the Guardian, to ward off fear; then Al-Muhyi, the
Quickener, to ward off all spirits and demons other than that which
I was busy summoning; then Al-Qadri, Lord of Power, to take
away my anxieties.

I etched in the sand the binary, tertiary and quaternary mystical squares and wrote the numerical values of the appropriate names of Allah, linking them with the twenty-eight letters of the Arabic alphabet and the twelve zodiacals. Around this I drew the square of Eve and resumed the incantation.

At sundown I wrote the name of the *djinn* on a withered leaf, scorched the leaf and dissolved it in water before drinking it. After this I fell into a swoon.

Again I was awoken in the night. This time I was roused by the sound of the desert singing. Have you ever heard the desert sing? It turns your skin inside out. It sings with one sweet, unbroken note, a note made by all the rocks and plants and the desert floor in unison. It sings to the moon (which had now reached its fullness). This sound will drive men mad, unless they are protected by the controlling rituals.

I did not go back to sleep. I drank some water and sat outside the cave on my prayer mat. I closed my eyes, sealed my lips and repeated the name silently to myself, with my tongue pressed to the roof of my mouth. On the stroke of noon I reached the count of 137,612. I had but to pronounce the name one more time. But I was terrified. Never without my teacher had I summoned the *djinn*. Would I be able to control it? Would I be able to bind it? My tongue stuck to the roof of my mouth, and my mind refused to repeat the terrible name for the 137,613th time.

I was paralyzed. I felt the sun's heat on my brow. The planet missed a beat somewhere. Sweat drained from me. I felt something out there, waiting with terrible, awesome patience. Then at last I spoke its name for the last time, and I opened my eyes.

Nothing.

There was nothing. No falling dust. No desert singing. Only the sun, like a blast-furnace in the sky. I waited for half an hour, astonished at my own sense of emptiness. My stomach was like the open plain of the desert.

The ritual had failed.

I got up, drank some water, ate a piece of seed cake. I felt crushed by the terrible weight of loneliness. Where was my brother Mehemet? How I missed him now. I felt ashamed that I'd tricked him into leaving me. I retired to the shade of the cave and lay down, immediately falling into a deep sleep.

When I awoke, she was sitting next to me. I woke with a cry on my dry lips. "Are you the *djinn?*" I squealed, scrambling back from her further into the cave.

"Of course not." She laughed. Her eyes were like the eyes of a lioness. Her smile was like light glittering on a stream. "Don't you know me? I'm the daughter of the goat-herd! You asked my father if you could marry me, and he refused. Well, I left him to come and live here with you. Here I am!"

She was indeed the same girl who'd made a fever of my imaginings all those months. And she'd grown even more beautiful. Her hair was as dark as the raven. Her smooth skin was the color of sand. I pressed my hands to my face and silently thanked God that she had been delivered to me.

I asked the girl her name. She was about to reply when a shadow fell over me. Something blocked the sun. I looked up, and it was Mehemet, who had returned from his errand. He looked suspicious.

"When did you come here?" he said, dumping his heavy bags of provisions on the floor. I could see he thought she'd been with me these three days.

But the girl leapt to her feet, and kissed him, and called him by his name. "I've just arrived, Mehemet. To be a companion. To learn whatever I can from the pair of you. Tell me I can stay here! Please don't send me away!"

It was obvious that Mehemet, too, was utterly captivated by the girl. Before he could say anything she was busy unpacking the provisions and set about cooking a meal. Mehemet looked at me and shrugged. The decision was made.

But the decision which remained unmade was whether she would choose Mehemet or myself. That night she slept a little way off from both of us. This was completely unlike the situation we'd experienced before. We could not both have the girl: we knew each other too well and knew it was impermissible in both our minds.

And yet we were equally smitten. No, sooner or later she would have to choose between us.

We began to compete. We behaved appallingly with each other. Under the guise of merrymaking, I would mock Mehemet for his squint, and he would berate me for the largeness of my nose. I would perform tasks to advertise my physical strength; he responded by straining his sense of humor. A deadly courtship was being conducted, which neither of us openly acknowledged. She stayed with us for some weeks, and every day, relentlessly, the skin was tightened across the drum.

One night she amazed us by dancing like a dervish. I think I'd always known what she was, but that night confirmed it. She whirled round and round, and the desert sand followed her turning feet in spirals of smoke. Her skirt flung outwards higher and higher as she went spinning, exposing the smooth flanks of her strong, sweat-soaked thighs. I thought the sand would catch fire. Her eyes were bright, like the shining carapace of a beetle or insect. Lust lifted its head like a cobra inside my loose pants. I'd never wanted a woman so much in my life. But there was Mehemet, also mesmerized. What could I do to get him away?

When she stopped dancing, the desert began ticking. It was the sound of falling dust I'd heard before. Suddenly I realized that, despite her having lived with us all these days, we still didn't know her name. She had an amazing ability to distract us or to make us forget it whenever the question was put.

When she finished the dance we applauded loudly, and I called her to sit between us. She was breathless. The human smell of her sweat was maddening. I could scent her woman smells from between her legs. I was determined at that moment, woman or *djinn*, to find out her name. I began to speak to her in soft tones, stroking her hair and reassuring her, fixing my eyes on her, until her own eyelids became heavy. She was falling under my influence, and I was about to ask her to tell me her true name when Mehemet broke the moment of trance by calling out a line of his poetry.

"The veil of the false self is an earthly darkness; but the veil of the heart is the radiance of love!"

She started suddenly and looked up at Mehemet. He was on his
feet, standing over us with his fists clenched. The moonlight shone
in the whites of his eyes, and on his teeth, making him seem like a
demon. The trance was broken, and I was furious. What did he mean
by barking out this cant?

She scrambled to her feet, seeming angry that I had almost
caught her. Then she turned to Mehemet, gently cupping his cheek
in the palm of her hand. "But are these your lines, Mehemet? Truly
you are a poet. Come and walk with me on the hill, and treat me to
more of your poetry. Ahmed, would you stay here and see that the
fire does not go out?"

She was telling me I was not wanted. After they had gone I sat
in a kind of fever, imagining them walking together under the brilliant moon as Mehemet spouted his appalling, portentous verse. It
was no good. I couldn't keep still. I had to follow them.

I came upon them resting their backs against a rock. I was able
to spy upon them from a short distance. The moon hung low, smiling upon them like a benevolent mother. Their arms were entwined.
She leaned across to him, and they kissed. And then again I saw his
tongue leap to her mouth and hers to his, even in the darkness, like
copulating serpents, and then their hungry mouths were locked together.

I gasped. I bit my knuckles in anguish. I beat my head against a
rock. I couldn't bear to watch anymore. I scrambled away from the
scene, weeping hot, venomous tears. I went back to the fire and sat
before it, shivering in a kind of frost, unable to get warm. I sat there
for a long time.

"You have let the fire go out." It was Mehemet. He was alone.
I didn't know how much time had passed. It was still night, though
the moon bathed us with its pearly light.

"Where is she?" I said.

"Gone to prepare a marriage bed," he said simply.

"So at last she's made her choice between us."

"Yes. You are not angry?"

I got up and embraced him. "Mehemet, my little brother, who
is dearer to me than everything, how could I be angry with you?

She has made her choice, and in choosing the finer thing she has chosen my brother. It is God's will. So be it."

Mehemet wept with relief and clung to me. He had been afraid that this would destroy our friendship. He cried uncontrollably, and he praised Allah that he'd been granted the love of both this woman and his wonderful brother.

I made him sit down. "But we have things to do," I assured him. "We must rebuild the fire, and we must arrange a wedding breakfast and prepare the groom for the wedding. When does she return?"

"At dawn."

"Then we have much to do."

I rekindled the fire and Mehemet laid out everything in the cave for a wedding breakfast. It was an hour before dawn. I helped him to wash and dress, and then I sat him down at the mouth of the cave.

"Let me make a prayer and a blessing for you," I said.

"Will you?"

"I will make a special prayer. Let us invoke the powers fitting to a groom. We'll make you worthy. I'll give you the strength of a lion to love her until you're both exhausted. And the wings of inspirational poetry, that you may whisper rare words in her ear with every thrust!"

Mehemet giggled as I drew a circle around him in the sand. "For protection," I said.

I began to whisper prayers in a soothing, reassuring voice. As I saw Mehemet's head begin to nod, I slipped in the key words. Mehemet had been my subject for hypnosis on many occasions, and he had allowed me to plant in his memory certain words to accelerate the process of hypnotism. His breathing became shallow. Within moments he was entranced. I brought him gently back to awareness.

"You are aware, little brother. You can see all around you. Look how the herald of dawn comes across the mountain top. How beautiful! But you cannot move outside this circle, not for anything. Even if a lion were to attack you. Indeed you cannot lift an arm, nor raise an eyebrow, nor twitch a muscle.

"More important, for the moment, you cannot speak. Not a

word, not a single syllable, not the smallest sound. Not even if an eagle were to swoop on you. Which is all the better because it means I won't have to listen to your appalling poetry."

Mehemet's eyes were now wide open and regarding me strangely. But he couldn't even blink. Yet in his eyes I saw the microscopic splash, signaling to me that part of him had detected my change of tone and was already struggling to escape from the hypnotic command. In that effort, I knew he would fail.

"Dear Mehemet, for some years I have had to tolerate the gibberish which you have offered as poetry. Enough is enough. Open your mouth. Let me see the chief organ of offense."

He opened his mouth and slowly thrust out his tongue. His entire body was stiffening in resistance. His eyes were fighting me.

"My, my. I see your tongue has turned black with the awfulness of your vile poetry. Let that be a lesson to you."

He gagged slightly, and his tongue flushed from pink to purple to black.

"Put it away!" I cried. "It's as vile as the filthy poetry it utters!" His mouth closed and his teeth bit down hard on the tip of his tongue. "What a sinful thing is a tongue, Mehemet. People should be more careful about the things they say and the words they speak. They treat words as if they were not real things. Yet you and I know they can be sins. Living *ssssins*, even after they have *passssed* from hearing. *Sssss.* Now what is *thissss*? What is *thissss* I hear? How *sssstrange*. It *ssssseeemsss* that tongue of yours has become alive in your mouth. A living *ssssin!*"

Great blisters of sweat broke on Mehemet's forehead. His eyes rolled in his head as he made a supreme effort to break from his paralysis. Now I could smell his fear. But something inside his mouth was writhing and lashing against his cheeks.

"Better let it out, Mehemet, before it turns in on you! Before it bites!"

He opened his mouth. I heard him gag. With mesmeric slowness, the black head of a hooded cobra unwound from his mouth, steadily emerging from between his swollen lips. Mehemet was still gagging. His entire body trembled. The cobra uncoiled from his mouth, swaying gracefully until at last it dropped to the sand at his feet. It lifted its head and proceeded to edge toward the circle scratched in the sand. When it reached the line, it was unable to cross. It hugged the curve of the circle and traced the full circumference, finally arriving back at its starting point.

"Isn't it beautiful, Mehemet?" I whispered pleasantly. "Study its markings. See it glisten. But look how it wants to escape the circle. We must make it go back where it came from."

The cobra slithered across Mehemet's foot and along the length of his thigh, pausing briefly at his groin. It climbed his arm and on to his shoulder. There it danced, inching toward Mehemet's still-open mouth. At last it slipped head-first between his jaws.

"But it can't live in your mouth, little brother. Or it will want to come out again disguised as bad poetry. No, no, it must go *inside!*"

Mehemet gagged and stiffened as the cobra's head eased into the back of his throat. The muscles of his neck constricted as the creature forced its way in, a centimeter at a time. A moment later the snake had filled his windpipe and was squeezing toward his gullet. Mehemet was choking. With a sudden force he lashed out with his legs and fell on his back. Still gagging for air, his body rocked with uncontrolled spasms. His eyes were darting wildly, until they rolled back in their sockets, all white. He thrashed at the ground, writhing, kicking. Finally the black tail of the cobra disappeared inside his mouth. Mehemet's head crashed against the desert floor. His fists beat the dust as his agony went on for several minutes. At last his body heaved in a final spasm and fell back, utterly lifeless, his dead eyes wide open. I lifted his head and looked into those dead eyes. They reflected the yellow and pink light of the breaking dawn.

I held Mehemet's lifeless body, wondering what to do. The sun peeled over the mountain as I sat. Some instinct made me look around. The girl was standing behind me. She was dressed, for her wedding, in crimson robes.

"There has been an accident," I said softly. "You know Mehemet was an epileptic. He suffered a fit in which he swallowed his own tongue."

She looked at me suspiciously.

"Examine him if you don't believe me."

"I don't need to," she said. "But I must have my bridegroom."
When she showed neither sadness nor emotion, I knew for certain that she was a *djinn*. But I had no fear, and I went with her into
the cave, where Mehemet and I had laid out a comfortable bed and
the wedding breakfast. There she undressed. Her skin was the color
of cinnamon. The smell of the dawn was on her. The yellow and
cerise light was on her shoulders. Her perfume made me swoon.

She spread herself for me. And at the moment of my greatest fulfillment, at the moment of penetration, she shed her earthly form.
For the next three hours I was driven almost out of my mind with
terror as she took me by the foot and flung me round and round
the planet. For the sin of intercourse with demons, with the *djinn*,
I have been paying ever since. Every night before dawn the *djinn*
returns to me and demands that I uphold my wedding promise of
that night by making love to her. If I give in, she turns into one of
her many abominable forms and terrifies me. Therefore every night
I must wrestle with her, holding her off until she becomes tired, or
until the light becomes too much for her.

That is the *djinn* with which I have to live, Tom. Would you like
more mint tea?

32

"Michael Anthony is dead,"
Kate had reported.

"Oh," said Tom.

Silence itched.

"He said I should go to Jerusalem. That day in the park. He described it to me, and he said if I went, a little bit of him would still be alive. In me. Shall we go to Jerusalem, Tom?"

"Why?"

"He said the city is like a fractured mirror: you can see yourself, but you get a shock at how it comes back to you. If we went, we could visit Sharon."

"I don't think so."

"Why does the thought of Sharon make you feel uncomfortable? Why won't you talk to me? I feel like I've lost you, and I have to find another way through. I feel like Mary Magdalene. Like I was a big part of something and then I was squeezed out to the edge, and I don't know how. Can't we go, Tom? Can't we go to Jerusalem?"

33

Magdalene. He called her the Magdalene. There was no rational basis for this. The name had suggested itself in his dreams. But as soon as he had named her, the figure haunting him, terrifying him, crying out to him in the streets of Jerusalem, became real. Ahmed had warned him not to name her; but she had named herself.

The faces of the Arabs in the Muslim quarter had softened and seemed friendlier after Tom's visit to Ahmed. The alleyways appeared less sinister, the shadows among the old stones less menacing. He smiled at people in the narrow streets, and they smiled back. The cobwebs of his own fear had been broken. After all, he reminded himself, this was an Arab city, Muslim since the seventh century apart from a very brief interruption during the Crusader period. Now the Arabs were pushed into a tiny quarter, ghettoized and perceived by Westerners as dangerous intruders.

At the Bethesda pool he turned sharply. Someone was following him. He quickened his pace along the Via Dolorosa and stopped suddenly. Two young Arabs passed by, talking loudly. He waited until the street cleared. He sensed someone hanging back in the shadows. Continuing along the Via Dolorosa, he passed into the Christian quarter.

It was not his phantom; the sensations were very different from those of the occasions when he was harried by the Magdalene. No scent, no mysterious quickening in the air. Something else. Reaching David's Tower at Jaffa Gate, he turned decisively. A man in a black suit stepped smartly off the Via into a side street.

A dress pageant was taking place inside the Citadel at David's Tower. He passed through the crowds beyond the gate and made his way up to the pedestrianized streets of the New City.

Sharon was away, working; counseling her alcoholic women and drug addicts. "They see visions," she'd said pointedly. "They have delusions. They're visited by phantoms." She wouldn't be free until the evening. He whiled away the afternoon at her flat, thinking about her. When she returned he pinned her to the door and tore off her clothes. She told him she hadn't made love that way since she was sixteen.

Afterwards he told her where he'd been and what Ahmed had told him. He was betraying no confidence, he'd decided, as Ahmed himself had told the story to Sharon.

"Cobra-shit," she said.

"What about the Masters, living in the desert? Or the Near Ones, as Ahmed called them?"

"I don't know about any Masters."

"Maybe he's referring to the Sufi mystics. They exist."

"Maybe. But Ahmed is a dope-head. I deal with these people all the time. You'd be amazed at what they come up with."

"Is none of it true?" asked Tom.

They lay in each other's arms on Sharon's bed, semi-conscious, drugged with coitus, brains still soaring, slurring their words.

"His friend swallowed his own tongue and died while under Ahmed's hypnotic influence. That much is true. All the rest is constructed out of his feelings of guilt. These phantoms he claims persecute him every night are created by his own imagination."

"But he believes they're real."

"And you think that makes them real?"

He thought for a moment. "Yes."

"So if I believe in fairies, that means they exist?"

"That's not what I'm saying."

She murmured something barely audible. She was drifting toward sleep. He stared into the visible darkness, knowing this question led, insidiously, remorselessly, to another one, about his own beliefs, about his faith. That faith had become like a magnificent edifice crumbling in the desert but watched on accelerated film as centuries of eroding wind holed it, cracked it, clawed it into dust. When it had gone, only the desert remained.

"What I'm trying to say," he tried again, not sure she was listening, "is that if enough people share a belief, then, to all intents and purposes, the thing is true."

He was talking about GOD and LOVE and TRUTH and other words styled in illuminated script. But were these things, after all, just writings in the sand? Monuments to Ozymandias? Buildings crumbling in the desert, eroded by memory?

Sharon, lying next to him, had fallen into a slumber. She hadn't heard a word. He peered at her in the inky dark. Who was this woman, and was there anything wrong in what they were doing? Did it offend his memory of Katie? Would she have disapproved? If not, then why did it still feel like an act of infidelity?

Like his first act of infidelity, committed against Katie while he was actually making love to her.

No, he couldn't stop his fantasies. It would have been like trying to stop his dreams. And, as he made love to his wife, the familiar fantasy unspooled. It was during the first sexual congress with Katie that he'd lost focus. In her stead it was Kelly McGovern. It was the class stockroom. The bleeding heart rose. He undressed her hurriedly, and Katie's full breasts diminished to Kelly's adolescent teats in his hands; her belly flattened out under his caress; her thighs trimmed; even her scent, her sex odor, changed; and virginity was magically restored. As he ejaculated into his wife, he heard his semen thump hollowly in the sterile cave of his fantasy. And, in the moment after, he knew absolutely that Katie knew.

From the time he and Katie had fallen in love, they had enjoyed a period of rich telepathy, no different from that of all lovers in the first thrill of connection: a telepathy apparent from the ability to second-guess their partner's next words, to feel their needs, to communicate in a shorthand which was almost a code, to detect hidden thoughts. Perhaps, by some special grace, their period of telepathic insight had been extended beyond the norm, but when it was taken away, as it was in that moment of cold ejaculation, he had known it was irrecoverable. The special grace had been withdrawn. It had felt like a death.

It was a death.

Katie had felt it too. The expression of hurt and bewilderment on her face had suggested it all, but they couldn't speak about it. Because where was the betrayal? It was all too abstract, beyond reference. But her eyes showed that she knew. A glint of hoar-frost chilled them as she glanced back at him, before turning a cold back, covering herself and feigning sleep.

He'd stayed awake that night for an hour, peering into the swirling dark. Yes, it had felt like a death.

He looked now at Sharon's sleeping form in the dark, her hair tumbling over her shoulders. He started. He'd thought her asleep, but her wide-open eyes were watching him. A disconcerting smile had settled on her lips. Her posture was odd. Her arm was drawn under her head and she seemed propped at an awkward angle. He leaned across her to switch on the bedside light.

The light fell across her and he shuddered.

It was not Sharon. In her place the Magdalene was sprawled naked across the bed. Her tattooed skin was dark, wrinkled, like the flesh of a dried fig. Long, gray hair hung over her withered dugs. Tattoos on her arms and legs and belly were unknowable symbols, brightly illuminated against her sand-colored skin. Her eyes were completely white, blind. She groped across the bed, reaching an arm toward him.

He was out of bed, slamming his back hard up against the wall. "What is it?" Sharon was saying. "What is it?" Tom was shivering uncontrollably. At last she managed to calm him. "It's me," she said. "Tom, it's me."

The apparition had gone. Sharon stood over him, fully dressed. She was still carrying a plastic bag full of groceries. Tom's eyes raked the room for signs of the old woman. He too was fully clothed.

"How long have you been back?" he asked.

"I just got in," she said, "and here you were, screaming."

Tom let Sharon hug him. But he was unable to explain. The room was still heavy with the familiar, spiced odor of opal balsam.

34

Ahmed felt strangely troubled for several hours after Tom's departure. He'd recounted the tale of his desert years because of an annual need to unburden himself; it was always the same around both the anniversary of Mehemet's death and what he'd come to see as his doomed marriage to the *djinn*. His reasons, though, were not completely selfish. He had an acute sense of—and sympathy for—Tom's suffering. He'd seen a *djinn* clinging to Tom's back like a blood-sucking creature. Sharon would have another name for it, in her arrogance, but he, Ahmed, had seen it for what it was. He had told Tom his desert story so that the Englishman might realize he wasn't alone in his suffering.

A new thought occurred to him. Were all *djinn* female? Or, if you were a woman, were all *djinn* male?

He shook his head, trying to cast off the idea, vigorously stubbing out a hashish cigarette in an ashtray. He returned to his table, flicking aside the checkered Palestinian headscarf he'd draped over the spiral scroll. He took out the initial notes he'd abandoned in disgust on discovering that the scroll opened with a genealogy. Ignoring the first three outer rings of the spiral arm, he recommenced his translation at a new and arbitrary point, following the text anti-clockwise toward the center of the spiral.

Ahmed translated methodically and automatically, transcribing the text into English almost without cognizance of the sequence of words he pencilled into his notebook. As an accomplished scholar, he understood that the ancient Hebrew language was without vowels and that the vocalization of the language required the reader to supply vowels according to the interpretation brought to the text. In turn, one's interpretation of the text depended on how the vowels were supplied. The relationship between reader and text was potentially more misleading than any number of *djinn*, and Ahmed had devised a working technique for mentally standing back from the words suggested by his scribbled notes. Anything ambiguous or questionable he placed in parentheses, to be resolved later. Only when he had recorded a few lines of translation did he attempt to render a coherent sentence.

(Just as) moths proceed from (out of) garments so does wickedness from women. So (it is) written. And if (a) menstruating (? yes) woman pass between two men, one (of they, them) will die. At 2,000 cubits from (every) temple must (stand) a house for the unclean to pray, for the unclean be (those with) plagues and scabs, the blind, those who recently (have, had) sexual intercourse, and bleeding (menstruous) women. So all (of this) is written.

Ahmed hardly raised an eyebrow at the misogyny of the text. Such sentiments were standard for both scrolls he'd seen previously and the writings of the Old Testament. Two hundred cubits, he estimated, would have been a walking distance of about half an hour, and this squared with what he knew of temple building and the usual dictates of the scribes. It was the next section that surprised him.

True (Righteous) Teacher (says) these things are not, and proceed from mouths of (false) and base. They (vile) Pharisees and scribes are Liars and hate women. Hate (fear) (they) menstrual blood, spread on land under (the) sight of moon for fertility. Blast vines. Fade cloth. Blacken (scorch) linen. Rust metal. Bees desert (their) hives. Rid fields of (pests). Calm storms at sea. Cure (boils? and something else). Make (good) a barren woman.

It can do all this? thought Ahmed. He reached for a smoke.

(They) (the Pharisees) despise sacred emblem of moon (worship) and women-priests. Spit at and make whores and harlots of they out of Canaan from the Temple of the Seven Pillars where (there) True Teacher found me against Liars. The Temple of Fountain of Blood and the sacred (profession, priesthood) he took me from (there) and from Ashtoreth saved me from (their) stones.

Who is this narrator? thought Ahmed. Who is telling this story? He re-read what he'd produced and proceeded further.

As for glorious things which are not (were not) spoken by True (Righteous) Teacher but by Liar Teacher, Spouter of Lies, they (went) recorded (as if) true. So that he (the Liar) will heal sick, resurrect dead but in his (Righteous) name. And he says (has said) to him you are LIAR OF JERUSALEM, Spouter of Lies, lying tongue and enemy. Then will (his) brother look East and I will. While he (Liar) looks West. For this did he kill him (have him killed—maybe this is a question) and (fulfill the) prophecy (of) Suffering Servant.

These short passages represented three hours' work, during which Ahmed had not looked up. Now he read his notes and instinctively reached for one of his slim, ready-rolled cigarettes. He inserted it between his lips before changing his mind, replacing the reefer on the table. He tried for a few more lines.

Old/former (Righteous) Teacher (made) prediction on middle day (of, presumably, Solar) year that Sons of Light rain down on Sons of Darkness (and) drive enemy from land. Unfulfilled. Fire not (did not) fall from heaven. For (crime of) false prophecy he (was?) executed. Disarray all through the people. He (new) Righteous Teacher came and (scoffed) at Pharisees and Liar who hated women most. Then (by) this (my?) marriage infuriated he them, more because (of) Canaanite wedding rites of Seven Pillars. When (by this) he saved his scribe, more (than anything) he offended the Pharisee.

Ahmed scanned his notes. *Saved this scribe?* In order to establish the identity of the author, he suspected he would have to go back to the beginning, to the outer arm of the spiral, and translate the genealogy, the long sequence of names at the beginning of the scroll, in the hope that it might eventually name the narrator. Other questions were swimming before him. Who was the Liar? Who

was the Righteous Teacher? But it would all mean nothing unless
he had a clue to the perspective of the person telling the story.

It was an uninspiring task, and tedious because of the unfamil-
iarity of names. A long lineage out of Canaan was established, ending, infuriatingly, with the name of the narrator's father and mother
and the conclusion of a marriage. It did become clear, however, that
the author of the scroll was female, for the scroll went on to unroll
the lineage of the male marriage partner, again unnamed. This
lineage-by-marriage was described as the "glittering" or "shining"
line, and the grandfather of the marriage partner was identified as
Jacob-Heli, a Jewish rabbi and member of the Essene sect.

Ahmed gripped the scroll at its edges. "Hey!" he said softly.
"Hey!"

35

Jesus could not have walked the Way of Sorrows, since the pathway through the city was different in his day. Pontius Pilate could not have said, "Behold the Man," from the Ecce Homo arch because it hadn't been built. The Gospels declare the Hill of Crucifixion outside the city walls, and while the current site lies well within, the original line of the city wall is disputed. There is even a persuasive theory that the Crucifixion took place rather in Qumran, which was known at the time as New Jerusalem. It hurt Tom to think of hordes of elderly Greek widows slobbering over the wrong sites.

Tom had gone up to the alternative site of the Crucifixion known as the Garden Tomb. He'd given up on authenticity and was prepared to settle for a bit of peace.

After finding him in a state of shock, Sharon had tried to work on him. He'd been defensive, unwilling to talk. He'd made her feel like a lockpicker. She'd become angry. Not just about what was happening to him in Jerusalem; she'd wanted to know all that had transpired in England. Her inquiries betrayed a prickling new sense of urgency. He was hiding, like one of her patients at the rehab center, she'd said. And she hadn't got time to play games.

It was a serious row, and it had startled him, coming so soon
after they'd recast themselves as lovers. She'd shaken him, literally
taken him by the shoulders. *What is it, Tom? Why won't you tell
me what's going on?*

Tom hesitated as he approached the Garden Tomb. Two would-
be guides closed in, beckoning, smiling. "Hello? English? Hello?"

"Fuck! Get out of my face!" The guides backed away, scowl-
ing.

Why won't they let me be still? he thought miserably. Why
won't they leave me for a single second? You daren't stop, you
daren't pause for a moment. He looked at the men, who were now
staring at him aggressively. He'd overreacted but couldn't help himself. "Piss off if you know what's good for you!"

He ducked through the entrance to the Garden Tomb and found
an oasis of tranquility. The circling predatory animals of tourist
Jerusalem seemed to respect its boundaries. No one asked him for
shekels; no one tried to peddle information or baubles.

Located next to the grubby Arab bus station, the place matched
the Victorian fantasy of the scene of the Crucifixion. It was Gen-
eral Gordon's passion. A quiet olive grove set about with jasmine
and oleander, it even offered, carved out of the yellow sandstone,
an excavated tomb. Tom took a seat in a shady bower, his eyes
closed, his head in his hands. Other folk strolling in the garden left
him alone.

Katie, I'm sorry I'm sorry I'm sorry. You would have loved this
garden. Why didn't we ever come here together?

He always seemed to be apologizing to Katie these days. In the
flux of memory, as in the frame of a photograph dissolving, the heat
of the Jerusalem morning retreated and he was on Dartmoor, walking with Katie six months before she died. They were glad to be
wearing stout walkers' boots and rainproof cagoules. A wind
whipped across the moor at right-angles, bringing with it rods of
rain. Portentous, bruise-purple clouds tumbled in toward them,
swelling visibly, filling the sky. They ran for shelter to an outcrop
of granite rocks; weird rocks, rolled like dough into flat, round
shapes piled one upon the other. The rain lashed them as they
crouched out of the wind, backs to the rock. Water drenched their

cagoules, ran from their noses. Their inner clothes became soaked; the creeping, insidious cold penetrated their bones. Katie squeezed his hand as they crouched.

"I love the moors when they're in this mood," said Katie. "I love them as much as when the weather's fine. More. I love their menace. Don't you? Don't you love it?"

"Yes," he said, in a way that meant "no."

She laughed at him, and tried to make him smile, and found a piece of wet chocolate for him, as if he were a little boy who needed cheering up. It didn't work. "Be happy," said Katie. "We're wet— so what? In an hour or two we'll be dry. What does it matter? What's more important than being somewhere with the one person you love most in this world."

"Right now, lots of things."

"Be happy. Tell me you love me."

"I love you."

"Not like that. Look me in the eye, as if this is the most important thing you will ever say in your life. As if it is the last thing you will ever say."

But the storm clouds had lowered crashingly, and darkened, and grouped around them, pressing in. Great curtains of rain lashed them, and he used it as an excuse to hide his eyes from her, turning away from her oppressive plea.

"Tell me, Tom. Look at me and tell me that you love me."

He opened his eyes to the matchless skies over Jerusalem, to the dazzling light. She'd wanted to come here. She'd wanted them to come here together, and he'd refused her that.

A small party of visitors was being guided around the garden by a silver-haired, quietly spoken Englishman. The murmuring voice had rescued him from memory.

"... We like to believe it, and for us it feels right. Golgotha means 'skull' or 'place of skull,' and if you look at that rock over there, you can see a skull-like shape. And he would have been crucified in a public place, as an example, and this was indeed a crossroads in those ancient times. Crucifixion, you know, was a long, lingering death. A man could hang on the cross for three days before dying, so long as his legs supported his weight. Unsupported, the sheer weight on his lungs would cause him to die of asphyxiation, and this is why as an act of mercy, the Romans would break the legs of the one crucified, to quicken his end. But it says in John they did not break his legs, and thus another prophecy was fulfilled, that 'not a bone of his shall be crushed.' And if you look over here, you will see the tomb, which for us, of course, is wonderful because it's empty . . ."

The small party shuffled off to examine the tomb cut in the yellow stone. Tom looked up and saw a man in a dark suit watching him from the entrance to the garden. The man slipped away quietly, disappearing behind the reception building. Tom got up and approached the reception, but the man had already gone.

He left the garden without making a donation.

36

Ahmed scratched his head like a man with an infested scalp. His efforts at translating the scroll were not going well. After leaving his initial endeavors overnight he had returned to it in a state of dissatisfaction. As a matter of habit, he retranslated his earlier work and found it steeped in error. In a single section he found he had seriously mistranslated at least seven nouns and detected four wild grammatical errors. Even allowing for the usual breadth of interpretation, he couldn't understand why his work had been so sloppy.

It was almost as if someone had come along in the middle of the night and rearranged certain characters of the manuscript. The thought chased him to a small ottoman chest, where he stored his collection of talismans.

Ahmed was a collector of talismans: a collector and a believer. He was the curator of a private and tiny museum of the objects. Many were attached to pieces of string so that they could be worn around the neck. Some were designed to be worn as bracelets or rings, and some were dirty concoctions of cloying, unguessable perfumes. Still others came in the form of desiccated creatures, such as scorpions or lizards. His collection included a shrunken human

head and a mummified finger. To people who knew about his collection he pretended an academic interest, and in the case of these
latter objects his concern was no more than that. But there were
other objects in his possession which, he believed, offered up gen-
eral protection against the incursions of the *djinn.*

The spiral scroll had reminded him of a certain medallion in his
collection which was of genuine Canaanite origin. He had obtained
it by stealth from the archaeological discoveries at Ugarit. He lifted
it carefully from the ottoman.

The medallion was a coin of smoothed and blackened bronze,
drilled and looped by a length of dirty string. It too contained a spiral invocation, engraved in cuneiform characters, unreadable to
Ahmed despite all his proud scholarship. He understood it to be a
prayer to Ashtoreth, rendered in spiral form so as to represent a
maze in which evil spirits may become lost and trapped. Ahmed
hung it around his neck and returned to work on the scroll.

After completing his revision, he rolled up his sleeves and at-
tacked a new section of the scroll with augmented vigor.

*He assembled new Council of Twelve (which) included Sicarrii
and Zealot but not Pharisee (and) not Saducee. Proclaimed Prince
of the Congregation. The Wicked Priest (Liar) of the Pharisee hated
(he) him because of the marriage in Canaan and his hatred of
women.*

*Then the thaumaturge Lightning (or the Fork of Lightning)
struck. He moved the (calendar) moon in the sky by (one) month,
thus Righteous Teacher no longer illegitimate. Then (I was) party
to the way of the Fig-tree. Lightning, under another name of
Bethany (made) the snake poison, and the Teacher by aloes and
myrrh to resurrect (him). Who comes to the prophecy will (make the)
fig-Messiah (flourish). Thereafter, the scriptures, and by these (the
same) means will the Suffering Servant resurrect. Of the Council of
Twelve, only he, Lightning-Simon, I and the Sicarrii know. I liked
not the plan. Lightning made a gift (bribe) to the Roman that he (his
limbs) be not broken in mercy.*

A shadow passed over Ahmed. He re-read his notes in a fever.
He scribbled rapidly in his notebook. A Teacher of Righteousness.
Persecuted by a "Wicked Priest." Married to the female narrator.

The fulfillment of prophecy = fig fruiting generations after planting, i.e. Old Testament. The Council of Twelve followers. The Suffering Servant/Prince of Congregation, possible death. Sicarrii = market-place assassins, sub-Zealot. Another name of Bethany, resurrected = Lazarus? = Simon Magus, i.e., the thaumaturge? Was he Lazarus? The Sicarrii who was in on the plan, Sicarrii = Iscariot? Sounds familiar, Ahmed? Sounds familiar?

37

Didit-didit-dididdid-did-did-didit."

"Christina, talk to me. It's Sharon. What have you taken? What did you take?"

Sharon, returning to the rehabilitation center that morning, found Christina back in the White Cloud Room. She took over from Tobie. One of the other residents had seen Christina popping pink capsules over breakfast, half an hour before Sharon arrived.

"How did she get hold of the stuff?" Sharon wanted to know.

"Smuggled them inside her, I expect, darling. That's the usual way."

"Leave her to me, Tobie. I'll handle it. Tell my daycare group they're on their own for a while."

Tobie went out and Christina began rocking, tapping her head against the cushioned wall. "Did-it-didit. Tobie pisses me off."

"Keep this up, and it's the nuthouse for you. We can't deal with this. We can't cope with you freaking out all the time. We're only here for nutrition and macramé, you with me?"

"Na-na-na, sha-na-na-na. You wanna know how they did-did-did-it? Sha-na-na."

Sharon had been through withdrawal, detoxification, highs, lows, trips and falls, uppers and downers, White Clouds and Screaming Blue Funks with Christina. Sharon had had a bad night herself and had slept little after arguing with Tom. It infuriated her that after working all day with recalcitrant clients at the rehab center, she then had to confront Tom about his making no effort to open up about his feelings; and she knew he wouldn't be able to face his bereavement until he did. He was brittle. Each piece of information came out with a tiny snap, as if she had to break each of his fingers in turn to get it out. He couldn't see that if only he would talk, or shout, or be angry, or weep, then he might stop being plagued by phantoms and accept the terrible thing that had happened to Katie.

"Sha-na-na-nan-nan-na."

"I'm tired of you, Christina." One thing she'd learned through all this therapy was to look after her own feelings. If she felt angry with one of the clients, the rule was to tell them or suffer later. It was a survival mechanism. Anyone who pretended to be calm, sorted, in control, balanced and unaffected by work of this kind lasted two years before they became one of the patients. The transition from therapist to client had, in more than one case, happened overnight. Depression and hopelessness were more contagious than scarlatina.

"I'm tired of all your games, and I'm sick of you never giving me anything back for all the help I give you. I don't have any more patience. It's all used up, so I'm going to ask Tobie to take over, or if she can't do it, someone else. That's it." Sharon stood up.

Christina didn't stop rocking. "Did-did-did, I'LL TELL YOU WHAT HAPPENED," she shouted when Sharon reached the door. "Did-did-did, I'll tell you tell you tell you." She began rocking slightly faster, tapping the back of her head against the cushioned wall.

Sharon came back and sat down again. "What pills did you take?"

"Never mind never mind never mind I'll tell you I'll TELL YOU HOW they did it. They did it. They broke his legs, yes yes, broke his fucking legs, that's how they did it, hey hey, I'm trying, hey, broke his fucking, he wasn't supposed to die no no, wasn't sup-posed to die he was just supposed to hang there, DO YOU UN-DERSTAND WHAT I'M TRYING TO just hang there until they took him down, not dead, no no not at all, just pretending to be dead so he could live, the whole thing he WASN'T SUPPOSED TO DIE but you know who, you know who THAT WAS SAUL, he told them to BREAK HIS FUCKING LEGS, he said break his legs, he's the one. He did it. That's how they did it! Did it!"

By now Christina was smacking her head quite hard against the padded wall. Sharon tried to contain the rocking by holding her. "Who? Who are you talking about, Christina? I don't know who you're talking about."

"Who? Who? Why, I'm trying to tell you, I'm trying, I'm TALKING ABOUT JESUS! JESUS! POOR JESUS! THEY BROKE HIS LEGS! THAT'S HOW THEY DID IT! JESUS! MY POOR JESUS!" Christina stopped rocking and collapsed on the floor, howling in anguish, her body racked with sobs.

Sharon tried to lift her, to comfort her. "It's just the drugs, Christina. You're having a bad . . . What did you take?"

"Nooooo-oh-oh-oh-oh-oh. Poor Jesus. Poor Jesus."

She was inconsolable. It was if she was experiencing everything she'd said at first hand. Her body convulsed; her howls squeezed out of her, choking her. Suddenly she stopped crying. She lay full-length on the floor, her head pressed to the nylon carpet, damp with her own tears. Then quite clearly she said, "I'm Mary Magdalene."

"Yes," said Sharon trying to soothe, "it's all right. And I'm the Virgin Mary."

Christina sat up, with an indignant expression on her face. She brushed her long brown hair from her eyes. Then she spoke in the same voice Sharon had heard invading the airwaves on the radio the previous morning. It was a voice she recognized with absolute clarity. It had brought her that morning to a standstill in the traffic, and again it chilled her to the core. *"Why are you trying to shut me out? It's me, Sharon, it's me. I'm trying to tell you what happened."*

"Christina!"

Christina's head lolled sideways. She tugged at her collar, as if it was hurting her. "I can't breathe," she said. The words were coming from Christina's mouth. But it was Katie's voice. "*I can't breathe I can't breathe I can't breathe.*"

"**I** don't know, darling. I've seen so many things here, all my certainties collapsed a long time ago."

They were in Tobie's office, drinking a second cup of tea. After hearing Christina speak in the voice of her dead friend, Sharon had backed out of the room and had yelled down the corridor. Tobie had been around, fixing a door hinge, and had come running. She'd taken one look at Sharon before escorting her into the office, charging someone else to sit with Christina: "Marcia, be a sweetie and step into White Cloud with Christina. Time for me to counsel the counselor."

But Tobie hadn't offered any counsel; she'd just listened.

"I don't know how it happened, Tobie. But somehow it's *carried across.* Tom can't come to terms with his wife's death, and it's infected me. The first time it happened I could put it down to imagination, but if you'd been there just now—"

"What happened, exactly? Tell me again."

"Christina was behaving in her usual freaked-out way, and then it was if a switch had been thrown, and she spoke to me in Katie's voice. Exactly as I'd heard it come across the radio yesterday morning. It wasn't *like* Katie's voice, it *was* Katie's voice."

"And what about this Tom? Are you fucking him?"

"Tobie—"

"Look, you don't know me after all this time? You think I'm judging you?"

"No. But if you're going to tell me that it happened because I feel guilty, then I'll scream."

"So start screaming. It might even help."

"But I don't feel guilty! I really don't!"

Tobie tapped the side of her head. "Not in here you don't." Then she moved her hand across her large breast. "But in here."

"I don't go along with that."

"Have you forgotten what you learned when you first came here?"

"Throw that at me, would you?"

"I'm not throwing it at you. I only ask you to remember we're all patients."

Sharon had found her way to the Bet Ha-Kerem rehabilitation center in the days when she finally admitted to herself she'd got a problem, and her problem was cocaine. It was a habit developed during eighteen months of high living with a rich property developer, and when the relationship ended, all she came out with was an expensive habit she couldn't possibly support. She sought help, and got it, at the Bet Ha-Kerem. Tobie noticed her ability to empathize with, and support, other clients. She had a real talent, Tobie had observed, and was doing more genuine counseling work than some of the paid staff. She was taken on at the center, at first in a part-time capacity, but she learned fast and her status advanced quickly.

Tobie was an inspiration. This little gray-haired, big-breasted Jewish mother, who irritated the hell out of everyone by calling them all *darlink*, was the wisest person Sharon had ever met. Her precepts were simple, beginning with the belief that all human beings have a tremendous capacity for lying and deceiving and that their first victim is invariably themselves. First stop lying to yourself, she told everyone, and then we have half a chance. More than that, she told Sharon, she should not hate people because they lie to themselves, but she should love them, because this self-deception was an emblem of their humanity. The effort to stop lying to oneself, she maintained, was the only suitable starting point for all notions of self-improvement.

When Tobie reminded her, "We're all patients," she meant exactly that. The other reason Tobie had taken Sharon on to her payroll was that Sharon reminded the old woman of herself: she, Tobie, was a reformed alcoholic.

"So what do you think?" Sharon said, softening.

"Tom is haunted, that's plain. From what you tell me, he can't face something concerning his wife's death. Now you've become lovers, you've shared his neurosis, if that's what it is. You thought you could get in his bed and help him; I know you. But you can't keep other people's emotions at arm's length: they're like sexually

transmitted diseases, *darlink*. They're worse than that: they get on
your back and stay there."

"You're beginning to sound like Ahmed with his *djinn.*"

"Oh, him. How is he? Do you see him?"

"He's much the same."

"All the trouble he caused us. It was after him I made this place
only for women. Still, you did a good job on him."

"I wonder."

"What are you going to do about Tom? Can't you get him to
talk?"

"God, have I tried! I know there's something there, but trying
to fetch it out . . . It's like trying to pull a big dog through a gold
ring."

"Yes." Tobie beamed. "Through his wedding ring, *darlink!*"

Sometimes Sharon wanted to kill Tobie.

That evening Sharon recounted to Tom what had happened. She was
building up carefully to the revelation about Katie's voice. She
wanted to use it to get him, finally, to talk to her.

"Christina told me some kind of story. It was all to do with Jesus
Christ on the Cross."

"It was a set-up," Tom blurted out.

"What? What did you say?"

Tom looked confused. "I don't know why I said that. It just
came out."

"What did you mean by a 'set-up'?"

Tom averted his eyes.

"Talk to me, Tom. Talk to me or else."

"I can't explain."

"Just bloody well try."

"The voice in my head. I told you, it started when I came to
Jerusalem. It just kept sounding in my head, like a tape left running.
The woman's voice. Then the identity of the woman seemed to
change. It would come on at me like a daydream, or in those moments just before falling asleep. I am the tongue, it said. But now
it's gone. It stopped a few days ago, immediately after we'd made
love for the first time. It was trying to tell me a story, a different

version of the Crucifixion. It was a set-up. They knew the Scriptures. They arranged for Jesus to fulfill all the prophecies to convince the people he was the Messiah. It was all rigged. But they didn't mean for him to die at all. I don't know. What do you want me to say?"

"It's OK, Tom. Just tell me everything."

"Anyway it stopped. Suddenly. After we made love, the voice stopped, and I thought it had gone. But the phantom came back. Remember that night you came back from work and found me screaming? I thought I'd been with you. But it was someone—*something*—else."

"Did the story involve the breaking of Jesus' legs while he was on the Cross?"

"No. Why do you ask that?"

"Because a client at the center said something about it. Even though she was pretty incoherent, she kept telling me that they broke his legs, and that it killed him."

"Without the support of your legs, your own weight on your lungs would asphyxiate you. I heard someone talking about it. They did it to shorten the suffering."

"Or to kill someone who wasn't supposed to die?"

"Yes, I suppose that would follow, too. But it specifically says in the Bible that they didn't break his legs. What has all of this got to do with me, Sharon? Why is all this stuff coming to *me?*"

It was time to tell him. "Tom, I think there's another voice behind the one you were hearing."

"So what are you saying?"

"Tom—" But Sharon didn't get the opportunity to say what she had in mind. The telephone rang. For a moment she wanted to ignore it, but she got up to answer.

"Yes? Oh? Yes. Right. Uh-huh. Yes. Is it? Uh-huh." She replaced the receiver with a soft click. "That was Ahmed. He sounded quite excited. Seems he's been doing some work on that scroll of yours. He wants us to go over to his place."

"Right now?"

"Yes." She sighed. "Right now."

38

You should know I worked all through the night on your dreadful scroll. I'll be honest with you; I didn't want to touch it. But I was being plagued by the *djinn*, and I thought several hours of scholarship might keep them away."

Ahmed, it was true, looked like a man who hadn't slept for the last twenty-four hours. His living quarters were unusually untidy. His desk was piled high with reference books and scholarly tomes. The scroll lay on the table in a ring of light under an Anglepoise lamp.

But while his features were exhausted, his mouth was animated. He smoothed his silky black moustache as he spoke. "Then what do I find? This blasted scroll of yours is infested with the *djinn*. Infested! They crawl all over the thing, sucking at it, feeding on it. And every time I translate something the *djinn* change it. I blink, look at it again, and it's something different."

"Ahmed, stop bull-shitting. Tell us what it says!"

"Bull-shit?" The Arab wagged an elegant brown finger at Tom but spoke angrily to Sharon. "Ask him! Ask your English lover! He knows! He knows it's not bull-shit!" Then he turned to Tom and very sweetly, formally, offered mint tea.

"Give him a beer," Sharon roared. "He'd much rather have a beer than your bloody awful tea."

"She knows I am Muslim. I don't drink beer."

Sharon leapt from her cushion and went to a fridge draped with another Palestinian checkered scarf. She held open the door, exhibiting a rack of Maccabee beers. She took out, and uncapped, three bottles. "He's a mean bastard."

"I love you," Ahmed told her, accepting one of his own beers. "Come and live with me. Be my love."

"I was talking about you to Tobie. She sends her greetings."

"That awful woman," Ahmed told Tom. "She nearly killed me with all her questions."

"She saved his life," put in Sharon.

"I'd rather spend a night tormented by a thousand *djinn* than have to face that woman again. Please say her greetings are not returned."

"Tell us about the scroll, Ahmed!"

"The scroll, yes. Did I tell you I worked all night on the thing? I hope you appreciate it. First, Tom, tell me about the man who gave it to you. Do you think he appreciated the fact that he had something very important?"

"Undoubtedly. He was very paranoid. Thought all sorts of people were trying to take it away from him. But since it passed to me I've had this notion I'm being followed around."

"You may be correct. At first sight the scroll looks like it was written by Jesus Christ himself."

"What?" Tom and Sharon said together.

"I said 'at first sight.' The author of the scroll introduces a family lineage which is unmistakably that of Jesus. His father was Joseph the Essene, his grandfather was Jacob-Heli and so on back through the line to King David. (Excuse me: I assume we're mature enough to discount notions of a virgin birth.) So at first I thought I was dealing with a manuscript written by your Messiah. Can you imagine my excitement? Remember, in Islam we count him among the prophets: I had to leave off smoking for an hour to clear my head."

"But it turned out not to have been written by Jesus?" asked Sharon.

"No. It became apparent that this lineage was declared through marriage. Don't be surprised. It's quite likely that Jesus was married. The Christian Church has always expunged it from the Bible, but the evidence is in the Apocrypha; and since Jesus was a rabbi, it would have been very strange if he were not married."

"The Magdalene," whispered Tom.

"Mary Magdalene," said Ahmed. "I believe so. But though the author of the scroll is a woman, she doesn't name herself."

"Go on."

"Do you recall that Jesus also had a brother?"

"James," said Tom. "The Bible mentions that he had a brother called James."

"Quite. But whoever wrote this document appears at first to be an enemy of James. She doesn't refer to him by name, and neither does she speak respectfully of him. She refers to this unnamed brother as the 'Difficulty' and the 'Ambiguity.' Now I must be careful in my interpretation of the text because everything is written in a kind of code. It seems that the author made a fragile alliance with this 'Difficulty,' i.e. James, against an enemy to whom she continually refers to as 'Liar' or 'Teacher of Lies.' They were involved in a power struggle over a religious cult.

"All this talk of 'Liars' and the 'Enemy' and the 'Righteous One' can drive you crazy because you don't know who they're talking about, and it keeps changing depending on whether they're talking about the past or the future. Plus in ancient Hebrew you don't know if you're reading 'the Teacher killed him' or 'he killed the Teacher.' You have to interpret. Let me read you something I translated, smoothed over for clarity."

Moving to his desk Ahmed found a piece of paper on which there were numerous scored lines and overwriting. He read: *When the glory of the fig-Truth within the Lie had failed, the Righteous Teacher's brother joined with the Lying Tongue and the factions of East and West were united against all. The Liar and his brother came to me outside the tomb. But I did not recognize him. Because he had*

joined with the Lying Tongue, who had given the order to break his
limbs. All the fig-prophecies had been watered. Each plant root. But
not the fulfillment.

Tom shivered. "Mary Magdalene. The scene in the garden, outside the tomb, where she fails to recognize the resurrected Christ."

"The fig," said Ahmed, "is a tree that has to be planted generations before it will bear fruit. Only later generations can benefit.
This refers to the maturing of certain prophecies. The author of the
scroll was party to an attempt by a religious sect to make the
prophecies happen. She was married to the central figure."

"What figure?" said Sharon. "Which prophecies?"

"It's all in the Old Testament Scriptures. The Suffering Servant.
The Prince of the Congregation. The Healer. The Messiah, mounted
on an ass. Listen to this: *"The Sicarrii, who helped along the Magus*
plan, killed himself in grief. The Council of Twelve dissolved in fac-
tion. I refused consort with the Pharisee who had executed the Right-
eous Teacher. My husband. My Teacher. My life.

"It's not clear," said Ahmed, "but some great plan to fulfill the
prophecies went horribly wrong. The scheme was thwarted, bungled even, and the Teacher of Righteousness was put to death. Then
the man who I think is James, plus this other man the 'Enemy,' the
'Liar of Jerusalem,' joined forces and tried, but failed, to recruit the
author of this scroll into a new movement."

"Yes," said Tom, getting up and going to the table. He picked
up the scroll. "They broke his legs while he was on the Cross. He
wasn't going to die at all. He would have survived and then returned
as if from the dead."

"You're running ahead of me," said Ahmed, "but that's what is
suggested in this scroll of yours. Remember Lazarus? That was the
dry run. He took some drug, some snake poison, which simulated
death. All they had to do was keep him alive until they could purge
the poison. There is a reference in the scroll to aloes and myrrh. Juice
of aloes is a strong purgative. Myrrh softens and relaxes the passage."

Tom waved the scroll under Sharon's nose. "Now tell me it's
all in my head. Now tell me I'm hallucinating. Now tell me it's only
guilt and if I talk about it, it'll all go away. Here it is, written here!

It's all written here! How could I have known that? How could I
have known?"

"You don't know anything," said Sharon.

"I know this: he wasn't meant to die at all. They had to make
sure his legs weren't broken as a Roman act of mercy. They failed.
They made a bid for power, and they bungled it. It went wrong.
That's all it was, and it went wrong!"

"Calm yourself," Ahmed protested. "You're getting too excited. You are frightening poor old Ahmed. Sit. Have a beer. Smoke
something. Only be calm." Tom put the scroll back on the table and
returned to his cushion, where he sat with his head in his hands.
"That's better," Ahmed said. "Now tell me how you know all these
things."

Tom looked into Ahmed's velvet eyes. "The *djinn* told me."

39

"How come," said Sharon, "you and Katie never had children?" They were drinking Maccabees at the Café Akrai, pretending to watch passing pedestrians.

Tom took a slug of beer. "How come you didn't?"

She placed a hand on his forearm. "No. That's not how it works. I ask you a question, and you answer open and honestly, with no trace of defensiveness. Almost as if I was a friend."

He looked from the hand on his arm to her upturned face. Her lips were clamped together, and her eyes were glistening with what might have been a growing anger. If she was angry, he didn't blame her. She was implicated. His mind flashed back to the moments before they'd left Ahmed's apartment.

As on his first visit, Ahmed had maneuvered Sharon out of the door ahead of him, so that he could have a brief word with Tom. "Does she know?" Ahmed had whispered.

"Know what?"

"Your *djinn* has split into two; and now it also rides on Sharon's back. Surely you must know this?"

He'd met Ahmed's steady gaze, wondering if the Arab was merely expressing a formula for the fact that they were lovers. Then he'd passed from shadow into sunlight to rejoin Sharon.

Meanwhile Sharon was waiting for a response. "Sorry. She wanted kids. I didn't."

"Why not?"

"To have children seemed to me like dying and beginning all over again. It was like facing a lover's leap. I couldn't do it."

"Was it a cause of conflict?"

"Only every day."

When Tom said "every day," it was true only of the later period of his thirteen-year marriage. Katie's biological clock stopped ticking and started chiming. He thought back to the time he'd met her at the party where he'd grabbed her foot.

"Her foot," he said, surfacing from his reverie.

"What?" said Sharon.

"Her foot. Did I never tell you the story of how I found her foot at a party? After she died, when her absence became really strange, one night in the dark I found myself holding on to one of her shoes. I even took it to bed with me. Like a dog, eh? Still clinging on to her shoe. As if she hadn't died—she'd just slipped her foot from the shoe."

He's opening, Sharon thought. "You must have loved her a very great deal."

An answer began to formulate a scowl on his lips, but before he spoke a shadow inserted itself between the neon light from the bar and their table. They both looked up.

The shadow was cast by a short, dark-haired man in a black suit. Sun-tanned, he carried a briefcase. His ingratiating smile looked as uncomfortable as his tight collar. "May I join you?" he asked.

Tom looked at Sharon. "This is the man who's been following me."

"Sorry," said the man. The smile was forced all the way to his slightly yellow back teeth. "May I sit down?" He placed his briefcase under the table. "You probably know who I am."

"No," said Tom.

He shot out a hand, making the sleeve of his jacket rise halfway up his forearm. "Ian Redhead." The wide smile followed, again held for a second too long before he added, "English." Tom accepted the handshake. Sharon followed up, languidly. The man was a bag of nerves. He sat down at last. "Of course, it's the scroll we're interested in."

"We?" questioned Sharon.

He spoke rapidly. "We think David Feldberg gave you the scroll. That is we had to wait to find out who'd inherited Mr. Feldberg's estate before making a generous offer on the scroll, but probate is still being sorted out, and anyway there's no sign of it among his possessions. We think he gave it to you."

"He did."

"That's a relief; I mean, to know what happened to it. Did he tell you we've been trying to buy it from him for years? Years. Do you still have it?"

"No."

"Where is it?"

"I sold it."

Redhead was crestfallen. "Who to? Who did you sell it to?"

Tom looked at Sharon. "What was the name of those people?"

"The institute or something or other?"

"Please don't say it was the Christadelphians."

"No," said Tom. "What were they, Sharon?"

"Catholics?" Redhead prompted. "A Jewish group?"

"Anglican, I think he said," Sharon offered. "Anglican."

"But they can't have been!" His voice keened. "Because I represent the Anglicans!"

"We've been lied to," Sharon said quickly.

"How much did you get?"

"Excuse me," said Tom, "but I think that's my business."

The Anglican agent slapped at the table. "I only mean I could have matched the offer. It was my responsibility to secure that scroll. I've failed. You don't know what this means."

"Sorry," Tom said.

Redhead looked up angrily. "Are you a Christian?"

"Yes, but I keep forgetting."

"You can't guess at the importance of that scroll to the Christian community."

"Or to the Jewish community?" put in Sharon.

"Are you Jewish? Is she Jewish? I'm not saying it's not important to the Jews. But it's even more important to us. Mr. Webster, I think—"

"You know my name, then."

"Mr. Webster, I think you're a Christian, whatever you say. I see the mark on you. Let me put something to you." He hoisted his briefcase on to the table, flicking open its brass locks. Tom half expected to glimpse bundles of banknotes, but the case contained a jumble of papers, crayons, colored pens and stickers. Redhead extracted a business card and handed it to Tom. He was about to close the case when something caught Tom's eye. It was a wad of large stamps, gaily colored with biblical scenes, gilt-edged, the kind children collect for attending church.

Tom pointed to the stamps. "I used to collect these."

"I do Sunday School." Redhead sounded almost apologetic. "Here in Jerusalem."

"I had a collection with one stamp missing. It was called 'The Day of Resurrection.'"

"What I was about to say—" Redhead closed his case, "—was that the Church is also short of some stamps in the collection. That scroll being among them. If in all conscience you can help me, please get in touch. My address is on that card." He stood up to leave, shaking hands first with Sharon. "Who knows? Maybe we could find you that missing stamp."

Then he was gone, leaving Tom and Sharon to outstare each other. "I hate people who talk in metaphors," said Tom.

"I think all he meant," said Sharon, "was that he might find you the stamp."

"What will you do?" Sharon asked. They'd had another drink since Redhead's nervous departure.

"I don't know. I really don't know."

"That remark he made about you being a Christian. It got to you, didn't it?"

"It made me think of Katie. She suddenly got religious some months before she died."

"Katie? She never had a religious vein in her body."

"I know. But you know how it is with old people, how they start to pick up on religion. Same with her. I'm sure she knew she was going to die."

No one had been more surprised than Tom when Katie had asked him, a couple of months before she died, to go with her to church. Her religious instincts had always resolved into a New Age mist. Gothic cathedrals exerted less of a pull on her than stone circles. Thus Tom was baffled when one morning she'd interrupted his reading of the Sunday newspapers by saying, "Harvest Festival."

"Harvest Festival?" he'd repeated. He was lounging in his dressing gown, unshaven and stupid.

She might have said "Tottenham Hotspurs, White Hart Lane, three o'clock."

"No, thank you."

"You used to have a faith. You always told me you used to have a faith."

"Used to. Don't now. Anyway I thought you were interested in Earth Mysteries."

"Oh it's all the same, Tom. It's just about being grateful."

"Grateful for what?"

"For God's sake! Are things really so bad?" Then she'd jumped on him, put her arms around him, kissed him. "Please come, please come, please come."

"Why?"

"Because something's about to happen, Tom. I can feel it. Like the sky is going to break open at any moment, and something the color of that tattoo is going to come out of it."

He stared at his tattoo so as not to have to look her in the eye. He didn't want to go to the Harvest sodding Festival and said so. To his astonishment, she cried. It had been a long time since Katie had cried to get her own way, but there she was gulping and sobbing as if he, standing over her, was the neighborhood wife-beater.

He could have capitulated, but it had become too much a mat-

ter of principle. In the end she went alone. When he saw her later
that evening, he asked her if she'd enjoyed it. She shook her head
and didn't speak to him for the entire evening. It was another small
death between them.

"I didn't want to go to the Harvest fucking—"
"What?" said Sharon. "What are you shouting about?"
Tom remembered where he was. "It's just . . . It's as if she knew
she was going to die."
"That's nonsense, Tom." Sharon recalled what Katie had said the
last time they were together.
"Come up to Gethsemane with me," he said urgently.
"What, now? At this time of night?"
"Yes, now." He stood up.
"What for? The gates will be locked. It's pointless."
"I have to do it. I want to light a candle for Katie. Will you
come? For her?"
When he put it like that, how could she refuse, though she didn't
want to go there at night? She hadn't liked it on the one occasion
she'd visited the garden by daylight; for her, as for many Jews, the
Christian sites were sullied by accusation and soured with associa-
tions of Jewish scapegoating since medieval times. The resonances
of betrayal and suffering made the Garden of Gethsemane spooky
rather than beautiful. She mistrusted it. But the place already triggered a strange energy for Tom. A bee from the garden had stung
him on the mouth—at least that was all she'd understood from his
garbled version of events that day.
No, she didn't want to go up there in the dark at all, but what
could she do when he put it to her like that? She drove across the
city, and he sat in the passenger seat in brittle silence. She parked
the car, and they walked up the incline toward the entrance to the
garden of betrayal.
As Sharon had predicted, the gates were closed, but a small yellow light burned inside the cave where Tom had met the Franciscan monk. Tom seized Sharon's hand, leading her up the hill away

from the gate until they found a place where they could clamber into the garden. Ignoring Sharon's protests, Tom went first, pulling her behind him.

A sickle moon cut through the wisps of passing cloud, offering a little light. The shining leaves of the ghostly olive trees were pressed like a hoard of silver coins at the mauve sky. Tom leaned a hand against one of the knotted, twisted olives.

"What are we doing here?" moaned Sharon.

Tom noticed something at his feet. Half buried in the dry earth at the foot of the olive tree was a small, standard-issue Bible. He rescued it from the dirt. It was quite old and almost rotted. Some visitor, some pilgrim, must have dropped or forgotten it, or had even left it as a votive offering. He opened it. The spine crumpled in his hand as it fell open. Tom wanted to see what random reading the Bible might offer, but instead saw a sleek, slug-like worm that had tunnelled a hole clean through the pages. The worm writhed from the hole, wriggling to the edge of the page and climbed on to Tom's thumb.

"Ugh!" He flung the Bible down in disgust.

"What is it?"

"A black maggot."

"I didn't see anything." Sharon too had examined the book to see where it had fallen open. All she'd seen was the white page.

"Come on."

As they approached the cave-shrine, they could see a monk in Franciscan habit sitting at an angled desk, busy with his pen. From his actions it seemed he was repeating the work of the monk Tom had met the day the bee had stung his mouth: ruling lines on a sheet of paper. But the monk was not the same man.

Tom thought he was looking at a child in a brown habit. As he drew nearer he realized the monk was dwarf-sized. Not only that, he was a black man. He must have heard their shoes scuffling the dust because he looked up from his work, cocking his head as if to listen. Tom and Sharon drew back to the cover of the trees.

The monk put down his pen, slipped off his high chair and wad-dled toward the cave entrance. They saw his eyes were almost all white with the sclerotic coat of the completely blind.

Tom made a comment. The monk stiffened and turned his head toward them. He was visibly straining to listen, the whites of his eyes oscillating wildly. He shouted something they didn't understand. Then, in English, "Anyone there?" They held their breath. "Man or spirit?" he called again. "Speak to me."

After a few moments he went back to his desk, climbed on to his chair and returned to his task of ruling lines.

"Can we go now?"

"Not yet," said Tom.

They withdrew between the olive trees, Tom leading Sharon to the spot where he'd encountered the Magdalene. "Here," he said, grabbing her roughly and kissing her.

Sharon laughed and threw her arms around him, then took his face in her hands. His tongue probed her mouth, and she felt dizzy with the pressure of his kiss. His hand popped the button on her jeans and she felt the zip slide with a soft tooth-rasp. He dug a hand inside her briefs and inserted his forefinger inside her.

Sharon writhed away from him. "No," she whispered. "Not here, Tom."

But he persisted pressing against her. Her nipples swelled against the pressure of his body. She maneuvered her lips away from his mouth to say, "Not here, babe. Come on, Tom. Let's go."

Tom ignored her. She jerked back, smiling at him, holding up her hands to signal "Enough." Tom's reply was to lunge forward, catching her by the belt-loop of her jeans, spinning her around and shoving her against the rough bark of an olive tree. In a moment he had hooked his thumbs into the waistband of her jeans and briefs, dragging them around her ankles. Using his weight to pin her against the tree he fumbled with his own trousers. He struggled to insert his engorged cock into her anus.

Sharon wrenched free and swung a closed fist at the side of Tom's head. It was a well-weighted aim. The blow connected heavily with his ear, knocking him off balance. He sank to one knee, nursing his ear with one hand and wiping his mouth with the other. His bobbing erection began to subside.

"What's wrong with you, Tom?" Sharon hissed, fixing her jeans. "What the hell is wrong with you?"

"I'm sorry. I'm sorry."

"Sorry? Fuck you!" Sharon stormed away toward the periphery of the garden where they'd crashed an entrance. Tom, still on one knee, watched her slip away through the trees.

He waited there for some time, crouched in the dark under the sickle moon. *What's happening to you? What's happening, man?* He was losing control, moment by moment. He knew what he'd just done, but he didn't know why. He'd been seized by a savage impulse. It had broken in him like a wave. Something was trying to break free inside him.

No, he wasn't possessed. How easy it would have been to say some spirit had momentarily possessed him; if it was not exactly he who had jumped on Sharon, it had certainly been *of* him. Some part of Tom was trying to break free and assert control, but with a slow, ripping sensation, like stitches popping one at a time. Each voice another popping. Each phantom another rip. Each hallucination or outburst another tearing free. He was scared of what was coming.

After a while Sharon came slowly and wearily back through the trees. She kneeled down beside him. Her anger had passed. She stroked a hand through her hair.

"I feel like I'm coming apart," said Tom.

"It's all right," she said in his ear. "It's all right."

A tear formed in the corner of his eye. She brushed it away with her thumb.

"No, it's not all right," said Tom.

"I'm here." She took his head in her hands, and she kissed him gently on the mouth. Then she opened her blouse and placed his hand on her breast. "This is what you want, isn't it, Tom?"

"Yes."

Sharon pressed her breast to his mouth. She cradled him and he sucked at her like a baby. Then she made him lie down in the dusty soil. Loosening his trousers, she placed her cool fingers on his cock, wetting her fingers with her mouth to lubricate him.

"I didn't mean to—" he shivered.

"Shhh . . ." She placed a finger on his lips. Then she slipped off her shirt, letting her breasts fall free before stepping out of her jeans and standing naked before him. He could smell her arousal, smell her sex on the night air, like a ribbon of scent winding around him, snaring him. There was another scent he recognized, comingled with her delicious cunt odor. It was a smell like balsam. He looked at Sharon in the darkness, standing over him, inspiring and yet terrible, like a figurehead on the prow of a ghost ship, and saw that it was not Sharon at all. It was what all this time he had most dreaded and yet most wanted.

"Katie. Oh, Katie."

"I had to come."

"Katie."

She kneeled before him, holding his face in her cool hands. "Don't cry. You don't know how difficult it's been. I've been trying to find a way to you."

She was warm, and flesh and blood. He tasted his own tears on her mouth. He kissed her, and she tasted exactly as he remembered her. "The old woman. Was it the Magdalene—?" he tried.

"It was me. Trying to find you. Don't talk, Tom. Love me." Katie sank back into the dust, gently pulling Tom across her. "Love me, Tom," she kept murmuring. "Love me."

She spread her legs apart, opening herself to him. Tom made to put his hand on her belly. But where her cunt should have been was something else. It was an open book, not resting in front of her body, but part of her living flesh. The open covers of the book were formed from the flesh of her inner thighs. Her pubic hair shaped a mysterious script on the pages. As if in a high wind, the pages began to flutter, fanning rapidly like a deck of cards. When they stopped fluttering, there was a hole where the pages came to rest, as if they had been eaten away by something rotten, corrupting.

"Please!" said Tom.

"Love me, Tom. Love me."

"Please!" he repeated, urgently.

"*De profundis,*" Katie hissed. She threw back her head and laughed a vicious, cackling laugh until her entire body convulsed and collapsed in on the book. It ignited in a noisy burst of flame, ash and cinders discharging in the air, leaving behind only a scorched odor trailing a whiff of balsam.

Tom threw back his head and howled.

When he looked up a shadowed figure was standing over him. It was the miniature monk, his white eyes oscillating wildly in his dark face. He pointed vaguely at Tom. "Man or spirit?" he shouted. "Are you man or spirit?"

40

Jesus Christ," Tom said to Sharon shortly after he'd met Tobie for the first time. "This just isn't going to work."

"Give her a chance," Sharon hissed. "Don't underestimate her. And remember she's doing this as a favor to me."

Tobie had stopped taking in men at the Bet Ha-Kerem, either as day patients or as residents, ever since the time Ahmed had run amok. During his period of intense crisis, Ahmed's party-piece had been to break into women's rooms at night, or to corral female day patients in some small room. Naked and in a state of considerable excitement, he would present his quarry with a blunt kitchen knife, begging her to hack off what he considered at the time to be the root of all his problems. Apart from frightening some of the women with this extreme request, Ahmed never harmed any of them and was at greater risk to himself than to anyone else. Tobie's chief fear at the time was that one of the women, in the swirling dark of her own crisis, might take up the invitation.

Sharon had to lean hard on Tobie to get her to see Tom. "Just see if you can get him to talk," she'd said. "He simply won't talk to me."

"I'm already working twenty-five hours a day. How can I?"

"Stay out of my day group. Leave the accountant alone. Get off the housekeeper's back. Stop interfering in the kitchen."

"Half an hour. That's all. I give him half an hour."

Sharon kissed her. "You're a sherbet."

"Get off me. Is he a walnut or an onion?"

Counseling shorthand came in fruit and veg. Some people peeled easily, like an orange, revealing a sticky, spongy mass inside. Others cracked with a struggle, like a walnut. Onions were tricky, pretending to reveal a layer at a time, but leaving you apparently no further on. Sometimes, when peeling onions, you were the one who ended up crying. "Onion," said Sharon.

Having persuaded Tobie to see Tom the Onion, all Sharon had to do was persuade Tom the Onion to see Tobie the Knife.

"No way," Tom had said.

But Sharon was determined. She reminded him of the condition in which she found him when she returned to the garden the previous night.

After he bruised her with his rough handling she stalked out of the garden, determined to drive away. But by the time she reached the car, her anger had lessened. She sat in the car collecting her thoughts, bent on giving him a piece of her mind when he arrived. Some time elapsed before she started to feel anxious. Then she heard his howl.

By the time she got to him, the little monk was struggling to help a naked, dust-caked Tom to his feet. Tom was blubbing Katie's name.

"Thank you," Sharon said to the monk. "I'll take him."

"He's very distressed," the monk said, his huge, unseeing white eyes trying to locate her somewhere in the sky.

"Yes. He is."

She managed to get Tom to dress himself, and the monk opened the gate for them.

*   *   *

"How much of last night do you remember, Tom?"

The fact was he remembered all of it.

"Admit you're in trouble," Sharon told him. "You won't talk to me. Talk to Tobie."

Sharon didn't let the matter drop and badgered him until he agreed to go in to work with her for an initial meeting. When Tobie called him *darlink* for the third time Tom developed a serious loathing for the woman. Then she claimed to be unable to see him until after Sharon had gone home in the afternoon. "Too busy, *darlink*. And Sharon's too busy to have you under her feet."

So he was sent away with an invitation to come back later. Before leaving the center he looked in on Sharon, who was talking with some women in the kitchen. They hushed when he walked in.

"Well?" Sharon inquired.

Tom shook his head. "It won't work." Sharon made her eyes into plutonium-tipped darts. "All right," he conceded. "Just the one meeting." He left, knowing that the other women in the kitchen were now quizzing Sharon about him.

He returned, as scheduled, moments before Sharon was ready to leave. She took him aside, kissed him and made him promise to give it a fair trial. Then she parked him in an immaculate, magnolia-painted room, with nylon carpet and nylon-upholstered, steel-frame chairs arranged in a circle, where he was told to await Tobie.

After fifteen minutes Tobie put her head around the door and waved a hand at him, manipulating her fingers like a spider. "Coming, *darlink*. Coming." Then she was gone again.

Tom fidgeted for another twenty minutes or so before Tobie showed up. By then he was feeling restless and irritable. He didn't know that Sharon's parting words to Tobie had been "Make him wait. Get him on edge."

Tobie sat down. "You want some coffee?"

"No," he said coldly.

"I do. I want some coffee." She was gone again for another five minutes, returning with a tray on which there were two cups. She sat down, rubbing her hands. "Is it comfortable for you? I don't like all these empty chairs. They make me think the room is full of ghosts."

"It'll do fine."

"You're sure?"

"Perfectly."

"Fine and good. Well, let's have this coffee before we begin. Black or white?"

Tom allowed the coffee to be pressed on him. Tobie made a grand fuss of offering him sugar, which he declined, and a ginger biscuit, which he accepted. Finally, with the coffee ritual over, cups and saucers were settled on adjacent chairs and Tobie was ready to begin. "Well, now, *darlink*. Here we are. Now what did you want to tell me?"

"Pardon?" said Tom.

"I understand from Sharon you have something to tell me. Fire away. Here I am." Theatrically, she put a hand behind her ear. "Look, I'm listening."

"You're kidding."

"Kidding? Why I should be kidding?"

"There's a misunderstanding. Sharon implied that *you* had something to say to *me.*"

"Honey, I don't know you from Adam."

Tom shook his head in disbelief. Tobie glanced at her watch. "I don't want to rush you, *darlink,* but we really don't have all night. Half an hour to be exact. I've got one of those ladies' birthdays to think about. We always make a cake and all those nice things, you know?"

Tom looked at her in disbelief. What was Sharon up to? Why was he here listening to this fussy old dame with the blue rinse and the birthday cakes? "Sharon thought it was a good idea, that's all," he said. She smiled sweetly, then seemed distracted by a small stain on her skirt, which she picked at in animated fashion. "She thought I should talk."

"Talk? What about, *darlink*?"

"She thinks . . . That is, Sharon thinks I'm going through some kind of crisis."

"Why does she think that?"

"Lots of reasons. Mostly last night. But—"

"Tell me about last night."

Tom sighed. "Well, I ended up naked in the Garden of Gethse-mane, that's the main—"

"And that's normal for you, is it, *darlink?*"

"Normal? Of course it isn't normal! I don't—"

"I'm only asking, *darlink.* So you agree there's a crisis?"

"Not a crisis exactly, more of a—"

"Well, if it's not a crisis, what is it? I mean *nekked* in the Gar-den of Gethsemane?"

"Look," Tom exploded. "You ask me to talk, and then every time I start telling you something you interrupt me!"

Tobie shifted her buttocks on her chair and patted her hair straight at the back of her head. Then she offered Tom a smile of dazzling sweetness. "Sorry, *darlink!*"

Exasperated, Tom started again. "Right. I admit, I went crazy last night up at the Garden of Gethsemane."

"Crazy? What's crazy? Maybe you had a few beers. Why not? Sometimes I want to take off my clothes and do crazy things. Don't look like that. Yes, even at my age."

"No, it wasn't a few-beers kind of craziness."

"Then what kind of craziness was it?"

"I don't know. The first thing was . . . well, I tried to rape Sharon."

"To rape her! I thought you were lovers! Aren't you fucking her already?"

Tom was unaccustomed to such candid talk from an elderly lady who looked as though she should be bottling chutney or jam.

She saw it. "What is it? I can't talk to you like a grown-up? Here, let's get one thing straight, *darlink.* Your daddy fucked your mummy, and your mummy fucked your daddy. As did mine and everybody else's. That's how we all get here. That's one of the two things you can be sure of. The second thing is that you gonna die one day. Everything else is up for grabs. Now, if we can't talk about sex or death like grown-ups, without thinking either's a dirty sub-ject, then we don't say no more, and you'd be better talking to a rabbi or one of your priests. Got me?"

Tom was suitably chastened. "Yes, we are lovers. And it wasn't exactly rape, but I wanted to . . . She was saying 'No,' and I was ignoring her, which, I must point out, I've never done before—not with her, not with any woman. I don't know why I behaved like that."

"What were you doing there?"

"Where?"

"Up there in the garden."

"I don't know. It seemed like a good idea at the time."

There was a long pause, during which Tobie guessed he wouldn't say any more about why he was in that place at that time. "Let's try a different question. What were you feeling when you were behaving like this with Sharon?"

"Bad. Just bad."

"No. That's how you feel about it now. Try that question again."

He thought about it. "I was feeling angry."

"You were angry with Sharon. What had she done to make you feel angry?"

"Not Sharon. She'd done nothing. I wasn't angry with Sharon."

"So who were you angry with?"

Tom felt hot. He was anxious. A dew formed on his brow. He tugged at his earlobe. "I . . . It's not—"

"*Darlink,*" she said, studying her watch. "I know I promised half an hour, but now I realize I have to dash." She rose and headed for the door. "Just as it was getting kind of interesting, don't you think? Come back tomorrow at the same time. And rinse those coffee things in the kitchen—be a good boy, huh?"

Tom stared after her in silent disbelief. After the door closed behind her he scratched his head and found himself collecting up the coffee cups.

He carried the cups through to the kitchen, where he found a woman with a curtain of long, dark hair and a face as white as the moon. She'd been one of those talking to Sharon earlier. Arms folded, leaning against the draining board of the sink, she appraised Tom coolly. She didn't offer to move aside as he swilled the cups under the tap and left them to dry on the draining board.

"I'm Christina," she said. "Are you Sharon's boyfriend?"

"Yes."

"I knew. I know a lot of things," Christina said. "I can see through you. I can see *right through* you."

"Good," said Tom.

He left the rehabilitation center quickly.

41

Sharon returned to her apartment grateful for the space afforded by Tom's session with Tobie. She could depend upon an hour or so of reliable solitude. It wasn't that she'd tired of Tom; on the contrary, she was alarmed by the strength of her feelings for him. What she'd considered to be a superior act of charity, almost a maternal concession, was drawing dangerously near to a lover's attachment. Now she was grateful for an hour to herself, to measure the situation.

It was Sharon's paradox that she used sex to keep men at a distance, as if to say: there, that's the closest you will ever come to me, the rest is not for you, now where are your resources? Sometimes it drove men crazy. It made strong men weep. It had earned her a great deal of reproach and many names. Slut. Bitch. Whore. Because masculine vanity, having recorded the sexual conquest, usually needed to win devotion too, to bear it away like a trophy. If devotion was not in train—and with Sharon more often it was not—men sulked or raged. Sharon's indifference was interpreted as deeply threatening.

*   *   *

"You and Tom were lovers, weren't you? At college?" Katie had
asked quite candidly on one of her visits to their home. Ostensibly,
Sharon had come to town so that they could watch a feminist play
together. Bored out of their skulls by old rhetoric, they'd abandoned the performance halfway through. Act Two, for them, took
place in a wine bar.

The question, put so bluntly, made Sharon blush. "Yes. But
only once. And it was a mess. We were drunk." Katie blinked at her.
Sharon tried to cool her blush with her hands. "We were both plastered. I'm not sure if, or how, we even managed it properly. Then
in the morning we woke up to the sticky smells of curry and garlic
and cat's breath. It wasn't romantic."

"Did it put you off each other?"

"Yes," she lied. "Yes, I suppose it did."

She regretted that lie. There was Katie wanting to level with her,
trying to surmount a potential obstacle to their relationship, an ele-
phant that lay sleeping between them, and she'd lied by giving the
answer she thought Katie had wanted to hear. In truth she'd been
disappointed by that boozy, lackluster night, but she'd never admitted it. Not to Katie, not to Tom and, for a long time, not even
to herself.

That wine-bar conversation had faltered when they were joined
at their table by two handsome, moisturized young men sporting
identical haircuts. "Great!" Katie exclaimed. "We're being chatted
up. Have a seat, boys. Let's hear your opening lines."

They teased the boys, who must have been ten years younger,
without mercy. With closing time approaching, Sharon dug her
nails into the thigh of the nearest boy. "You know that time when
the chicks go to the loo to talk about you?"

"Eh?" he said, wincing. "What?"

"And you buy us tequila slammers while we're out, eh? Well,
make 'em doubles."

Then she marched Katie off to the toilets. "What are you up to?"
Katie giggled, lowering her knickers and speaking from the cubi-
cle.

"Are you on?" Sharon called from the other stall.

Katie only giggled louder.

When Katie came out, Sharon was pretending to inspect an eyebrow in the mirror. "I said, 'Are you on?'"

"What do you mean?"

"Back to their place. You can tell Tom I dragged you off to a nightclub."

Katie stopped laughing. She caught Sharon's eyes in the mirror. "No, Sharon. That's not how it is."

Sharon regretted that even more deeply. She particularly regretted it because Katie knew Sharon was testing her. She knew Sharon wasn't remotely interested in the two hairstyles waiting out in the bar. She knew Sharon was trying to get her to betray Tom.

Katie knew, and she knew. But that other terrible, complex telepathy which exists so acutely between women could never be admitted, and Sharon had no choice but to brazen it. They emerged from the toilets to find large tequila slammers awaiting them on the table.

"Well," Sharon said, tipping back her tequila. "I was all set for a stormy night, but my friend here says no, and we girls stick together." Sharon hadn't forgotten the expression on the face of the boy who'd obviously paid for the expensive cocktails.

That episode was possibly the only tiny blemish which lay between Sharon and Katie, and it was overlooked, if not forgiven. "You shouldn't make a religion out of sex," Katie said to her on the way home.

"Why not?" she snapped back. "The Christians have."

It was three years since that night. In her Jerusalem apartment, with an hour to kill before Tom's return, Sharon kicked off her shoes and lit candles around the room. She darkened the place by drawing the blinds. It was a ritual she'd developed for unwinding from the stresses of her job. This time what she really wanted to think about was Tom.

Mozart's *Requiem*. It was her favorite piece of music for getting rid of stress. Her principle response to the piece was not religious; rather, she found something within it which could spool her in until she lost all awareness. Often she would fall asleep, or drift between sleep and waking in the shadow of consciousness, while the music played. The remorseless argument of the *Requiem* would marshal her down a corridor of slippery black vinyl, almost as if she were being conducted down the spiraling grooves of the disc spinning slowly on the turntable, grooves deepening and growing more steep-sided as she surrendered. And as she was ushered along the vertiginous continuum, stroked by the outer fringes of sleep, fanned by the wings of dreaming, the music was transmuted, becoming splintered light for a moment before resolving back into sound, but this time as a single voice, seductive, familiar, insisting: *Help him. You must help him.*

Tic. Tic. Tic.

The sound made Sharon open her eyes. She was dozing in her chair. The stylus was skating at the end of the still rotating disc. The dull, amplified click repeated over and over. She knew she must have dozed, but she was dimly conscious of words whispering in her head. The candles had burned down slightly. Soft yellow light pulsed from unwavering flames. The record player continued to click provocatively.

Tic. Tic. Tic.

She padded over to the hi-fi, lifted the stylus arm and switched off the unit. Turning, she stiffened suddenly, letting the stylus crash back on to the cherished black vinyl.

A woman stood in the doorway between the bedroom and the lounge. She was naked, looking away from Sharon into the heavy book she held in front of her. Faded tattoos followed the contours of her tanned skin. Her face was lined like a map of the city, and her eyes were like chips of polished black stone.

"Katie?" Sharon whispered.

But it wasn't Katie. The figure continued to read, her lips moving slightly as if mouthing words from the book. She seemed oblivious to Sharon's presence. Then she turned a page. The vellum wrinkled and folded in her hand; the page transformed into a soft white bird, its feathers marked with ancient script. The bird hopped from the book, wheeling toward Sharon. Another page was turned, changing instantly into a second bird; then another; then another. The birds winged around the room before flying, one by one, from the open window.

42

"This evening, before you came home, I dreamed of the Magdalene."

"You too? Are you sure it was a dream?"

"No. I'm not certain. I was dozing in the chair. I got up and she was there. I blinked my eyes and she was gone."

"Was it a *djinn?*"

"Maybe. Perhaps it was something else pretending to be a *djinn.* I don't know what a *djinn* is."

"I'm beginning to."

"Do you think it watches us in the dark?"

"Yes."

"Do you think it watches us when we make love? Was it watching us just now?"

"Yes. It crouches in the dark, and it watches. I don't care anymore."

"Ohhh . . . When you kiss my belly like that . . . Make love to me again. When you make love to me, the *djinn* can't get inside me. I'm afraid of them getting inside me."

"You're not afraid of me being inside you?"

"Never. But I'm afraid of love getting inside me. I'm afraid of letting myself love you, Tom."

"Is love a *djinn?*"

"Yes, I think it must be. Love is a *djinn,* crouching in the dark, waiting to get inside you."

"No. The *djinn* is what comes when love is gone, when it's seen enough."

"You're right. Love gets bored. Love gets tired. It wants to go somewhere else. But when it comes out it leaves a terrible hole, a gaping wound, bleeding, hollow. A place for *djinn* to live. That's why I'm afraid of love. Don't make me love you, Tom. Don't make me do that."

43

So what about Katie? Why won't you talk to anyone about Katie?" Tobie was nothing if not direct. She slurped coffee and clattered cup on saucer. At this second session Tom had been ordered to make the coffee himself in the kitchen and was upbraided when he'd failed to add biscuits to the tray. "Ginger snaps, *darlink*. In the cupboard you will find ginger snaps, or I can't work."

As well as ginger snaps Tom had found Christina in the kitchen. She was seated at a Formica table, her long hair hanging on either side of an untouched glass of water. "Hello," Tom had said brightly. She'd ignored him, hadn't even moved her head to acknowledge him. When he returned to the room in which the first meeting had taken place, Tobie had rearranged the chairs. Now there were two chairs facing each other and a third adjacent to the other two.

"Why the spare chair?" Tom asked lightly.

Tobie shrugged. "Could be for someone, could be for no one. What about Katie?"

"What about her?"

Tobie reached over and put a tiny pink hand on his arm. "You know this notion of release, it's not a joke. It's very important."

"Yes."

"So tell me about her."

"What do you want to know?"

"Where does it hurt, *darlink*? Where does it hurt!" Tom looked nonplussed.

Tobie looked tired. "This is why I don't bother no more with men. You are all too stupid. Why do I waste my energies? So you can pretend you don't know what I'm talking about? Only for Sharon I do this. OK. Have it your way. Let's start with the funeral. What can you tell me?"

"She was cremated. The usual thing. Quick job. Some vicar she never even knew. Standard verses. Curtain closed. Done. Wheel in the next."

"You sound bitter."

"What else could be done?"

What else indeed? thought Tom. Death placed you in the grip of ritual forces which either did the job or left you profoundly dissatisfied. But it was the institutional efficiency which had dismayed him most about Katie's funeral, the punctilious execution of the event. There was something terrifying about the way in which the vicar had swung into the ritual, a smooth meshing of gears, a dynamo whistling, some well-greased words swished across the face of the thing like dependable old curtains. You felt like you were at a hanging but all you saw was the trap door falling open. Then you were led away and pushed into a car with a noiseless engine. A kind of silence took over. The dispatching job was done, but it touched no one. It settled nothing. It was like watching a film of a funeral; God, it was even raining when you came out. Afterwards everyone came up and mouthed feeble words of consolation before going home; but you, you were left with the feeling that there was still somewhere a body dangling from a rope, struggling, kicking, screaming.

"How did she die, your wife?"

"A tree fell on her."

"Not a normal way to go."

"She was driving. There were gale-force winds. Not uncommon in England in the autumn. It blew a lot of trees down. One of them landed on her car as she drove home from church."

"Was she alone in the car?"

"Yes."

"Pretty bad luck."

"Bad as luck gets."

"So why do you feel shitty about it?"

Tom looked up. "I'm not finding this easy, you know."

"I know that, *darlink*. I'm not finding it easy either. Being grown-up about these things isn't about it being easy."

Tom plummeted into an abyss of silence. If he was waiting for Tobie to drag him out of it, she resisted. Perhaps five minutes went by, but it was impossible to tell when each second rounded and fattened itself in the howling vacuum. At last he looked up at her, finding her gentle, sea-gray eyes resting patiently on his. "What?"

"You were about to tell me why you feel shitty about all this."

The door opened. Christina walked in and without asking for, or receiving, permission sat down on the third chair. Tom looked at Tobie.

"We have a kind of open system, *darlink*. Everybody helps everybody. It means nobody is the patient, nobody is the doctor. Christina and all the other women here have experiences and insights which can be of help."

Christina was staring dead ahead. If Tobie was suggesting she might act as one of his therapists, Tom was beginning to wonder how low he'd sunk.

"Low enough," Christina said.

"What?" said Tom.

"You heard."

"I heard, but I didn't—"

"Oh, fuck."

"Don't be aggressive," Tobie soothed.

"He's the one," Christina said, "he's the one who's being hostile."

"But I didn't—"

Christina ignored him and turned to the older woman. "I'm trying to be grateful, Tobie, really I am. But listen to what he's giving out. How can anyone be grateful? His mind is way outside his skull. Fuck it, if he's going to be like this, I'm going." Her chair fell backwards as she stood up and left the room.

After the door had closed Tom looked again at Tobie, who was patting the back of her hair. She said, "You were about to tell me why you feel shitty about all this."

Odd. She seemed to repeat the words in exactly the same tone of voice she'd used before Christina had interrupted. Tom looked at the chair. It had righted itself, but he hadn't seen Tobie pick it up.

"You looked confused, Tom."

"What was she talking about?"

"Who, *darlink?*"

"Christina. What did she mean about being grateful?"

"You lost me, honey. What does Christina have to do with this?"

"She just came in and—" Tobie was looking blank. "—and knocked the chair over."

"Nobody came in, *darlink*. Not Christina, not anybody."

Tom looked hard at her, suspecting some kind of game. "Wait here." He got up, left the room and stalked along the corridor to the kitchen. Christina was still in her place at the table, staring ahead, the untouched glass of water before her. "Did you just come into the room? Answer me."

Christina didn't move. Tom put his face aggressively close to hers. She didn't blink. Then she drew her lips back across her teeth, somewhere between a sneer and a smile. Tom went back to the room.

"Now you look upset," said Tobie. "Tell me what's upsetting you."

"Hell! I saw—or I *thought* I saw—Christina join us. She was sitting on that chair. She said something to you about feeling grateful or not feeling grateful."

"Was it that?" Tobie pointed to a hand-drawn sign on the wall which said:

*Be Grateful to All Those You Meet Here for
Giving You the Chance to Work on Yourself.*

Tom sighed.

"So you met Christina, huh? Sharon's very good with her. Let me tell you about her: she's like a radio station, picking up all this stuff from the airwaves. Only when you tune in you don't know what you're going to get. Interference. Pirate stations. Police calls. She's got a dial that won't stay still, no matter what we do. No, Tom, she didn't come into the room just now. But someone did. And we think we know who it was, don't we, *darlink?*"

"Do we?"

"Yes. Oh, yes, we both know who it was. Don't we?"

"She was driving home from church. It was a Sunday."

"Was she religious?" asked Tobie.

"Not until the last few months of her life; not at all before then. I was the one with vestigial religious beliefs. She used to take the piss in the early days. She and Sharon both. In fact, it was Sharon who weaned me off religion at college."

"She would. But we're talking about Katie, not Sharon." Tobie wouldn't let him run away from the subject.

"It was incredibly windy that morning. Even before she set off."

Tom remembered the color of the sky, like heated steel buckled under a hammering. He recalled the autumnal tree tops waving furiously as she climbed into her car. She'd asked him to go with her again. It had become a ritual by then. Every Sunday she would ask; he would refuse. "Coming?" "No." But that morning the request had a special tone, a renewed significance. The question pealed like a bell. That morning she'd applied her make-up with a particular haste, plastered it on, trying to cover up what was cracking underneath.

Then the car wouldn't start. He recalled waiting behind the door with a sinking feeling as the starter motor brayed hollowly in the yard, again and again. The overnight rain had dampened the electrics. He was afraid she might change her mind and stay at home. Finally he'd put on his shoes and had gone out to help. Throwing open the bonnet, he'd sprayed the terminals before trying the thing himself, muttering under his breath, "Start, damn you, just start."

At last the motor had coughed into life, dirty exhaust smoke pulled ragged by the wind as he revved the engine. She'd taken over from him in the driving seat without a word. They didn't exchange a kiss. They didn't even meet each other's eyes. She drove away. It was the last time Tom had seen her alive.

"You didn't want to go with her?" asked Tobie.

"I wouldn't have gone anyway."

"Anyway? What do you mean anyway?"

"I had to . . . I had an appointment that morning. I had to see someone, but even if I hadn't, I wouldn't have gone."

The church Katie had started attending was some twelve miles from their home. There were nearer options, but this was a medieval sandstone church, part Saxon, part Norman, which they'd discovered while out walking. Katie had fallen in love with its leaning belltower and the bizarre inscriptions of its seventeenth-century gravestones; with the rain-chewed gargoyles outside and the interior carvings dreaming under centuries of wood polish; with the cracked baptismal stone font and the odors of dying flowers; with the pyrotechnics of stained glass; and with the weight of expended prayers, embedded in the stone walls like stacked hymn books.

And most of all she'd been taken by its greatest treasure, something preserved under the belltower only because the rampaging iconoclasts were unable to reach it or were too sickened or dispirited by their own vandalism. Standing in a trefoil perpendicular niche in the east wall was a rare statue of Mary, the patron saint. Shielded from the weathering of centuries, it was not Mary the Virgin, not the Mother, but the darker Mary, the shadow one, the sexual Mary. She was represented with flowing hair and clad in a gown, holding a vase of balsam in her outstretched hand. She gazed south-east, it was said, in exact compass alignment with the city of Jerusalem.

The Magdalene, watching from the tower.

"I've thought of something," Tom said to Tobie. "It hadn't occurred to me before. The church she'd started going to, it was the Church of Mary Magdalene."

"Is that significant?"

"No. Yes. God, I don't know."

"Sounds like it might be."

"If you say so."

"Let's try another tack. Who were you going to see that morning when she died."

"No one. It's not important."

Tobie looked at her watch. "We're going to have to call it a day at that, Tom. Rinse out these cups, won't you? And maybe tomorrow you'll be ready to tell me who you went to meet the morning your wife died."

Tom found the kitchen empty. He was relieved Christina was gone. He carefully rinsed and dried the cups, and—because Tobie had scolded him for only completing half the chore on the last occasion—put them away. As he left the building he found Christina sitting on the steps in the sunshine.

"Hey, you," she called. He hovered on the steps above her. She looked up at him, shielding her eyes from the sun and said, "Katie says hi."

44

The black water lapped at Sharon's thighs in some parts of the tunnel. She was wading in shorts and plastic sandals. The pencil beam of her torch was refracted by the stream, creating an illusion of smokiness on the surface of the water. She flashed the light on the walls and at the roof just above her head, all of it hewn out of the living rock. Jagged brown stone gleamed dully.

There was a splash behind her. Ahmed, missing his footing, swayed against the wall. Nothing was said, and they waded on for another two hundred yards in silence.

"How is it you never came here before?" Ahmed wanted to know.

"Not my idea of fun."

Hezekiah's tunnel was built to bring water from a hidden spring into the city at the time of siege. It was the only place where Ahmed would agree to talk to Sharon about the *djinn*.

When Sharon had left work that evening, kissing Tom before he went into one of his dark sessions with Tobie, she had on impulse visited Ahmed rather than returning home directly. As usual, he hadn't answered his door until her fourth knock. He'd shaved his head. She made no comment about this. It was something he did from time to time, claiming that the *djinn* tended to hang on to a person's locks and that this was why monks and nuns and other holy persons cut off their hair when taking sacred orders. She did remark, however, that he was looking a little tense.

"I've smoked no hashish for a week. No alcohol, nothing. Not even tobacco."

"It'll do you good. And keep the *djinn* away."

His bitter laughter had brought on a fit of coughing. "You know nothing. Without all this the *djinn* multiply by the second. You know nothing."

"I think I've had an attack of the *djinn*, Ahmed."

"I know," he said seriously. "I've been expecting you to tell me."

Ahmed had two ways of talking about the *djinn*. Mostly it was in the form of lively banter, as if continuous reference to demons and spirits was a terrific long-running joke between him and everyone else, as if he too knew it was nonsense but was nonetheless playing the game of never letting on. Then at other times his voice would soften and become lower, and others began to wonder if the joke was on them. "I've seen it."

"Something's happening. I don't understand it. I know it's tied up with my feelings for Tom."

"You're still fucking that bastard Englishman when you could have me!" he had shouted angrily. "Look at you. It's disgusting! You're in love with him!"

"Maybe."

"Watch out for love. That's the worst of all the *djinn.*"

"Be serious, Ahmed. I want to talk with you."

"I am being serious. But I don't like to talk of the *djinn*. It's the surest way to make them appear."

"Ahmed, what have you been telling him? What have you been filling his head with? Whatever it is, it's spilling over to me."

"So, now you begin to believe in the *djinn*. You had it coming. You want me to help your friend, huh? All right, maybe I will, but we don't talk about it here. I don't want this place swarming with them tonight. Come on, we're going for a walk."

"Can we walk the wall? I love walking the wall." She always felt unsafe unaccompanied.

"Are you mad? The wall is crawling with *djinn*. It's their favorite place in all the city. Some of them are even disguised as Israeli soldiers. No, there's only one place in this city where we can talk about them safely."

"But where?"

Ahmed had pressed a hand on her arm. His tones had become hushed again. With his shaved head and smouldering eyes he looked crazed, psychotic. "I'm going to show you how to make the *djinn* appear. You won't ever see this again. Believe me, you won't want to."

Exasperated but disinclined to argue, Sharon had followed Ahmed out of the apartment. First they'd driven back to her place to grab some suitable clothing, then to the tunnel, where Ahmed was well known. The supervisor had greeted Ahmed and assured him that the last tourists had gone through some time ago. He was about to close, he said, so no one would come up behind them. Sharon wondered how much time Ahmed spent down here.

The tunnel, Ahmed had told her, took about half an hour to pass through before emerging at the Pool of Shiloah. They sloshed on, the water level rising and falling, the sides narrowing and widening, the ceiling occasionally making them stoop. Light from their torches shivered on the damp walls. Sharon stopped when she saw a light up ahead.

"What is it?" Ahmed breathed.

She pointed and the tiny light ahead moved and went out. Ahmed passed her in the tunnel, and she followed behind. Then she saw the light again, and froze. "There's someone up there," she hissed.

Ahmed turned patiently. "Don't be an asshole. It's your own light, reflected."

When they reached the halfway marker, Ahmed pointed to the spot where the ancient engineers had struck pick against pick, digging from opposite ends. "This is the safest place in the city. Here we can make the *djinn* appear in relative safety. I say 'relative.' Here, give me your torch."

He turned out both lights, and they were plunged into primeval darkness. It was cool in the tunnel. But for the occasional trickle of water from the walls, it was silent as a tomb.

Ahmed spoke out of the darkness. She heard his feet wading through the unseen water. He was circling her slowly. "This is the oldest part of the city. Old as the Canaanites. Older. There was a settlement here long, long before David came and gave the city his name. It was built—"

"Why are you circling me? You're being creepy—"

"SHUT UP, YOU BITCH! SHUT UP! Say nothing! Now I have to start again!"

Sharon was shaken by this sudden outburst. She began to doubt the wisdom of coming here. She always exhibited a breezy over-confidence with Ahmed, where other people were scared by him. Until this moment she'd always believed he would never do anything to hurt her; but now she sensed he might be experiencing some new kind of crisis. The indications were there: the shaved head, the sudden withdrawal from his drugs, this new volatility.

"This is the oldest part of the city," he said again, moving around her, wading gently through the water as he repeated the words, identical in order. She could hear his soft breathing between each sentence and the swish of his shins drawing through the water. "It was built around this spring, the Gihon spring, because the people from that time recognized this place. It was, and still is, the navel of the earth. It is a place of seed power. Just as a seed is wedded to the memory of the plant which created it, so it this place wedded to the memory of its origin. The Hindu calls this place a *chakra*. The Aboriginal calls it a *jiva*. I call it the cradle of the *djinn*. The city of Jerusalem is built over this place. My people tell how the rock under the Golden Dome is a giant plug to stop the energies of this place pouring out on to the earth."

Ahmed had drawn closer as he circled. She could feel his breath on her neck. She wanted to tell him he was frightening her, but she was afraid to speak.

"But it leaks. Vapors stream from this place. The city is like a vast mind constructed over the abyss, intoxicated by vapors of its own dreaming." Ahmed began to back slowly away into the darkness. His voice retreated, diminishing, becoming no more than a soft whisper. "Drugged and dreaming. And this is the place where the *djinn* are breathed into life. Here they are dreamed into existence. Here they come into being."

He was gone.

There was nothing but blackness. She strained for the sound of his breathing but heard nothing. She listened hard for the sloshing betrayal of his movements further on up the tunnel, but there was nothing. All she could hear now was her own breathing and her own heart beating.

"Ahmed," she tried, lowly. Then, louder, "Ahmed!" Her voice volleyed through the cavern, startling the rock.

"You bastard, you'd better not have left me—" Her voice writhed and withered in the crannies of the rock. He'd taken both torches. She waded on a few yards and, for a moment, became disoriented. Which way had they come in? Was he telling her the truth when he'd told her they'd reached the halfway point? She waded again and screamed as she crashed into the wet rock. Groping with her fingers, she located the plane of the wall. She found herself gripping it with her fingernails, as if gravity had shifted and she was in danger of falling.

Then she became aware of another presence in the tunnel.

She heard a low breathing, and her skin seemed to pull itself inside-out, like a glove. She tried to speak. It came out as a paralyzed croak. "Ahmed?"

There was no answer. But something stood in the water just a few feet away from her. Something solid and imposing, a cold, hard presence. Another shocking wave passed across her skin, a rinse of acid. Bile rose in her mouth. She sensed the thing fattening, approaching. Her hands were gripping the wall.

Her nostrils flared at a familiar odor as two pencil beams of light were flashed on, cross-directed at the water. Taking shape out of the black stream, and rising to meet her, was a life-sized stone statue. It was a medieval representation of a woman with flowing hair, carrying a vase of ointment, carved from eroded gray stone. Sharon reached out to touch it. The stone seemed unspeakably cold. Condensation, like congealed breath, gathered on the cold stone cheeks of the gray visage.

As Sharon's fingers touched the damp stone cheek, warmth leapt from her fingertips and the thing transformed. No longer stone, it was living flesh. Now it was an old woman, black veil thrown back. It was the tattooed Magdalene, dripping water, arm outstretched, holding forth not a vase of ointment but a dead white bird in the palm of her brown hand.

Sharon stumbled back against the wall, a strangled cry escaping between her teeth. But as the image of the Magdalene swelled before her and rose steadily out of the water, a ripple in the stream seemed to break it, and the vision re-formed a second time. "Christina!" Sharon breathed, confronted by her client from the rehabilitation center. Christina was standing in the water, in jeans and T-shirt, smiling at her beatifically, almost maniacally. Christina failed to answer Sharon's cry. She was already changing again. She was becoming Katie.

Katie's hands were cupped on either side of her mouth. Her face was contorted with rage, and she seemed to be calling, trying to make herself heard across time, but no sound was coming out. Sharon put a hand to her own choked throat. "What? What is it, Katie?" she whispered. But Katie, tortured in her own silence, continued to call silently across the abyss.

A ripple passed across the phantom, and there came in Katie's place another stone idol, this time like a Canaanite goddess carved in yellow stone. Sharon had only a moment to witness it before, with kaleidoscopic reinvention, it was transformed yet again, this time into a vile, inhuman form, upright and reaching toward her, something half-reptile and half-insect like some primal seabed creature, shining like a beetle, fibrillating limbs groping at her. When it metamorphosed for a final time its face was Sharon's own open mouth contorted in a silent wail.

Sharon was paralyzed, unable even to give voice to her own scream. Then Ahmed was holding her, soothing her, trying to calm her. She could not make sense of any of his words. As he ushered her away from the spot, she was still looking wildly around for signs

of the ugly spirit that had reached out at her from the liquid darkness.

When they reached the Pool of Shiloah at the end of the tunnel
she sat down, exhausted beyond tears. Her own reflection in the
pool had returned to normal. Ahmed sat by her, occasionally
stroking her shoulder.

"What was it?" she said.

"It was the *djinn,* of course."

"Is that what it looks like?"

"I don't know how it looked for you. It takes different forms
for everyone."

"But the last thing I saw: was that what it really looks like?"

"I can't tell you. Only you give it its form. All of its forms. Only
you."

"But if you can make it appear like that, can you make it go
away?"

"I can't do that. I'm too much in love with my own *djinn.*"

She looked into his eyes. She couldn't tell now if he was utterly
crazed or wise beyond understanding. Then she saw her own reflection in the pool, gazing back at her.

45

Whom had he gone to see that day? The day Katie died, the day Katie had uprooted a tree, magnetized it, charmed it out of the ground, conjured it out of the wind, prayed for it to fall on her head, offered herself, martyred and sacrificed. He blamed her for her death. She'd wanted it. Willed it. Made it happen. So he would pay the penalty.

With whom did he have an appointment that day? This was Tobie's signing-off question, uppermost in his mind as he made his way back to Sharon's apartment that evening. Maybe he would have answered it too, if it hadn't been for the little old Jewish Gorgon's *certainty* about herself. She knew it. She knew it instinctively, almost immediately, the way people unconsciously home in on a wound, accidentally stroke a bruise or brush against a cut you might be carrying. The dumpy, barrel-breasted, blue-rinse *witch* had *known,* and she hadn't even disguised it.

If it hadn't been for her smugness, her self-satisfaction, the effortlessness of the woman in going to the point, he might even have told her. But right now he wondered how he'd even allowed himself to be talked into the thing. And what sort of a place was it? What kind of therapy did they offer the inmates of the center? All this shit about letting anyone sit in on the session as you spilled your private guts. That flake Christina. Why was he supposed to let a smack-head eavesdrop on his grief? Why should he even have to sit in the same room as that kind of piece of shit? Because the blue-rinse *darlink* Jewish mamma thought it was a nice liberal idea to get everyone to help with the washing-up.

He was furious. His fingernails dug into the palms of his hands as he stalked the arid streets in the evening sunshine. Two young Hasids, beards tucked into their necks, heard him talking to himself and glanced up as they passed. He glowered back at them.

He wouldn't tell her. He couldn't. For one thing she would tell Sharon. Neither of them could possibly understand. They were women. They didn't have the capacity to guess at what he was having to deal with. Their reactions would be predictable, prefigured.

What did women know about it? What gave women the moral right to make any judgment about the behavior of men and the depths of their desires? Ah, but they did know! At least on some intuitive level, without knowing its force, they all knew how to provoke that desire from an inadmissibly early age. Those girls at school, from the moment they arrived on their first day, were already blushing with astonishment as they sensed its latency. Senior schooling coincided with puberty; that was no accident. By the second year they were learning how to control and direct its sublime force. By the third year they were luxuriating in it, and after that the apprenticeship to sexual power was over. It had all been tested out on those poor-bastard adolescent boys, lagging behind in the maturity stakes but with hormones boiling and bubbling and popping until they were hallucinating in the classroom, like kids on spiked drinks at a teenage party. And all the while, in the pink classroom clouds of unruly pheromones, the air whistling with mismanaged signals, these poor dumb boy-oxes were expected to study!

Those fourth-form girls, like Kelly—Kelly McGovern, with her bleeding-heart rose motif and crisp white blouse, and provocative skirts, and immature legs wobbling on heels. She knew how to stand an inch too close while he marked her book; how to leave two buttons open at the top of her blouse so that in leaning forward her

white breast would quiver like a fledgling dove wanting to fly free
of the restraining net; and how to glance back over her shoulder with
a nascent smile before returning to her seat, a smile acknowledging
that he'd dealt the correct or approved response, a smile suggesting, impossibly, that she was manipulating him. . . .

Yes, the previous year there had been another teacher at the
school, Mike Sands, able and committed and with an eye to the hi-
erarchical ladder, who had fallen that way. Rumor of his affair with
a fifth-former soon became an open secret. The incredulity of the
rest of the staff was translated into outright hostility, and in the matter of a week he was transformed from popular and respected colleague to staff-room pariah. The female staff seemed to take it per-
sonally, speaking about it with bitterness, as if they had themselves
been violated; the male teachers added to that their contempt for his
weakness, but their occasional confused stabs at humor betrayed an
agenda of hidden envy.

"The poor man," Katie had said when Tom told her about it.
The poor man? Everyone else had other words to describe him, but
Katie was the only person from whom he'd heard any expression
of sympathy.

"Poor man? He's a shit," Tom had said. "He abused his position. He took advantage. He deserves everything he gets." He'd
heard his own voice keening.

"All he had to do," Katie said, "was to leave her alone. That's
all. But he couldn't. And he's still falling." Katie often surprised him
by the things she said. "It's sex, isn't it? We can't deal with it. That's
why our religions hate it so much. It wants to save us from ourselves. If we don't have any certainties, we can't trust ourselves."

"It's a battle," he'd agreed.

"Is it?"

"Oh, yes." He'd tried to sound ironic, but she heard only the
essential seriousness.

Mike Sands offered his resignation before they fired him. Tom
never heard whether he ever got another teaching job after that. He
was gone, but his name haunted the staff room for a while. Then
another term went by, and one morning Tom arrived at school to
find a set of preposterous accusations chalked on the blackboard.

It wasn't true. It was all nonsense, and he'd sorted the matter, resolved it, found the boy responsible and understood his obsessive jealousy over the McGovern girl. He'd explained to the boy that he knew Kelly was experiencing a teacher-crush. He'd been kind. He'd let the boy get off with a warning.

But he couldn't help looking at Kelly in a new way. Almost literally, she seemed overnight to have acquired an aura about her, a vividness, a golden light. Her attentions began to distract him, even to disturb him. When she dawdled at the end of his lessons, always the last one to leave, he couldn't help but notice how her haversack, slung from her shoulders, seemed to ruck the hem of her skirt, offering an extra expanse of thigh as she left the room. And how on closing the door behind her, she always glanced back, to register his gaze.

Jesus, he'd thought, she's fifteen years old and she's pulling my strings.

One day Tom had been boring himself, teaching comparative religions at the end of a tiring session, and Kelly had approached him with a question.

"Why don't we do the Song of Songs?"

The other students filtered out of the classroom. She'd asked him about the Song of Songs and he hadn't got a flicker of an answer. "Pardon?"

"We've done all this about Hindus and Muslims and Buddhists. Why can't we do the Song of Songs?"

"It's not a religion, Kelly. It's a book of the Old Testament. A marriage song." He pretended to hunt through his desk drawers for something he'd mislaid, so that he didn't have to meet her eyes.

"I know. My sister's boyfriend is at college; and he told me it's too mature for R E teachers."

"He would, wouldn't he?" He looked up. She flicked her copper-colored hair and moistened her pink lips with her tongue. It was a totally unselfconscious act. The dull electric light shone yellowly on her upturned face and on her lips. "Wait," he said, getting out of his chair hurriedly. "I'll get you a copy and you can take it home and read it."

His keys trembled in his hand as he unlocked the stockroom

door. His only thought was to give her a copy and get her out of the classroom. He couldn't stand to be alone with her. He couldn't stand it.

Inside the stockroom he felt out of danger, yet knew all the time she was just on the other side of the door. He flicked on the light and cast his eyes along the rows of obsolete textbooks. He looked for something with suitably large print and a dry commentary, preferably toned down by depleted modern language, suitable for a fifteen-year-old siren with a crush on her R E teacher.

He was reaching for a shelf when the door opened and she came inside. Gently, slowly, she closed the door behind her. She stood with her back to him, holding the door handle.

He had a hand on the shelf. "What are you doing?"

She let go of the handle and turned from the door. Her legs were crossed at the ankles, and her hands were clasped lightly in front of her thighs. Her eyes were cast down.

"It's not a good idea," he said, "for you to be in here." It came out in a whisper.

"Why?"

"Because it doesn't look good."

"Why not?"

"Please go, Kelly."

"I don't think you want me to. I think you like me."

"Yes. But it would be better if you went. Really."

He knew then that he'd already said far too much. He'd admitted everything. All he'd had to say was "Get out," and he hadn't. Now he felt paralyzed. It was coming from her. She radiated sexual tension, infecting him, transmitting it to him. His arms seized. His fists clenched. He could smell her breath on the air in the tiny store cupboard. He could almost taste it, sweet with desire, sour with fear.

All male schoolteachers, he knew, had entertained this stockroom fantasy. Many would deny it; very few had been faced with it. She kept her eyes averted as Tom, still leaning against the bookshelf rows of school-issue Bibles, swallowed hard and tried to control the rushing noise in his ears. His eyes fell on the gentle swell of her breast underneath the bleeding rose. Her breathing was short, and he realized her terror matched his own. He understood that they were both out of control. Then, for the first time since entering the stockroom, her eyes met his. If she hadn't, if she'd kept her eyes averted, the moment might have passed and they would have been saved from themselves; but instead she looked up, squinted at him, gold light like tiny barbed hooks in her eyes, and his hands were on her waist and his tongue was pressed inside her mouth. They kissed for a long time, locked. She almost let herself become limp in his arms, until the paralysis drained from them.

"This can't happen," he said. "I don't love you."

"It's all right."

"It's not all right. It's not. It's all wrong."

It was like trying to stop a train by waving from the side of the track. She remained utterly passive, gazing into his eyes as he unbuttoned her skirt and tugged it down. She gasped as he hooked his thumbs into the band of her tights and pants and drew them down to her ankles.

They heard the classroom door open. They froze. There were footsteps. Her unblinking wide eyes gazed into his. Someone opened a desk drawer and closed it again. More footsteps. The classroom door opened and closed again.

"Wait," he said. The keys were still hanging on the other side of the stockroom door. He reached around for them and locked the door from the inside. He scattered a pile of exercise books from the seat of an old armchair. Pressing her into the chair, he pulled off her shoes and the indecent knot of tights and knickers at her ankles. She fumbled at his trousers. He led her hand to his already engorged cock. She held it lightly, tenderly.

He was on fire. The smell of her confused his senses. He could taste her mood. Her desire for him was a clear, sweet bell. There was a smell from her, a smell that made him think of a fiery balsam. He heard words from far off: *A garden enclosed is my sister, my spouse!; a spring shut up, a fountain sealed.*

She shuddered again as he touched a finger inside her. He was surprised to find how moist she was, and he suspected she was not a virgin. "God. God."

"It's all right," she said. "I've done this before. It's all right."

Jesus, now she was coaching him! He kissed her again, and then he unbuttoned her blouse, releasing her girlish white breasts from the unnecessary bra, kissing each in turn. His kisses poured down her belly. He dearly wanted to push his tongue inside her, but he didn't know the depth of her experience, didn't want to frighten her or do something that might repel her.

Awake, O north wind; and come thou south; blow upon my garden, that the spices thereof may flow out. Let my beloved come into his garden, and eat his pleasant fruits.

Instead he wet his finger before inserting it inside her again, and she flinched with pleasure. Her eyes blazed in awed fascination with what he might do with her. Her lips were slightly parted. She took short gasps of air as he probed and stroked.

My beloved put in his hand by the hole of the door, and my bowels were moved for him. I rose up to open to my beloved; and my hands dropped with myrrh, and my fingers with sweet-smelling myrrh, upon the handles of the lock.

Then her fingers tightened around the head of his cock, and she impelled him toward her. He parted her thighs wider, sliding a hand under her buttock before he penetrated her. She bucked and squealed and he had to put his hand over her mouth, and she bit into his fingers.

"Don't," he said. "Don't make a noise."

"It's all right. I won't again."

He made love to her gently and aggressively in turns; above all he wanted it to be a good experience for her. He meant to withdraw from her before ejaculating, but she was tight and burning hot inside, and he couldn't bear not to stay in her.

When he did withdraw, he dressed hurriedly and guiltily. She did the same. Then he unlocked the door, checking that no one was around.

"Look," he said after she'd stepped out from the stockroom, "look—"

"It's all right," she said. "I won't say anything to anyone. Now I know, I won't tell anyone."

She picked up her rucksack from his desk and hoisted it on to her back. This time her skirt didn't ride up and though she was smiling, she didn't look back over her shoulder at him. He watched her walk down the corridor and out along the playground, like any schoolgirl going home after a day's lessons.

How could he tell Tobie or Sharon about that? What could they possibly know about it? Women's needs were a complex mystery to men; yet they always presumed to measure and circumscribe the equal and opposite mystery. How could they ever know? They had never stood in the same howling wind. They had never put their hand in the identical flame. How could they ever guess how men live with Nature's cool hand cupping the genitals and flexing an elegant, jewelled finger one hundred times a day to tickle the ready glans? What did they know about any of it? They could never understand that male sexuality was so far out of control.

For a moment he felt the deep, tidal roar of the rage of the Old Testament patriarchs against women for their inordinate power to confer and withhold sex; to tease and to deny; to manipulate; to humiliate; to shame and to condemn.

46

I'm not going to see Tobie anymore," Tom announced when he arrived back at Sharon's apartment. "I'm not having any more to do with her."

"He's angry," said Sharon.

"He used to say hello," said Ahmed, reclining in Tom's favorite chair, swigging a Maccabee.

"I thought you didn't drink beer." Tom opened the fridge and helped himself to a beer before slumping on the sofa next to Sharon.

"What has she done to you?"

"Nothing. That's just it. It's a waste of time. All you do is talk, endlessly, in circles. There's this idea that it helps. It does nothing. That place is full of addicts, right? Well, some of them are just addicted to talk."

"You are right," said Ahmed, waving his bottle. "And that old woman, she is the worst. She will try to peel your head like an orange."

Tom winced. "Anyway, I'm not going again."

"So you keep telling us."

"Be like me," said Ahmed. "Stay away. That place is like a waiting room for *djinn*. Sharon and Tobie lift them off this and that person who comes to the place, and then the *djinn* just wait around for someone like you and me, Tom, so they can get on our backs. Believe me, it's not a healthy place."

"You're crazy," said Sharon.

"You laugh at me? Didn't you see enough today? Didn't you? Hey, Tom, this one, she thinks working up there has made her immune. But now she's changed her mind."

"What's he talking about?"

"Nothing."

"Nice haircut, Ahmed," said Tom.

"Is he laughing at me? Yes? I make a prediction. One day you too will have this haircut." The Arab glared.

Sharon sensed a serious mood swing. She changed the subject. "Ahmed has made a further study of the scroll. He's got some more things to tell you. I'll get you another beer."

"It's difficult work." Ahmed's voice had become uncharacteristically muted. "As the spiral of words approaches the center, it becomes smaller and more difficult to decipher, and the information becomes denser. But I think it's important.

"Last time I told you how there was faction in the movement after the death of Jesus on the Cross. The Magdalene was marginalized as Jesus' brother James tried to lead the new movement. They tried to get Mary to recognize James as the resurrected Jesus outside the tomb. At first she wouldn't go along with it. But a third force came along, described by Mary as the running-dog of Caiaphas. This man was a Pharisee, one of the religious police. Mary describes him as a woman-hater, an opportunist and a liar who had converted to Christianity and built a following by scapegoating the Sicarrius—Judas Iscariot—for his part in the plot which went wrong. Together James and this man went to Damascus. On the road this man—the Liar—was plagued by demons or *djinn* pretending to be the ghost of Jesus. From then on the Liar claimed to be speaking with the authority of Jesus.

"Though she does not name him, other than call him the Liar or Hater of Women and so on, I believe this man was Saul, originally one of Jesus' persecutors, who became Saint Paul. Mary describes a second conflict inside the movement. The Liar, because he

hated women, tried to discard any of Jesus' teaching which he
didn't like. James and the Magdalene established a temporary truce
to drive the Liar out of Jerusalem. They succeeded, and he went
west. In Ephesus they beat him, and in Crete they drove him back
into the sea, knowing him for what he was. Then he went to Corinth
and to Rome, looking for converts among the gentiles."

"If the Liar was Paul . . ." said Tom.

"Then the Liar succeeded. He became the great Apostle. The
presiding genius of the Christian Church. To this day."

They broke his legs. They broke his legs. "But if that's the same
man," said Tom. *They broke his legs.* "I mean if that's the same
man—"

"What?" said Sharon, waving a beer under his nose.

"Nothing," he said declining the beer. "Nothing. Look, I'm
tired. I'm going to turn in, if you folks don't mind. I'm not feeling
too good."

He left Ahmed and Sharon talking in the lounge and undressed
in the bedroom. He was shivering violently, and suddenly he felt
very cold, as if he had a fever. He pulled the thin sheets over his
shoulders and curled up. With the sound of Ahmed's voice murmuring from the lounge, he fell asleep.

47

When he woke up, Tom felt cold. The wind howled outside the window and shrieked in the branches of the ash tree across the road. He sat up, casting wildly around the room. The body next to him shifted. Katie blinked up out of her sleep. He was at home. He was in England. Katie was in bed next to him, snuggling after his warmth.

"What is it?" Katie murmured. Sleep pasted her eyes half shut. She exuded comforting, human smells of slumber and sleeper's breath.

"Katie. Katie."

"What's wrong?"

He got out of bed and crossed to the window, tearing open the curtain. The verdant treetops outside were taking a buffeting. The street was wet. Gray slate tiles on the houses opposite glistened with slick rain. Raindrops stippled the window pane.

Katie struggled upright in bed, her face engraved with concern.

"Katie, I had this dream. You wouldn't believe the dream I had. Come here, let me hold you. You were dead. You were killed by a falling tree. And I was in Jerusalem with Sharon. And you were haunting me. And Mary Magdalene was haunting me. Oh, Katie!"

"It's all right. I'm here. I'm here."

"I can't tell you the half of it."

"Were you upset? Upset because I was dead?"

"I was falling apart. In Jerusalem. It was all so vivid."

"I'm going to make some coffee." She pulled a dressing gown on. "Perhaps it was a sign."

"A sign?"

"Jerusalem. Mary Magdalene. Maybe you should come to church with me for a change."

"Church? What? Yes, maybe I will. Maybe I will. I feel so strange."

Her eyes lit up. "Really? You will? Hey, something must have got into you."

He heard her padding downstairs, the sound of the kettle filling, crockery lifted from a wall cupboard: familiar, domestic sounds.

He looked out of the window again. He could taste the moisture in the atmosphere contrasted with the aridity of his dream. Traffic hissing along the wet road was light. The unpeopled streets spelled out Sunday. Wind whistled round the house.

Along the street came the boy delivering newspapers. He was reading a comic as he walked, following his route automatically, dipping a careless hand in his paperbag. It was all wonderfully banal and reassuring. Tom heard the newspaper inserted through the letterbox, dropping on the mat. He flexed his toes in the deep pile of the bedroom carpet before pulling on a bathrobe and shuffling downstairs.

He flipped open the Sunday newspapers. There was something wrong with the front page. The masthead was unreadable. The banner headline was written in a foreign script, something like the Hebrew lettering from his dream. Then Katie came up behind him, snatching the paper from his hand. She opened the door and summoned back the paper boy.

"Try to look at what you're giving us," she said with a stiff smile, handing the journal back to him.

The boy colored. "Sorry," he tried. He fished in his bag and brought out their usual Sunday paper wedged with supplements.

Tom checked the date. It was 30 October: in the dream, the date his wife had died.

He nudged open the door of the lounge. The curtains were still closed. An unfinished bottle of red wine stood on the coffee table; wine dregs solidified in the two crystal glasses. Slumping into a chair, he held his head in his hands. He felt like he'd been dreaming for months; his mind was still awash. He felt slightly feverish. Fragments of the dream began to swim back to him. An Arab. A Jewish woman. Something about a scroll in a spiral shape.

"Are you all right, Tom?" Katie was standing over him with coffee, wisps of steam coiling from the mugs.

"Yes. Yes, I'm—"

"Did you mean what you said about coming to church with me?"

He shook his head. "I can't. I've arranged to see someone. I can't get out of it." The words tumbled out before any thought, almost as if scripted. It was what he said to her most Sunday mornings. It had become a reflex. The disappointment in her face was unbearable.

"For a moment I thought you meant it," she said, getting up to draw the curtains.

Tom had a momentary horror of what he might see when she flicked back the curtains. It was with some relief that their tiny rose garden and patio looked unchanged and that the redbrick wall at the rear stood unchallenged. "Wait. I've changed my mind. I will come."

"Really?"

"Yes, really."

It was the weight of the dream, in which she had died. He'd dreamed that she'd died on her way back from church that very day, the 30th of October. A storm had caused a tree to topple on to her car. Even though it was only a dream, he couldn't stand to let her go out alone. He would go with her and divert the return journey. It was true that he had an appointment; but he would have to deal with that later.

In the dream he'd been responsible for Katie's death. He'd inflicted a thousand tiny wounds on her. She'd felt his love for her begin to dwindle, and from that moment on her own death was imminent. It was a double-death. When love died, she died. Katie had willed it. "I'd die without your love," she used to say. She'd meant every word of it.

In the dream he had had a tattoo on his leg, Katie's name on a backdrop of vivid color. He inspected his ankle. There was no tattoo.

The gale was gathering strength as they drove out of the city toward the Church of Mary Magdalene in the country. Trees were bent at acute angles, like survivors of some catastrophe still trying to shield themselves from the wind. Snapped branches and leafy twigs littered the road. Few other cars seemed to have ventured out.

Katie drove. "You're very quiet," she said as she changed gear.

"I'm still thinking."

"I know," she said soothingly. "You're trying to put it right."

"I'm sorry. I really am sorry."

"Don't. At least you're here."

When they reached the church the sky was swollen, colored like a bruise. The sandstone church tower leaned into the wind like a rigged ship tacking against formidable racing clouds. They got out of the car. The lych-gate bobbed slightly in the wind. The great yew tree in the churchyard creaked and waved, and even the effaced headstones seemed insecure, each like a tiny boat moored in a dangerously swelling harbor.

"We'd better get inside, out of this wind," Katie said, locking the car.

They approached the sanctuary of the church. A lofty, aluminum double-ladder was drawn alongside the porch, leaning against the tower and reaching up to the trefoil niche sheltering the effigy of Mary Magdalene, as if someone had been trying to save or steal the statue. The fierce wind rattled the ladder against the sandstone wall of the tower. A claw hammer was hooked around one of the lower rungs, swinging slightly. Tom had a bad feeling. His sense of dread redoubled as Katie reached for the iron ring of the church door. She opened the door a fraction before turning to him. "Come on," she whispered. "Don't wait out there."

Tom hovered outside the porch, the wind snatching fistfuls of his hair, rattling the aluminum ladder against the tower. "I can't," he said. "I can't."

"Don't be silly, Tom. Come on." She slipped inside the door, leaving him alone outside the porch.

The freezing wind shrieked round the sandstone church like a predatory spirit. The sky darkened further. It was not yet noon, though it could have been night. Something moved at the periphery of his vision. He looked up. There was nothing but for half a dozen stone gargoyles grinning down at him, eyes popping, tongues drooling. Rain water dripped like saliva from the tongue of one of the carvings. He turned away, running a nervous hand through his hair, unable to move backwards or forwards. When he looked back up at the Magdalene effigy, what he saw made him step back. The Magdalene had shifted position. The eyes were lowered at him; her arm, once holding a vase of ointment, now seemed aligned at a new angle, pointing at him.

"I can't do it, Katie! I can't come in!"

As he shouted, he heard a low growl from the throats of the gargoyle creatures, and in a second all six heads were yammering and barking at him like rabid dogs.

"Katie!"

Above the sound of the barking gargoyles he heard his wife calling to him from behind the great oak church door. "You know what to do, Tom! You know what to do!"

Tom looked at the ladder and hammer. Grabbing the hammer, he proceeded to climb. The ladder creaked and shifted slightly. The wind snatched at him as he drew abreast of the lowest row of gargoyles. The first gargoyle slavered and spat as he aimed a hammer blow directly at its face. The hammer punched into the soft sandstone, and the figure exploded in a small cloud of dust. The second and third gargoyles went the same way.

Panting and weeping, he continued to ascend the ladder to a second row of heads. But as he climbed the gargoyle heads had changed. Tom was paralyzed as he gripped the rungs. The first was the face of David Feldberg, begging him to take the proffered scrolls. The other gargoyles had also been transformed. They were the heads of the scholar Ahmed, and of Tobie from the rehabilitation clinic.

"Please, Tom," they cried. "Please!"

"Don't be fooled, Tom!" came Katie's voice from within the church. "Don't be fooled!"

Still weeping, Tom launched the hammer at the first face, pulverizing it. Then he dealt two swift blows to the last of the faces. The wind snatched at the exploding dust. Chippings of stone spiraled to the ground, falling at the foot of the ladder.

"Come inside!" shouted Katie.

A mighty gust of wind roared around the angle of the tower, heaving the ladder on to a single leg, pushing it away from the wall. The ladder swayed momentarily in dark space before it clattered on to the sandstone. Tom recovered. He was but a few rungs from the Magdalene. The wind blasted him full in the face, hurricane-strength as he struggled up the remaining rungs, squinting into the full force of the gale. His breath coming in short gasps, he reached out to touch the effigy. The moment his fingers contacted the cold stone, the wind lashed like a giant paw, smashing the ladder from beneath him and flinging it into the darkness of the churchyard. Tom felt himself falling, spiraling endlessly down into blackness.

He landed on his feet, inside the church. He was standing just inside the oak door.

A small congregation, perhaps a dozen or so people, was gathered near the altar. Only Katie, who stood with them, seemed to notice him. She smiled.

"What are you doing here, Katie?"

She shook her head, finding the question ridiculous. "The morning, Tom. We're watching for the morning."

Katie turned away. Surveying the walls of the church, Tom saw the desecration. In three places the ochre-colored walls had been paint-sprayed with spiraling words. In each case the word LIAR was sprayed in letters of diminishing size. As he looked closer he saw the words LIAR LIAR LIAR repeated in the scrawled spirals, until the letters became obliterated in an ugly paint blotch at the spiral centers.

Tom approached the altar. A low murmuring was coming from

the congregation. A stone spiral stairway had appeared in front of the altar, and, led by the vicar, the congregation was descending to a shadowy crypt. Each step was engraved with mysterious runes and Hebrew letters. Tom caught a whispered chant as he stood behind Katie. She shuffled toward the stairway, falling in behind the others. "Liar, liar, liar."

He joined in the chant. "Liar, liar, liar."

48

"And so in this dream," said Tobie, "did you take any pleasure in punching out all these faces?"

"Yours," Tom said emphatically. "I remember being particularly satisfied when I got to you."

Tobie laughed girlishly. "How did I know, *darlink!* How did I know you'd say that?"

"Do we really have to have the Undead listening in on this?" Tom flicked his head toward Christina, who'd been in on the session from the beginning. She sat with her chair reversed, her hands folded under her chin. Since the start of the session she hadn't once taken her eyes from Tom, and she hadn't said a word.

"I don't allow clients to abuse each other," Tobie said evenly. "You can be as candid as you like with each other, but no abuse."

Someone put a head round the door and asked Tobie to take an urgent phone call. "Talk to each other, children; I'll be back in a moment. Talk."

After three minutes of enduring both Christina's silence and her unblinking gaze, Tom said, "At least we're all agreed you're actually *here* this time. I was beginning to think you were another phantom. That was quite a stunt you pulled."

Christina said nothing. She blinked once, very slowly. Tom shook his head. Under the lank curtain of hair, and behind that pale, ravaged face, Tom thought Christina must have been an attractive woman, once. Her punishing anorexia had left her with a teenager's figure.

"I know you want to fuck me," she said sullenly.

"?"

"I know it."

"I'd rather fuck a corpse."

"You've been doing that already."

Tom glowered. Christina didn't even flicker. They sat in silence for a few more minutes, until Tobie returned.

"Have you two made the most of each other? Have you been talking?"

"No," said Tom.

"Yes," said Christina.

"Good," Tobie said. "Good."

"Ask him about schoolkids," Christina said, getting up off her chair. "He fucks schoolgirls."

Tom's eyes incinerated her as she left the room. Christina tossed a backward glance at him over her shoulder.

"Well," said Tobie.

Tom was still glaring at the closed door.

"Don't be alarmed, Tom. I warned you, Christina picks things up. She doesn't know any more, take my word for it. She picks up fragments, and that's all she knows. I have an idea it's related to her sickness."

"Sickness? What sort of a place are you running here?"

"Let's say I'm no longer surprised. Was that who you had to meet that day? A schoolgirl?"

Tom nodded.

"You'd been having an affair?"

"She was one of my pupils. I met with her that day to end it. We mostly met on Sundays, when Katie was at church. It was only a few occasions. I knew it was madness, but I had a kind of fever for her."

"Why were you going to end it?"

"I was meeting her to tell her it had to stop. I'd come to my senses. I realized what I was doing, to her, to Katie, to myself. I was going to leave her alone. In my own mind I'd resolved it."

"And Katie was killed that day."

Tom wiped away a single, hot tear. "I went through all that with Kelly. I felt sick. Hollow. Then I came home and I went to bed. I was awoken by the telephone. It was the police. A tree had fallen on Katie's car on her way back home. A tree. Blown down in the gale."

"And it's hard not to personalize a thing like that."

"I know what you're thinking of me. I know how you must see it. Well, maybe everything you think of me right now is correct—"

"Stop it," Tobie interrupted. "Stop it right there." She leaned out of her seat to place her two hands on his forearm. For the first time it occurred to Tom how young were Tobie's eyes. Where so many people of Tobie's age had eyes like dried beads, shrunken by the loss of life's novelty, hers blazed with sympathetic light. "First thing, Tom, I don't judge. I'm not here to do that. I got too much in my life I've done wrong to judge anybody. Understand that, for my sake. I see you suffering and I want to say, hey, I suffer too. You see, talking about it is the only way I think I get you to stop judging yourself. Because that one is the worst judge of all."

"It didn't stop there. She'd known about it. You see, some kid at school, a boyfriend of Kelly, he got jealous. He knew, or guessed. He started writing things about me on the blackboard at school. I caught him, and I dealt with it, so I thought. But then someone else—I don't think it was him, maybe it was Kelly—started sending letters to Katie, spelling it out. Katie confronted me one day, and I admitted it. Of course, she was terribly hurt. But I promised that I wouldn't see the girl any longer.

"Then after . . . after Katie was killed, the writing on the blackboard started up again. I would turn up in the classroom at the beginning of the day to find the board covered with filth and abuse, sometimes words I'd never even heard of. Shocking things. Then weeks would go by and it would happen again. It couldn't have been the original boy because he'd moved to a different school.

"And it was always on a Friday morning. One time I had a hunch it was about to happen again, and I contrived to stay in my classroom overnight to see if I could catch someone. It was easy to dodge the cleaning staff. There's a stockroom . . . a store cupboard at the back of the classroom, and anyway I had my own keys. I locked the classroom door and I settled down on a chair in the stockroom with the door slightly ajar. I stayed awake all night. Perhaps I dozed before the first staff and kids arrived, but when I went out of the stockroom, there it was, the usual litany of filth, chalked in huge letters on the blackboard. And the classroom door was still locked.

"But now I knew who was doing it. I should have known it was her all along. The handwriting, when I came to examine it, was hers, but in printed form. It was Katie's. She was doing it."

Tobie blinked impassively.

"I couldn't take it anymore. I gave in my notice. I needed to get away. The only person I could think of running to was Sharon, here in Jerusalem. But Katie followed me. She tracked me down. She's here. She won't let me go, Tobie. She won't let me go."

They sat quietly for a while, Tom with his eyes averted. At last Tobie said, "I think we came a long way today. I think it's enough for now. I'm going to make you some tea before you leave, but I want you to promise me something. Promise me you'll repeat this to Sharon. She's very worried about you, and you don't talk to her. Will you do it?"

Tom shrugged.

"That's not good enough. I want a promise. Now will you promise me, Tom?"

49

Rabin and Arafat were talking. The leaders of the Israeli government and the Palestine Liberation Organization were on the verge of agreeing to an historic compromise. The Jews and the Arabs were talking, but Sharon and Tom were not.

Tom was becoming more and more remote. Tobie had told Sharon that he had begun to open up during their "sessions" but felt sure there was still more for him to face. Sharon had deliberately stood back from these developments, hoping to give Tobie operating space and Tom breathing room. She hoped—beyond hope—that Tobie could wean him away from Katie and that she could have him to herself.

But the opposite was happening. He was slipping away from her. Day by day. Even during their lovemaking, in which she'd surprised herself with her invention and ardor, he clung to her like someone who felt himself physically fading. Sometimes as they made love he seemed to gaze at her with a kind of awe and terror, as if, with a moment's loss of concentration, one of them might be turned into an insect. He couldn't seem to abandon himself to her, not even at the crucial moment. And that was what she wanted from their lovemaking, from their orgasms: she wanted total surrender, annihilation, transcendence. She wanted unconditional love.

She wanted these things because she was sick of lying to herself. She had spent fifteen years pretending she wasn't in love with Tom, and she was tired of it. It had exhausted her. She had pretended all this time to Tom. She had pretended to Katie during the years of their marriage. And she had pretended to herself. That last lie was perhaps the biggest and the most hurtful to endure.

Sharon knew she had lied because she hadn't dared. The inability to dare had come from the terrible realization, as a young girl, that love must be suppressed, disguised, cowled. She'd learned at an early age that to reveal to someone the open fire, to brandish the torch in their face, was to terrify the object of one's love, so that they leapt back from the flame. Give all and you will receive nothing. Unmitigated love is met with unmitigated contempt. No one, it seems, either wants or can find a use for utter devotion and surrender.

Except Messiahs, demons and gods.

At fourteen years old Sharon had learned this vicious, universal lesson on giving herself unconditionally to a man more than twice her age. He had taken her virginity and left her only with a sense of outrage that her dedication was not reciprocated. At some deep level, in some protective sanctuary where the soul retreats to lick its wounds or die, she'd vowed that never again would she expose herself to so much hurt. And she'd done what almost everyone manages to do: she'd checked the instincts of love. She'd reined love in. She'd smokescreened it, dissembled it, thrown a cape over it, so that its brilliant and unbearable light shone only weakly; and had been so successful in her art that she'd even come to disguise the thing from herself.

Thus when she first met Tom and a fist closed round her heart, she hid behind a ferocious cool; and when still later he accidentally tumbled into bed with her one night and the fist tightened, she drowned her instincts in alcohol; and when he got married and she felt her breath becoming shorter, she calmly unclenched the fingers around her heart by befriending his wife Katie, even though she knew Katie was not right for him in the way she herself was right;

and finally when she heard Katie had died in a terrible accident, she appalled herself with the way in which indecent hope and thanks mixed with grief. For a while she hated herself and once again smothered her true feelings under a morass of cynical doubts and actions. And when the almost unthinkable had arrived, and Tom had come to Jerusalem—come to *her*—she had gone out and found a man, any man, a young Arab man, as an antidote to the snake poison of this terrible, paralyzing, heart-gripping affliction, contriving even that Tom should stumble in on her.

The head and the heart. How they loved to play their games. How they loved to cheat and lie and steal from each other.

And on this day, with the sky a boundless blue soaring over Jerusalem, with golden domes winking, and towers calling, and faith rising like heat ripples, Rabin and Arafat were talking. The Jews and the Arabs were breaking bread, and Tom was slipping away.

Sharon reminded herself she had an errand to run. Tobie had asked her to deliver an envelope to a former client who lived up near the Me'a She'arim. After delivering the letter, Sharon turned back toward the ghetto. She was curious as to how the ultra-Orthodox right-wing Jews were going to respond to the political breakthrough. There had already been demonstrations against the agreement, just as some of the Palestinians, led by the fanatical Hamas, were demonstrating in Gaza.

A sign confronted her at the entrance to the ghetto:

DAUGHTERS OF JERUSALEM: DRESS MODESTLY AT ALL TIMES.

It was painted in peeling gold lettering on a black board.

DO NOT PROVOKE OUR WORST NATURES.

Modesty, she knew, meant exposing neither her knees nor her ankles, nor her arms, and not even her elbows. She stood outside the entrance to the ghetto in a blouse which was capped at the shoulders, baring her arms, and in a skirt which reached only to her knees. She'd been inside the ghetto before, suitably attired. But at that moment she felt a sudden anger that this particular group of Jews could unlawfully annex part of Jerusalem, imposing on all who entered the terror of their misogynist rule. Must we be responsible for the boiling cesspit of your lust? she thought. Must women carry your demon?

Her own demon told her to go in.

Inside, the Me'a She'arim was like a film lot. Narrow streets, with dozens of antiquated stores literally spilling their goods on to the pathways. Hasidic Jews scurried by, almost every one wearing eighteenth-century Lithuanian aristocratic garb. I'm a Jew, she thought. I love this country. But what have I in common with these people? More than once she'd sat up all night at Ahmed's house, arguing with crazed fundamentalist Arab friends of his who were no madder than these Jews. Two women passed by, eyeing her askance. Their heads were shaved. She knew they would have wigs—wigs!—in their wardrobes for special occasions. An old man with a Methuselah beard growled at her from a shop doorway, or maybe he was just clearing his throat. She stopped and smiled at him. He growled again.

"Was I walking too fast?" she said in good Hebrew. "Or too slowly?"

The old man said nothing. She went farther, finding a knot of young men standing on the street corner, discussing the peace talks. She heard the words "traitor" and "betrayal."

"Rabin and Arafat are the peacemakers," she said loudly. "You should give thanks to God. These men are risking their lives for peace!"

The young men stared at her in astonishment, their eyes swimming behind their spectacles. She walked on, feeling the drills of their eyes in her back and her buttocks.

Get out of here, she told herself. *What are you trying to do?*

She passed deeper into the ghetto. Ghetto! How odd that the rest of the world used the word to describe a place from which it was difficult to escape, where here they made it a cultural fortress, a place where outsiders, time, even history, could not get in.

Get out. This is no place for you.

She leaned her back against a wall sprayed with religious graffiti and took out a cigarette. As she made to light it, something cracked hard against the wall beside her head. Her unlit cigarette fell to the ground. There was a puff of dust in the air from the wall, and at first she thought she'd been narrowly missed by a bullet. Then she saw a stone had fallen at her feet.

Get out! Move!

But she shouted defiantly, "I'm a Jew! This is my country too! You don't represent us!"

As she looked around she saw a cluster of bearded and bespectacled young Hasids, all staring at her beadily. The stone could have been thrown by any one of them.

Is this what you wanted? Is this it?

She turned and walked back out of the ghetto by the way she came in.

Back in her car, she held a handkerchief to her face and wept. Not because of what had happened in the ghetto, or because she was frightened—which she was—but because of Tom.

Tom couldn't love her because he was possessed. He was possessed by the idea of his dead wife, and ideas, Sharon knew, could claw people apart like demons. Ideas were like spirits—no, not *like* spirits, they *were* spirits. Some were good angels and some were unclean spirits. They manipulated you, tempted you, wrestled with you, led you by the nose. They could harm you. Love was a spirit— who would deny it? A good angel or a filthy wind? How else could you explain human behavior? When the angel-demon of love was in you, your temperature rose, your hands wouldn't do what you told them to do, you would find yourself walking to places you knew you shouldn't go. You lied in your own heart, as she did over Tom.

And Tom didn't have room for the angel-demon of love because he was possessed. He was like the city, Jerusalem. A city that proclaimed love from every tower and curved dome, every spire and slender minaret. And yet it had no room for love because it was a city possessed by the unclean influence of fundamentalism in all quarters. Self-obsessed religious rages and theological fevers. The towers and walls of Jerusalem were crawling with diseased demons, with *djinn*, ranged around the battlements, defending the walls against the armies of love, armies who looked eerily like the defenders themselves. . . .

So with Tom. He was an occupied zone. She couldn't come near him. She couldn't tell him, so she sat in her car outside the walls of Jerusalem, and wept.

50

So. There we have it," Tobie said. "The mystery is solved. There's really no more to be said."

Tom was distracted. He was distracted by the thought that Sharon was just about to leave the building, and his brain was on fire with some of the things she'd said to him the previous night. That morning she'd already left for her work at the rehabilitation center before he'd had an opportunity to talk with her. They had a Weather-house agreement. Tom would go for his sessions with Tobie only at the time Sharon was leaving; that way they could put a distance between Sharon's professional interest in his progress and their relationship. But it was becoming more and more difficult. He knew that Tobie and Sharon talked: confidentiality was, according to Tobie's precepts, just another level of hiding. He, in turn, talked with Sharon about the sessions. But the previous night Sharon had said some things which had astonished him.

"Huh?"

"I said it's really all over. Yesterday you told me everything, and you told me Katie had been responsible for writing those things on the blackboard. What more is to be said?"

Tom looked at Tobie's smiling face, scenting a trap. That afternoon they'd been joined not only by Christina, but by two other women—Rachel, whom he'd never seen before, and Rebecca, who was a resident at the center. Rachel had sympathetic brown eyes and soft, black curls; but for the deeply engraved lines of harassment, she could have been a model. Rebecca looked like a potential serial killer. The three younger women leaned forward in their chairs as if expecting imminent revelation. Tobie lounged back in hers, knees together, hands relaxed in her lap.

"Why does that sound as if you don't mean it?"

"Don't I mean it? Is there some reason," said Tobie, "why I shouldn't mean it? Katie wrote on the blackboard, even though she was dead."

"You may not believe in ghosts," said Tom, "but there are plenty of people who do."

"I believe in ghosts," said the serial killer.

"And me," said Christina.

The third one, Rachel, smiled sweetly.

"Did I say I didn't believe in ghosts?" said Tobie. "Did I?"

"Yes," Tom said bitterly, "you probably have some neat theory which admits them without having to believe in them. No doubt you can rationalize them away. I say *ghost.* You say *guilt.*"

"Neat theory? *Darlink*, there's nothing neat in my life, I promise you. But if you want to know what I think about ghosts, it's this. We laugh, don't we, at those medieval ideas of ghosts and spirits and demons. Modern psychology has words for these: 'hallucination,' 'projection,' 'transference.' This is the modern orthodoxy, and that's the litany. It all comes out of the disturbed self, doesn't it? But in two hundred years, maybe they discover some new orthodoxy, and they have more understanding about energy, spirit forces which can influence people. Then they titter and laugh at our simplistic twentieth-century psychology. So, Tom, why don't you give me some credit for having a fucking imagination just once in a while?"

Tom was taken aback. It was the first time Tobie had sworn at him, and the first time she'd dropped the sweet-little-old-lady persona. Now she looked quite angry. The three other women, too, were staring at him as if they thought it was high time he behaved himself.

"I'm sorry—" he tried.

"Don't be sorry. Be precise. We got more sorry here than we can use."

"That's true," Christina added, obscurely.

"And the truth is, Tom, we're getting a little bit impatient."

"What more do you want? I told you everything yesterday. I made a clean breast of it."

"Big deal," said Christina.

"Yeh, big deal," said the serial killer.

Tom was astonished at the way the mood had suddenly turned against him.

"After all," said Tobie, "there's more than just your feelings at stake here. Other people are suffering too."

Sharon? Did she mean Sharon? The previous night Sharon had excelled herself. She had, against all her best instincts, made her apartment beautiful for Tom, cooked him a meal, filled the place with lighted candles and told him the *truth*.

"Always?" Tom had said, after fifteen seconds of stunned silence.

"Always."

"Even from college days?"

"From the first day I met you. Almost everything I have ever done since then was either to impress you, or to be near you, or to run away from you. It's horrible, isn't it?"

"Is it?"

"Hiding it, I mean. All that time. Hardly a day going by without me thinking about you in one way or another. Having to pretend to be pleased when you were married. Having to pretend not to have hope for myself when Katie died. Everything in between."

"I can hardly believe what you're saying to me, Sharon."

"You'd better. You don't know what it's taken to get me to say this. You've been inside me, possessing me, haunting me like a spirit, all this time. And yet you weren't even responsible."

"I don't know what to say."

"You don't have to say anything. You don't have to do anything. I just had to tell you, that's all. I had to change what I was doing and tell you."

"Does it feel better?"

"It feels better and it feels worse."

They had gone to bed, but too much lay between them: the weight of Sharon's revelation, his own confession in Tobie's sessions, the ghost of Katie paradoxically drawing ever nearer as he tried to talk it out of existence. These things were like a set of daggers hovering in the dark, angled toward his head. When Tom was unable to make love, Sharon had cried hot, bitter tears.

"Yes," Christina echoed Tobie, "other people are copping the fall-out."

Rachel, who until this moment hadn't uttered a word, smiled sweetly and said, "What we're suggesting is this. What if we do believe in ghosts, and yet what if it wasn't Katie at all who wrote those things on the blackboard?"

Tom looked from one to the other of them. Rebecca and Rachel gazed at him, fascinated. Tobie watched him closely, head cocked. Christina blinked dully.

"Tell us what was written," Tobie said softly.

Tom cleared his throat. "It was just filth. Juvenile filth."

"Tell us exactly."

"You know the kind of thing. 'Teacher fucks' and all that—"

"Here." Tobie was holding out a felt-tipped marker pen. She nodded at the gleaming white board behind him and pushed the pen into his hand. "Show us."

"Is this necessary?"

"Don't be afraid. Nothing you write up there can shock us."

"Hell, no," affirmed the serial killer.

Tom got up stiffly and stood at the board. He shook his head briefly, as if to distance himself from the unnecessary ritual. Then he calmly wrote the word "FUCK" on the board in large letters. He looked back at the group. Tobie nodded approval. Then he wrote "TEACHER FUCKS VIRGINS."

"You told me," said Tobie evenly, "that it was written in Katie's handwriting. Could you make it look like that?"

He shrugged, wiped what he had written and wrote it up again in rounded, feminized but decisive letters. Then, more rapidly, he wrote, "KELLY MCGOVERN SUCKS MR. WEBSTER'S

COCK." Then he started scribbling faster, as if with a pent-up
anger. "SHE TAKES IT UP HER ARSE. HE COMES IN
KELLY'S CUNT." His hand scuttled across the board in an ac-
celerating frenzy, filling the available white space. It was almost as
if his hand was a detached thing, independent of the rest of his
body, scrabbling across the white space like a broken-winged bird
or an insect looking for cover. The white space was filling up with
angry, demented lettering. He began to fill in the spaces between
letters. He was sweating profusely, scrawling more and more juvenile filth and abuse across the first slogans. Finally, when the board
came to resemble a tangled black nest, indecipherable, his arm fell
limply to his side. He turned to his audience. "Satisfied?"

"Yes," said Tobie. "Very."

"Can we go now?" said Christina.

"Yes, you can go now we know."

Christina and the serial killer got up and left, as if they'd been
doing him, or Tobie, some huge favor by sitting in on this exhibi-
tion.

"What do you mean, *now we know?*" Tom's voice keening.

"I think you know too," said Tobie. Rachel, who had stayed,
smiled sympathetically.

"What do you mean? What are you saying?"

The two women looked back at him in silence. Then the light
dawned.

"I get it," Tom nodded, smiling. "You're saying that I did it.
You're saying I wrote the stuff on the blackboard, is that it? Is that
what you're saying?"

"It seems to me," said Tobie, "that you're the one who is doing
the saying."

"You're crazy."

"Guess we all are, Tom. A little bit."

"You're saying I did this to myself?"

"Tom, face it. You felt responsible for Katie's death. Maybe, you
think, if you hadn't seen this girl, you would have been with Katie.
Or maybe you should have gone with Katie that morning. Whatever. You blame yourself. And you can't forgive yourself, can you?
Oh, maybe it would have been better if you'd loved Katie."

"Shut up, Tobie."

"Yes, that's the hard part. The really hard part. If you'd loved Katie, it would all have been different. You could have grieved differently. Things would have been different. But what you really can't forgive yourself is the terrible sin of *not* having loved her. You think that's what killed her. You think that from the moment you stopped loving her, she began to die. The double-death. Death from lack of love. Didn't she say that to you: 'I'd die if you ever stopped loving me'? Didn't she say that? Well, you have to believe me, Tom: you don't have that much power. Yet, still, every day you go on crucifying yourself, all because of the unforgivable crime of not loving her enough "

"Fuck you, Tobie."

"Self-crucifixion, Tom. It's all the rage in this place."

"I said, 'Fuck you.' "

"You'll think about what I said. You haven't any choice." Tobie got up. "At least your hostility is a little more out in the open. I'm going to leave you with Rachel here for a moment. She's got something to say."

Tobie went out, closing the door behind her with a quiet click.

"Did you see that?" Tom shouted at Rachel. "Can you believe that woman?"

"Sit down," said Rachel. "Sit down beside me. I've got something to tell you."

Tom slumped into a chair across the room from Rachel, so she got up and pulled a chair close to him. "I was one of Tobie's patients. She asked me to come today, to talk to you. I was addicted to pills, I had eating disorders, all of that thing I went through. Some of this was caused by phone calls I used to get. Obscene phone calls from some anonymous man, almost every night I spent alone. I reported it to the police, changed my number, did everything. Still they continued. Then the phone calls became letters, addressed not only to my home but to all the people who were close to me. The letters offered graphic accounts of all of my sexual perversions. In lovingly rendered detail. I liked orgies. I liked to be whipped. I liked to eat my lover's shit. Of course it was all lies, but can you imagine how my mother and father felt about receiving this kind of stuff through the mail?

"I can't tell you what I imagined I would do with this man if I ever found out who it was.

"Anyway, you know what I'm going to say. It was Tobie who showed me that I was the one who was sending the letters. The phone calls may have been real to start with, I don't know. But I never had one when anyone else was with me."

Tom was only partly listening to Rachel's story. He was recalling the night when he stayed behind at school, hiding in the store cupboard at the back of the classroom, with the door locked. He knew he had slept, and the words had appeared on the blackboard while he had slept.

"The point is," Rachel continued, "I'm here to tell you it happens. Of course, I didn't want to believe it. I *couldn't* believe it. I hadn't even heard of half the bizarre practices I'd dreamed up for myself in those letters. But when it was shown to me, when it was pieced together, when I finally admitted to myself what a dark side of me was doing, then I started to get better.

"That's all I have to tell you, Tom. And I can't stay any longer: I've got a family, and I have to go back to them now. But Tobie asked me to tell you my story. Talk to her: she's a great healer. A bit odd, but a great healer." Rachel stood up, offering a handshake. "I want to wish you well."

Tom accepted the handshake, limply, without a word. Rachel hesitated, then stroked his shoulder affectionately.

" 'Bye," she said. "I'll tell Tobie I'm leaving. She won't want to leave you alone."

Rachel went out. Tom sat alone in the crushing silence. Tobie's words were still echoing inside him. The searchlight of a terrible truth had been turned on him. It burned like lime.

The sound of a door slamming further down the corridor jolted him back to awareness. He leapt off his chair and dragged a cupboard away from the wall, wedging it in front of the door.

Tom was barricading himself in.

51

Sharon arrived back at her apartment to find the message light winking on her answerphone. Before playing back the message she opened the fridge and pulled out a Maccabee, uncapped it and bumped the fridge door shut with her bottom. Unable to face him, she'd managed to get out of the center just as Tom had arrived.

It had been a terrible day. Exhausted from a night of crying and lack of sleep, she'd been little use to anyone at the center. Tobie had been in an irritable mood, and all of the women resident at the center had given her premenstrual hell. She had never understood how it was that women living in institutionalized proximity all managed to synchronize their menstrual cycles; but it had been true in college, in the kibbutz and in the rehabilitation center, and it was not a natural advantage. She slumped in a chair.

Now she was going to have to face Tom, having unloaded on to him the full weight of her obsession. Revealing everything, she'd sensed immediately, was a mistake. She was still inwardly cringing. She'd been prepared for several different reactions but not for the dumbfounded silence which had followed her announcement. Tom had simply frozen.

After work that evening she had gone to Ahmed's, where she had confessed it all again. Ahmed had been in a strange mood, lying quietly on his floor cushions, nodding his shaved head, listening to Sharon's emotional account of everything she'd said to Tom.

When Sharon had talked herself into silence, he'd said, "So, you have suffered as I have suffered."

"How have you suffered?"

"We're the same, you and I. We're both damned by the fact that we are liked by the person we love. It's hell to be liked when we would be loved. It would be easier to be hated."

She looked into the Arab's liquid eyes and realized about whom he was talking. "No, Ahmed, don't say that."

"It's true. I've always felt this."

She got up. "I'm sorry, Ahmed, I have to go. It's all too much. I can't take all of this."

"You see how quickly they run from our love? From you and me both?"

"I'm sorry."

"If he says sorry to you, you'll know if he means it."

Ahmed hadn't got up to see her out. She'd hurried away through the Arab quarter and had sat in her car for half an hour before returning home.

The answerphone light was still blinking at her. She put down her beer, got up out of her chair and touched the play button.

"Hi, Sharon, it's Tobie here. Be a sweetheart and come over here as soon as you can. Your Tom has gone White Cloud."

52

The hammering on the door receded. The voices calling to him quieted. After dragging the cupboard against the door, he'd stacked chairs and Formica tables in support of it, and those outside were unable to push their way in. He sat against the wall as the sound of their battering became distant, almost two thousand years distant.

She sat quietly against the wall next to him. He hadn't seen her come in. One of her thin legs was drawn under her, and Tom could see she was wearing nothing under her white cotton dress. She was perspiring. The white cotton stuck to the buds of her nipples and clung to the curve of her thigh. Her immature cunt was exposed to him, a scented cloud of pink flesh and fluffy, copper-colored hair. It was Kelly McGovern. Kelly from his school class.

Her lips were parted slightly in an expression of disappointment. "Why didn't you?"

"Kelly. How did you come to be here?"

"Why didn't you let it happen?"

"Kelly, I'm sorry. I'm sorry."

"There's nothing to be sorry for. It didn't happen, did it? It never happened. It was all in your head. A schoolteacher's fantasy.

I wanted it, but you never let it happen. That day in the stockroom. Everything in our human nature had brought us to that moment. But you kissed my hand and sent me away."

Strange light enveloped her, gray and gold. "Sometimes," said Tom, "sometimes I think that was the more serious sin. Sending you away. Was that where it all started to go wrong?"

"Those meetings with me. Sunday mornings in the park. You never laid a finger on me. Do you know what you were doing? Crucifying yourself on your own lust. You impaled yourself on your fantasies. You even came to believe it yourself. You had to punish yourself for something you never did."

"She knew I wanted you. It killed her. The knowledge killed her."

"No. You're wrong. It was all in your head."

She placed a hand on his arm. Her touch of cold fire, the smell of her perspiration, the perfume of her underage sex terrified him. "I've been trying to tell you what happened," she said. "You've been running away from me. All this time, I've been trying to tell you. I need you to know."

He tried to speak, to beg her to leave him alone, but his tongue dried in his mouth. The words wouldn't come. She leaned across him, revealing her tiny breasts where the damp cotton dress fell from her shoulders. Her left breast bore the tattoo of the bleeding-heart rose. He reached out to trace the tattoo on her skin, but when he put his hand to her breast he found a living rose in his hand. His finger pricked on a hidden thorn. Three tiny beads of blood bubbled on his finger.

Instinctively he put the speckles of blood to his mouth. She kissed him, put her tongue in his mouth. He closed his eyes. He knew that what she was saying was true. Nothing had happened that day. He'd sent her away, even though he'd wanted her more than life itself. It was all true. He surrendered to the kiss.

When he opened his eyes she had changed. Kelly was gone, and he was kissing Katie. He tried to resist, but the tiny flecks of blood on his mouth had bonded hard. His tongue was glued to hers. The flesh of his lips tore as he tried to pull away. The ethereal light had shaded into gold and violet. Katie hugged herself closer to him.

"Love me, Tom," she murmured through their locked kiss. "Love me, love me!" The rose in his hand had blown. Withered petals dropped through his fingers. Her mouth tasted of ash.

Then it was Sharon, and not Katie at all, who was trying to calm him. "Hush, hush." The kiss unlocked. "Be calm," she said.

"Sharon? Is it you? I'm falling apart."

"Hush, hush. It's all right."

But the light around her brightened, and Sharon was a huge white bird, a giant dove in his arms. A dribble of crimson blood from his mouth stained the white feathers of the bird's breast. Its eyes and its beak were terrifying chips of polished black stone. And in a moment the bird had been transformed again into another woman, dark, strong and beautiful.

The smell of balsam was on her. Her hair, falling in a shimmering, black cascade, was thrown across one shoulder, streaming perfume. Her oiled skin was the color of cinnamon. Her toenails were painted pink, and she wore anklets decorated with tiny bells. Her bare forearms were tattooed, each with an unnameable mythological beast. He knew she was the Magdalene. Not the woman who had dogged him through the dusty alleyways of Jerusalem but the resplendent young Mary Magdalene.

"Listen," she was saying, "you must listen." She held his head in her hands, forcing him to meet her eyes.

"I'm afraid. I've been afraid of you."

"I've been trying to tell you what happened." She spoke in a rapid, soft whisper. "Katie asked me to help you. I put my scroll in your hands. The crucifixion. The crucifiction. I was only a woman against many; because I was his wife there were some who followed me, but what chance did I have? I was written out, exiled to Qumran. Do you know what it's like to be written out?

"It was while I was toiling in the balsam factory of Qumran that I wrote my scroll. I could see which way it was going to go. I told how we knew the prophecies by heart. We made them happen. We even knew how to survive the Cross, with snake poison, and aloes, and myrrh. But it was the enemy, the Pharisee, the hater of women, who broke us. He hated our love. He suspected our plot. He ordered my love's legs to be shattered on the Cross to hasten his end, to spoil the prophecy. Our persecutor, Saul, adapted and discarded Jesus' teachings, replacing them with his own misogynist frenzies. This is Saint Paul, Apostle of the Lie.

"My love had one great teaching: that the source of all human trouble is the heart. But Katie asked me to tell you this, Tom: the miracle *did* happen. After his death he became pure spirit, haunting his own Church. He waits, like the *djinn*, haunting all of the liars who judge and preach and hate in his name, like a dim memory in the mind of the Christian who has forgotten he is a Christian."

With the ball of her thumb the Magdalene stroked a tear from his eye. Then she stepped out of her cotton robe and kneeled before him. More tattoos adorned her upper thighs; fabulous creatures decorated her breasts, writhing over her navel, representing the seven spirits cast out of her. The carnal priestess. Temple prostitute. The unnatural light about her shimmered red and violet, gold and gray. She undressed him diligently, and when that was done she leaned across him and slipped his erect penis into her mouth. Then she straddled him, sliding herself down his shaft, burying his head in her long hair until he almost swooned away. He surrendered. He lost sense of himself.

Her body stretched and shimmered like a single coil of tensile steel. She devoted sinuous, expert attention to him until suddenly her body cracked like a whip, again and again. Her breath came shorter and shorter, and then she stiffened, tightening her grip around him and squeezing his balls until he ejaculated inside her, her painted fingernails tearing the skin of his back as he bucked and shivered.

He fainted. He felt his consciousness fold down, like a star withdrawing its rays, and then opening again. When he came to, she was still clinging to him. Her hair, damp with sweat, stuck to his face. He was still inside her, his orgasm spent, and as he withdrew he noticed the smear of menstrual blood on his flaccid cock. Her perfume had changed. He disentangled himself from her. It was not Mary Magdalene.

"You," he gasped.

"I knew you wanted me. I knew. Did it. Did it." Christina smiled at him.

"But how did you get in?"

She indicated an open window at the back of the room. Meanwhile the chairs and tables barricading the door tumbled to the floor. There was the sound of scraping from behind the door. A cupboard was heaved aside.

"Not this," murmured Tom. "Not this." He pulled his trousers on. There was no time to find shirt or shoes before the people at the door broke in. He swung a leg through the open window.

Sharon was at the front of the group of women bursting into the room. "Tom, come back!" she cried.

"Christina!" shouted Tobie, gazing down down at the flushed, naked woman giggling on the floor.

"Did it. Did it. Diddit."

"Come back, Tom! Come back!"

53

With the evening *adhan* sounding from the mosque and the light outside his window fading from turquoise to lemon-gray, Ahmed crafted yet another in a long procession of hashish cigarettes, an unbroken chain going back to Sharon's departure two hours earlier. As he lit up, puffing with dispirited satisfaction, there came a hammering at the door. The knock was delivered three times. Knowing this to be the call of the *djinn,* he declined to answer, instead drawing luxuriously on his giant reefer. With the sweet sounds of the *shahada,* the declaration of faith, tumbling through the skies from the mosque, this was anyway an unusual—or audacious—time for the *djinn* to be calling. In any event, he never went out after nightfall, such was the risk of physical confrontation with any number of *djinn* in a city as insane as Jerusalem.

But then a fourth knock came, hesitant at first, then decisive. Ahmed stirred, blinked, rubbed his eyes. Hauling himself to his feet, he teetered to the window and looked down.

Either he was hallucinating, or the Englishman stood at the threshold, bare-chested and without shoes. Ahmed had to refocus. "Are you a man or *djinn?*"

"Throw me the keys."

Ahmed wasn't sure he wanted to. He withdrew from the window to consider, then relented and tossed down the bunch of keys. The keys glimmered in the half-light, cutting an arc through the air. In a matter of seconds the Englishman had unlocked the door and had bounded up the stairs.

Ahmed accepted the proffered keys and stepped back. Tom was wearing only a pair of trousers. His feet were blackened, sooty, filthy. Sweat and dust caked his chest. His hair was wild and stuck out at odd angles, and his eyes darted from object to object around the apartment, refusing to settle.

"Allah,"' said Ahmed. "You look more like the *djinn* than the *djinn*."

"Talk. I want to talk."

"Tea? Oh, to hell with the tea. Have a beer. Here, hold this."

Ahmed handed Tom the smoking reefer while he rummaged in the fridge. Tom looked at the thing before taking a lungful, biting back the smoke and holding it in his lungs. When Ahmed returned with a beer, he offered to give it back.

"Keep it," said Ahmed. "I'm sick of the stuff. I'm giving it up. Sit."

Tom sat cross-legged on a cushion. Ahmed winced at the dirty feet on the spotless fabric. He'd joked about the Englishman looking like a *djinn,* but it was true; he actually looked like someone on his way to becoming a demon. Ahmed speculated on the possibility of someone making that transformation within a normal lifespan. He had not heard of it but suspected it was possible.

"What are you looking at?" said Tom.

"Pardon me. Was I staring? I have been distracted of late. You want to talk about the scroll?"

"To hell with the scroll. I don't want it. It's yours. I'll make a gift of it to you if you tell me what I need to know."

Ahmed knew when to tread carefully. "Tell me what you need to know."

Tom sucked greedily on the reefer, holding back the smoke before exhaling. "I want to know how to get rid of a *djinn.*"

Ahmed surveyed him steadily. "No one knows how to get rid of a *djinn.*"

"But you must have some ideas. You must have tried things yourself."

"Please. Be calm. I never tried to get rid of my *djinn*. She is my penalty. My penance."

"What? Are you in love with your own suffering?"

"Am I alone in that?"

Tom looked defeated. He got up and prowled the room. Seeing the scroll pinned out on the table, he peered into the spiral of unknowable words.

"I advise you not to go too near that thing. It's vibrating with *djinn.*"

"I lied about the girl," said Tom. "Remember when we traded stories? I lied. I didn't lay a finger on her."

"I suspected it."

Tom sat down again. The reefer was smoked out. He hung his head in dismay. Nothing further was said. He shifted, letting his head fall back on the plump cushions behind him. The two sat in silence, twilight thickening into dark outside the window, occasional sounds of strollers drifting up from the cobbled street outside.

He is falling asleep, thought Ahmed. He's exhausted. I must give him something. He moved across the floor on all fours. Taking the Canaanite talisman from around his throat, he gently hung it around Tom's neck. Squatting back on his heels, he began whispering to him. "The *djinn* inhabit an infinite number of personalities, each a different facet of you. You must search through your dreams for the good *djinn,* and ask the good *djinn* to make intercession for you. Offer a gift, and then pray. This is all I know."

Tom had drifted away. Ahmed left the Englishman to sleep.

Tom drew up outside the church. The passenger seat beside him was empty. The gale squealed like a hellcat, almost tearing the door from its hinges as he climbed out of the car. Rain lashed at his face. The lych-gate creaked. The church tower leaned precariously into the wind. Once again it seemed like a ship, imperiled by a cruel

ocean, a ship of lost souls. Gravestones like jetsam awash on a dark
sea in the wake of the storm-lashed ship. A giant yew tree moaning
and splintering like a broken mast. A single bell tolling in the darkness.

Where was Katie? He made his way through the swinging lych-
gate. She should be here. She should be with him. Branches torn
from the trees were bulleting around the churchyard. A crow trying to alight on the church tower was flung up into the black sky.
He stared up at the tower. The wind dragged scratch marks through
its soft sandstone.

An aluminum ladder formed a triangle against the perpendicular of the tower. A claw hammer was hooked over a lower rung.
Tom looked up, and there was a motion in the trefoil niche below
the tower's castellations. The Magdalene statue had gone. Katie was
there, her hair torn by the wind, her white robe drawn like fine silk
across the curves of her body. Clouds like black smoke rolled across
the sky. Her toes gripped the niche in the crumbling stone. She was
looking down at him.

The storm became more ferocious with each passing second. He
knew he should take shelter, but he was afraid to progress beyond
the porch. Suddenly the church door was torn open, ancient oak and
iron cracking angrily against stone.

"Come down, Katie! I can't go in! Not without you, Katie! I
can't go inside!"

But the wind picked up the ladder like a straw, flinging it into
the blackness of the graveyard. Katie had no way down, and now
the wind was digging out the mortar between the stones of the
tower. Dust was sucked from around the stones immediately below
Katie's feet and then from individual bricks. The tower was top-
pling. Katie spread her arms wide like a bird and flung herself toward him. He saw her fall. His eyes were fixed on hers like mag-
nets as she plunged through the air, her dive bringing her directly
above him. Eyeball touched eyeball.

There was no impact. At the moment of contact, the scene dissolved and he was inside the church. Katie was gone.

Slogans were scrawled on the wall in ugly spirals. LIAR. The
congregation at the altar was shuffling, one behind the other, down

a spiral descent under the floor, steps engraved and painted with black Hebrew letters. David Feldberg was among them, smiling at him. Katie was nowhere around. The vicar was Michael Anthony, the absconded priest, beckoning him to follow.

"I can't come! I have to watch for the morning!"

Michael Anthony seemed to become annoyed. The rest of the congregation stopped shuffling and looked around, irritated at whatever was holding up their progress.

Instantly Tom recognized that something about the church had changed. In every representation of Jesus Christ, in every painting or carving or stained-glass portrait, the image of Jesus had been supplanted by that of a woman, naked, sexual, bloodied and suffering on the Cross. Mary Magdalene had taken his place as the one crucified. Her sacred colors were scarlet and purple, gray and gold.

"Intercede for me," he said. "Tell her I know what happened. Tell her I know everything."

Michael Anthony looked anxious, as though he didn't understand what Tom was trying to say.

"You must intercede for me," Tom persisted. "Pray for me. Ask her to leave me alone. Tell her I'll make known the contents of the scroll. Tell her I'll do it for her. And give her this."

Tom opened his mouth and forced his fingers into the back of his own throat. With an easy spasm he vomited into his own hands a fat, live, buzzing bee. The bee rolled in his cupped hands as it was offered to the priest.

Michael Anthony accepted the insect, nodding now as if he understood. He began stroking the bee with his forefinger, backing toward the congregation who had resumed its shuffling descent into the spiral well.

The bee buzzed intermittently in the priest's hands. Tom thanked the Magdalene with a brief prayer before backing out into the storm raging outside the church.

The buzzing sound of the telephone woke him. He sat upright. Ahmed was in the bedroom and was talking, to Sharon it seemed, on the telephone.

"Yes, he's here now." The Arab spoke in an undertone. "No, he's asleep. I think he's exhausted. No, no, he's not going anywhere."

Tom hauled himself up from the cushions. He smudged his face with his hands, trying to collect his thoughts. A silk shirt rested over the back of a chair. He slipped it on. In the hallway he found a pair of Ahmed's running shoes. He quietly let himself out of the apartment while Ahmed was still reassuring Sharon that he wouldn't let Tom out of his sight.

54

Wide-eyed, Tom studied himself in the mirror, his locks tumbling to the barbershop floor. The Arab barber's scissors whispered at his ears, clipping miraculously close to the skull. The barber snipped with ostentatious style, keeping the scissors in constant clipping motion as they hovered across Tom's head or wafted through the air. The scissors flashed in the mirror, swooping like a strange bird trying, but failing, to settle.

When he'd finished cropping, the barber set in with his electric shaving tool, guiding it across the crown in neat tramlines.

Katie stood at Tom's side, a hand resting lightly on his shoulder, watching the shaving in the mirror. Her hair was plaited. Her eyes were sea-gray. "I'm sorry," she said. "I'm sorry I did that to you. I had to find a way through to you again. I had to come through the others. How else could I find you? You lock me out. Both you and Sharon lock me out."

"What do you want?" said Tom.

"The prices are on the wall," said the barber, not deviating from the careful line of his electric shaver.

"I want your love," said Katie.

"Why?"

"So that no one is cheated," said the barber. He switched off his electric tool and began stropping a cut-throat razor to complete the job.

"Because I love you. I will always love you."

"Can I trust you?"

"If you can't trust your barber," he said flashing his razor, "who can you trust?"

"You can trust me," said Katie.

"How does it look?"

"It looks well," said the barber.

"It looks well," said Katie.

Tobie walked by the barber's shop in the Arab quarter and saw a man with a shaved head paying the barber. The man looked familiar, but she pressed on, anxious to find Tom. She didn't feel entirely comfortable in the Muslim quarter of Jerusalem at night, but she'd arranged to follow Sharon to Ahmed's apartment.

After Tom had barricaded himself in the room at the rehabilitation center, Tobie had awaited Sharon's arrival before forcing her way in. Finally, heaving their way inside, they'd found Christina naked on the floor and the rear window wide open to the night. After that Sharon had returned to her own apartment, hoping to find Tom there. When he failed to appear she'd telephoned Ahmed. After instructing Ahmed to detain him, Sharon had contacted Tobie and asked her to rendezvous at Ahmed's place.

Tobie was furious with herself that she'd failed to predict Tom's reaction. In all cases she made a careful judgment about how much pressure to bring to bear and about how much truth an individual could face. Perhaps it was a difference between men and women, she reasoned. The last time something like this had happened was in Ahmed's case, when he had run amok, after which she had sworn never to admit men into the center.

If Tom had been a woman, she would at that point have broken down, cried and looked for sisterly comfort from the women around her. Tom had instead opted for flight. Tobie detected some volatile element in a man's sexual chemistry which, when threatened, would always foil her most carefully constructed therapy. The capacity for self-deception was, despite all myths to the contrary, more tenaciously protected in men than in women. In any event, she could never have predicted Christina's role in the crisis.

As she made her way along the narrow street, she stopped abruptly in her tracks. Retracing her steps, she drew up at the barber's shop. The man with the shaved head was at that very moment quitting the open front of the shop.

"Tom," said Tobie evenly. "We've been worried about you."

Tom froze. He looked away to his left and seemed to listen a moment, as if awaiting inspiration. When he looked back at Tobie, his eyes were blazing black holes, all pupil. "Hi, Tobie. No need to worry."

Tobie hesitated. "Look, Tom, will you walk with me? I'm a little nervous of being in the quarter at night. Maybe you'll accompany me?"

"Where are you going?"

"I thought I'd look in on Ahmed. Why don't you come with me?"

Tom paused again before answering. "No can do, Tobie. I have to be somewhere else."

"Where? Where do you have to be?"

This time there was a long silence. Tom allowed himself masses of space before speaking. To Tobie it was a common symptom but always disturbing. "The Me'a She'arim."

"Me'a She'arim? Why do you want to go there, Tom? You don't want to go to the Me'a She'arim."

Pause. "Yes, yes. I've got a score to settle. There's someone I must see there."

"A score? What's going on, Tom?"

"There was a man there in the Me'a She'arim. He threw a stone at Sharon. We can't have that, Tobie. We can't have that sort of behavior."

"Hey, come with me, sweetheart. Let's go find Sharon and Ahmed. Let's go where it's cozy. Come on, take my arm and walk with me."

Tom was already backing away, breaking into a run. "Can't do it, Tobie. Got a score to settle. Catch you later."

He was gone, vanished into the shadows of the narrow alley-ways. Tobie knew it was useless to try to follow him, so she let him go, quickening her steps toward Ahmed's apartment, where Sharon was waiting.

"He's gone to the Me'a She'arim. Hello, Ahmed; it's been a long time since we saw each other," said Tobie.

"The Me'a She'arim? Don't stare at her, Ahmed. Where's your hospitality?"

Ahmed couldn't take his eyes off Tobie. "I apologize, you terrible old woman. Sit. Sit. You must excuse me; it's not every day the worst woman in the whole world visits my house. Can I offer you something?"

"We don't have time for that. I just ran into Tom down the street; he looks pretty frightening. He's shaved his head, and I think the sooner we persuade him to come home with us, the better."

"You're right," said Ahmed. "He was here earlier. He stole my shirt and my shoes. All the time he was here he was listening to his *djinn*. Don't you look at me like that. I tell you, his *djinn* was talking in his ear all of the time. He is now well under the influence of his *djinn*."

Sharon said, "But you told me he was going to the ghetto. What does he want there?"

"He said he had a score to settle. Some man threw a stone at you, and he was going to put it right."

"It's true, one of the Hasidim threw a stone when I was there the other day. I must have told him about it."

"Those Hasidim will cut him to pieces if he tries to cause trouble in the Jewish ghetto," said Ahmed.

"Let's go," said Sharon. "Ahmed, will you come?"

"Are you crazy? I, a Palestinian, come to the Me'a She'arim? Don't joke."

"You'll be with us."

"Worse still. And, anyway, it's night. I never go outside after nightfall."

"We need you," said Tobie. "We've got to find him."

"What do I owe this Englishman? He stole my shirt. He stole my shoes." Here he looked at Sharon. "What else has he stolen of mine? I can't do it. Believe me, if I could come with you, I would. But it is night, and I would risk everything. My *djinn* would be out there, waiting for me."

"I'm asking you," said Sharon. "Ahmed, I need you to come."

"But the night," pleaded Ahmed. "But the night."

"*De profundis,*" Katie said, walking at his side, her right hand resting lightly on his left shoulder. "Up from the depths. I have told you everything. Mary's scroll has been opened to you. Now you know how it was done. Now you know how the Liar deceived us. You know how we were cheated. Now you know who is the real Liar."

She was carefully steering him through the alleys of the Arab quarter. The towers and the Golden Dome were illuminated at his back, and the church spires were lit up before him, wrapped in an exotic shawl of deep sable. People drifted by in the streets, insubstantial as wraiths, quiet as the dust. Passing into the busier thoroughfares, they felt a tension thickening the air, a sourness clogging the oppressive heat. Too many young men thronged the street, all talking in hushed but animated tones. They skirted a pair of nervous soldiers. The conscripts were in a state of twitchy, heightened alert. Something had happened or was about to happen.

"What's going on?"

"There will be a riot," she said. "Come on."

When they reached the city wall near Solomon's quarries, Katie gripped his shoulder. They stopped. She was pointing up at a soldier in silhouette, patroling the wall. The soldier had his back to them. As he moved quietly along the parapet, cradling his automatic rifle, Tom saw the unmistakable swish of a tail from between the soldier's legs.

Impossible!

But there it was again, a glistening, black, curving length of demonic tail stroking back and forth. A fist squeezed Tom's bowels. A sick wave washed over him.

"Hushhhhh." Katie held his face in her cool hands. He felt his gaze being commanded, held and stilled by her mineral-ocean eyes. "You are seeing the *djinn* for the first time," she said.

Perspiration prickling on his brow, Tom looked up again at the soldier on the wall. The soldier seemed to become instinctively aware of him, began to turn slowly, his face hidden in the dark but rotating slowly toward them. The demonic tail twitched again, and the face began to emerge out of the shadows.

"Quickly." Katie pushed him into a side alley. "You must not let them know you see through them. Never. Do you understand?"

But Tom was quivering, terrified by the physicality of the *djinn*. He staggered against a wall, vomiting. Katie placed a hand on the small of his back and propelled him through the alley. They emerged at Damascus Gate.

It was a relief to be outside the Old City. The air seemed to sweeten, to lighten. Damascus Gate was busy with people, and the road was heavy with traffic. Her hand rested lightly on his shoulder again as she guided him toward the Arab bus station. He stopped to look back at the wall, spying two more soldiers on the parapet.

"The soldiers," he said.

"No, they are not all *djinn*. The *djinn* disguise themselves as soldiers, just as they disguise themselves as ordinary people. But you know that."

"Yes. I know that."

She guided him to the service station, where he bought a fuel container, filling it with three liters of petrol. He also bought two plastic bottles of orangeade. At a short distance from the bus station he stopped to drink. He felt feverish, and he was sweating profusely. He consumed half of one of the bottles of orangeade and emptied both bottles into the gutter. Transferring the petrol into the orangeade bottles, he discarded the remaining petrol, along with its container.

Together they began to walk back in the direction of Damascus

Gate. "The Liar hated all women," said Katie, "seeing us a source of uncleanness. He also hated Jesus because of his affection for all women. When Jesus cast out the seven demons from Mary Magdalene, he recruited her from the Canaanite temple into his own. He wanted women to be priests, the equals of men; but the Liar hated all of this. The Liar despised his own flesh. He despised every human frailty.

"After the Crucifixion, the Liar saw his opportunity. He usurped the Church and moved it to the West. Mary's punishment was to be written out. It was as if her tongue had been torn out. No, it was not the Liar who was converted by Christ on his famous journey to Damascus. It was the Church of Christ which was converted by the Liar."

"We're not going to the Me'a She'arim, are we?" said Tom.

"No. I just wanted to buy us some time. And we've already arrived."

They had come to a stop on the corner of the road known as Derekh Shekhem, directly opposite Damascus Gate, and had drawn up outside the doors of the great church of St. Paul.

"The Liar's Temple. Paul, hater of women. Despiser of the flesh. Reviler of earthly love. False prophet and Apostle of the Lie. Scourge of the female. Father of the *djinn*. Liar of liars."

Tom gazed up at the face of the church of St. Paul. Darkness enfolded its walls like black wings. He mounted the steps and went inside.

Sharon, Tobie and Ahmed made their way through the streets in silence. The two women had linked arms with the Arab, who proceeded in a state of terror. They passed knots of agitated young men who stopped talking as they drew near and surveyed them with hostile glares.

"What are they saying?" asked Tobie. "Is something happening?"

"You know the *intifada*," said Ahmed. "Something is always happening."

"But the peace talks—"

"Not everyone is in favor of Arafat. You know Hamas will try to break the talks."

The air was spiced with the sense of impending insurrection. The shadow of violence was cast ahead of the event. The walls enclosing the streets sweated with anticipation. The drainage channels flowed with sour rumor.

"Allah, can't you feel it? Let's get out of the Old City," pleaded Ahmed. "The place is crawling with *djinn*. They are waiting for corpses."

At Damascus Gate Ahmed looked up at the sweating parapets and shivered. For a moment the others thought they wouldn't be able to get him through the gate. He was rooted. Neither would he tell them what he saw. He was like an obstinate thread unwilling to pass through the needle's eye.

A detachment of soldiers entered the city by the gate, forcing back the small crowd of youths hanging around under the archway. This fresh commotion and the accompanying cries of protest broke the spell, and Tobie and Sharon managed to usher Ahmed through.

It was only a few minutes from the gate to the Me'a She'arim ghetto. They turned alongside the church of St. Paul. Sharon looked up to glimpse the shadow of a man passing through the door of the church, clutching something to his chest.

"We should hurry," said Tobie.

"Why am I doing this?" wailed Ahmed. "Why?"

"Because you love Sharon," said Tobie.

"You are the worst woman I've ever met," said Ahmed.

At the entrance to the ghetto, Sharon paused under the sign "DAUGHTERS OF JERUSALEM: DRESS MODESTLY AT ALL TIMES." "Shit. Look at what I'm wearing." A pair of shorts exposed the sandy expanse of her thighs just above the knee and was topped off by a sleeveless blouse. She looked hopefully at the other two, neither of whom had anything they could offer her. Tobie at least was wearing slacks and a sweatshirt.

"It can't be worse than wearing a Palestinian face," said Ahmed.

"It can," said Sharon. "The daughters of Jerusalem have proud and haughty necks."

"What?"

"Forget it. Come on, we don't have time to worry about it."

They stepped through the wrought-iron archway and into the ghetto as if it were Dante's Inferno. Inside they patroled the streets, utterly conspicuous, trying to exude a confidence none of them felt. The bearded, behatted and beshawled Hasidim passed by with side-long glances, but they were left alone. One old man came out of a small shop and, spotting Sharon, dropped a bag of red apples on the ground. They rolled into the gutter. It was a histrionic gesture, a the-atrical piece of protest.

"I know some people in here," said Tobie. "They might help us."

"Don't be long," said Sharon. "I want you near."

Tobie dived further into the ghetto. Sharon and Ahmed stayed close to the edge, walking slowly along a lamp-lit street. An elderly Hasid with a stooped back and a flowing white beard stood in a doorway, eyeing them hawkishly. When they drew abreast of him he suddenly bellowed, *"This is not New York City! This is Yerusha-layim!"*

"Stay close," said Sharon.

"You stay close."

"Should we hold hands?"

"Yerushalayim!"

"Not a good idea."

They hurried away from the old man, who was still screaming after them, turning a corner to get out of his sight. Instantly they realized their mistake. A huddle of younger Hasidim stood under a street lamp a few yards away. To go forward would take them right past the men; to retreat would have seemed weak. They chose to go on. The young men swung their heads, their locks shaking, the light from the street lamp reflecting in their glasses.

"Lot of shit in the neighborhood,'" said one.

Sharon crackled something in Hebrew, which Ahmed missed. It silenced them for a moment. Then, as they passed, one spat at her feet. "Whore."

"Ignore it," Ahmed whispered. "Tom, where are you?"

They put the young men behind them, hoping to find a way back to the ghetto entrance. Instead they turned into a dead end.

Another back street curved the wrong way, leading them past more
shops and hostile clusters of men gathered like crows under weak
street lamps. They all seemed to bare their teeth from behind lux-
uriant black beards.

"Get us out of here," said Ahmed.

"I'm trying. I'm trying."

They passed into a quadrangle: on one of the walls the slogan
"JUDAISM AND ZIONISM ARE DIAMETRICALLY OP-
POSED" was sprayed in foot-high letters. Sharon paused, trying to
figure out the way back. "There's nothing for it. We're going to have
to retrace our steps."

"I don't think so," said Ahmed.

Sharon followed Ahmed's gaze. The way was blocked by a huddle of Hasidim who had followed them into the quadrangle. The
Hasidim were quiet, singularly menacing in their long black frock
coats and their broad-brimmed hats. Every one of them wore spectacles, as if glasses were also part of the ultra-Orthodox uniform.
Their eyes were magnified and excited behind the spectacle lenses.
A second street running from the quadrangle was filling up with
black-garbed spectators.

"Time for negotiation," said Ahmed.

Someone shouted out the Hebrew word for "whore." A different insult, saved for Palestinians, was directed at Ahmed. Out of
nowhere came a volley of small stones, cracking on the wall behind
their heads. It was impossible to see who was doing the throwing.
The groups of men seemed curiously immobile. Then Sharon
glimpsed a lifted arm and felt a rock strike her leg. It was a heavy,
bruising blow. She gasped, staggering to one side. Another rock
came hurtling through the air, missing Ahmed's face by a small
margin.

In a matter of seconds bricks and stones were raining down on
them. Sharon felt her cheek sliced open by a sharp edge. Stones fell
against the wall behind them. As she raised her hands over her head
she saw Ahmed felled, down on his knees, crouching, trying to
protect himself from the hail of rocks. Then he scrambled upright,
braving the missiles to throw himself around Sharon, desperately
trying to shield her with his own body.

They both went down.

The volley of stones stopped as quickly as it had started. They heard shouting, first in Hebrew, then in English. As they peered through the cracks between their fingers, a tall young Hasid was charging toward them, bellowing in anger. Sharon thought he was going to swing a kick at them. But when he reached them he stopped, turning to face their tormentors. His hat had fallen to the dust. His black beard was full, and his hair was thinning to baldness. He was red-faced with exertion, and his corkscrew locks were shaking from rage. He spread his arms wide in a gesture protective of Sharon and Ahmed, who were still crouched on the floor behind him.

"Cowards!" He was shouting back at his own people. "Cowards! What are you doing? Throw your rocks at me! Is there one of you who is good enough to throw those rocks? Just one of you?"

No one answered. The crowd remained silent. The bare-headed Hasid protector threw back his head and released an almost inhuman roar of defiance. He turned and glowered at Ahmed and Sharon. Sweat glistened on his brow. His eyes shone like hot pitch. He turned back to the crowd. "One of you! Is there not one of you whom God has made good enough to throw a rock? If there is, throw it at me!" He picked up a stick, and in a frenzy he scratched something in the dust before hurling the stick aside. "Go home! Go home, and let these people go!"

No one moved. The man chased the first knot of spectators, who broke ranks and began to disperse. The second group also broke up and began to drift away, hastened by the enraged Hasidic Jew, who charged into them, bellowing, daring any of them to challenge him.

Then Tobie was there, helping Sharon to her feet. The rescuer was a friend of hers. Sharon was cut about the face and arm. Ahmed too was wounded. Their rescuer came back across the quadrangle to pick up his hat. "Don't bring these people here again, Tobie."

"It was my fault," said Sharon. "I brought the others here."

"You're Jewish," he said. "You know these people are like children. You provoke their worst natures. I'm sorry. Don't come to the neighborhood again."

He escorted them to the entrance to the ghetto. Tobie spoke rapidly in Hebrew. "Get them out of here," said the man, dragging off his spectacles and mopping his brow with a white handkerchief. "Just get them out of here."

Tom entered the darkened doors. A host of candles flickered throughout the vast church as he closed the door behind him. Votive offerings, each burning with a soft, whispered prayer. False prayers, thought Tom. Each light a lie.

A solitary worshiper was kneeling at a pew close to the altar rail. The man's head rested on his folded hands. Tom's footsteps echoed up to the vaults as he took a place well behind the worshiper, clutching his plastic bottles to his chest, waiting for the worshiper to leave.

The candles of the lie burned slowly. Occasionally the flames shivered in a draft. Tom thought of Katie, patiently waiting outside. She hadn't had to tell him what to do. He had known.

Mary Magdalene had shown them the truth. Mary the saint, *djinn*, angel, demon, inspiration. Above the altar hung a Cross bearing the body of the betrayed Christ. But it was not Judas who had betrayed him. It was Paul. Remember, Tom thought, his own hands clasped before him in simulated prayer, religious truth depends on the version of events which survives. Mary's version had been written out. She had been excluded because she'd refused to recognize the man who was not Christ in the garden outside the tomb. Because Mary had known that the coming of the Messiah was a planned, stage-managed event, subverted by Paul, the Apostle of the Lie, hater of women.

Stop crucifying yourself, Tom, Tobie had said. Stop crucifying yourself.

He could atone. He could destroy the shrine of the enemy for Katie. The Usurper. The Liar. Mary Magdalene was the truth. Paul was the Lie.

The worshiper at the front shifted position. He's not going to leave, thought Tom. He looked again at the man hunched over in prayer, and began to sense something wrong. Something about the man's posture, leaning at a slight angle, alerted him. He began to get a bad feeling: a dead weight, a lead sphere, swelling in the pit of his stomach. The feeling began to escalate.

The door opened behind him, admitting a draft of air, triggering a moment of hysteria among the moth-white candle flames before it closed. Someone else entered the church and sat in a pew behind him. When he looked around, his perspective had changed.

He no longer found himself seated at the back of the church. Now he was crouched in a pew under the altar rail, in the position of the solitary worshiper. As he looked over his shoulder to the back of the church, his original position was taken over by the figure who had just entered. Hugging his bottles of petrol to his chest, Tom failed to make out the features of the shadowy newcomer now bent over a pew. Tom's gaze returned to the altar. The church began to sweat. Stone slabs oozed. Wooden benches seeped. Altar cloths, plaster saints, the golden Cross, all began to weep sticky malevolence. The lead sphere inflated inside his stomach. He wiped his eyes with the ball of his hand.

His perspective suddenly switched again. A blink of the eye whisked him back to the seat at the rear of the church; he was gazing once more at the solitary worshiper by the altar rail. He got up and took a few steps toward the altar, slowly approaching the hunched figure there. A taste of metal coated his mouth as he drew up behind the figure. There was ringing in his ears. He swayed under a momentary giddiness. Beneath the pew in which the gray worshiper sat hunched, Tom saw something fat and coiled, glistening with oily luster. The thing gleamed darkly in the shadows. It flicked lazily, snake-like.

Tom stepped back. The thing moved again, extending to full length before recoiling. Now he could see it was no snake. The thing looped through the back of the pew and was joined to the worshiper's body at the base of the spine. It was a tail.

"The *djinn*," he breathed.

Struggling against the horror rising in his gullet, Tom heard something behind him. He darted a look over his shoulder. Near the entrance to the church another gray figure was rising from the pew he himself had occupied moments earlier. The tailed creature beside him had gone.

Somehow they'd reversed positions again. The figure from the back of the church approached him, its black tail clearly visible, swishing lightly against the carpeted length of aisle. The advancing demon carried something close to its chest. Two plastic bottles of sloshing yellow liquid.

The creature in the aisle was closing in on him, breaking into a run. Backing away, Tom's perspective switched again; this time the *djinn* pursued him from the altar-end of the church. Each time Tom's mind registered and resisted the change of perspective, the perspective switch was thrown again, until he was sandwiched, hunted from both ends of the church simultaneously.

He was being propelled into a collision with a *djinn* which had his own face. The double-demon ran at him, bearing down.

At the moment of impact, all sound was stilled. The candle flames stopped burning without being snuffed out. Each light was like a tiny white flower, blossoming, expanding its halo until the individual bulbs of white blotted into each other, forming a single wall of blinding light. Behind the wall of light was a distant screaming, gradually amplifying, growing to occult pitch, the sound at first splitting the wall of white light with hairline cracks before shattering it, so that time poured through the breach and the candles began to burn again with individual light. Tom felt the scream issuing from his own throat. The petrol-filled bottles tumbled from his grip and rolled across the floor. He staggered into a wrought-iron stand bearing a dozen burning candles. It toppled on to the plastic bottles of petrol.

Tom stumbled outside the church, holding his throat, gasping for air. No one was around. Katie had gone.

"It was you, Katie," Tom said to the thickening darkness outside the church. "It was you all along."

There was the sound of riot emanating from the direction of Damascus Gate. Tom heard gunfire, one, two shots. Smoke was coming from inside the church through the open door. He scrambled down the steps, dragging himself to his feet. No one was around to notice the conflagration from inside the church. Tom ran off toward the commotion at Damascus Gate.

When Sharon, Ahmed and Tobie arrived at Damascus Gate via the Ha Nevi'im road, a near riot was in progress. A throng of demonstrators was being pressed back under the Crusader arch of the gate by a small detail of beleaguered soldiers. The crowd was forced back across the bottleneck of the concrete rampart spanning the dry moat. Meanwhile more Arabs were pouring into the crush from the street under the battlements of the wall. The sweating faces of the throng were illuminated by the ropes of fairy lights strung from the battlements, and the young Arabs arriving at the rear of the crowd began funnelling Ahmed, Tobie and Sharon in toward the arch.

"This is bad," said Ahmed. "This is bad."

"Something's on fire," said Tobie, pointing at coils of smoke issuing from the church of St. Paul. "They've set fire to the church."

They heard some people talking. A demonstration by Hamas supporters in East Jerusalem had resulted in the killing of a soldier. The soldiers had returned fire, shooting dead a young girl. The people were in an angry mood, jostling the line of uniformed Israeli conscripts trying to hold the gate.

"Let's get out of here," said Tobie.

"There!" shouted Sharon jubilantly, pointing at a figure pressed against the wall beneath the Crusader arch. "Is that your shirt, Ahmed?"

Ahmed nodded his head in dismay. It was Tom, wearing Ahmed's silk shirt, his head shaved.

"We've got to pull him out of this," said Sharon.

But there was no way of making progress through the crush. Rumors began to sweep through the crowd. The Jews had set fire to St. Paul's to blame the Arabs. The Christians were burning a mosque in retaliation. Ahmed began to panic. "I can't stay here," he hissed. "Look at these people. One in five of these people is a *djinn!*"

Tobie took his hand. "Stay close."

"I'm afraid of the night," said Ahmed.

"Me too," said Tobie. "Me too."

Suddenly the cordon of soldiers gave way, and there was a roar as the crowd breached the line. People fell to their knees under the crush. Two men jumped down into the dry moat to escape the press of bodies. Fighting broke out to try to make room for those who had fallen underfoot. More Arabs came up from behind, enclosing the three of them in the melée. It was hot. Tension and incipient violence hung over the crowd like smoke from a burning tire. There was a clatter of boots from overhead as a fresh detail of soldiers took up positions on the wall above them, training machine-guns on the crowd through the battlements.

Sharon grabbed Tobie, who was still holding Ahmed. She gave them a tug. "Come on."

They followed the flood of people through the gate. The first cordon of soldiers had retreated inside and were backing up into the Arab *souk,* followed by the demonstrators, who were chanting now, crying the name of God, fisting the air, bellowing slogans, ululating. The three of them were flushed through the gate into the square inside the old walls.

"God is great!" a young Arab screamed into Tobie's face.

"Not on days like this!" Tobie screamed back.

Ahmed held his head in his hands.

"There!" shouted Sharon, seeing Tom swept around a corner, away from the *souk.* "He's broken free. Come on."

But a cohort of troops jogged up toward them from the direction of Herod's Gate, bellowing at them to get back. They pressed themselves against the wall as the soldiers pushed past, herding the crowd back into the arch of Damascus Gate. Sharon abandoned the others, running toward the spot where she'd sighted Tom. Tobie and Ahmed followed.

Tom was frightened. He'd joined the crowd in the bottleneck of Damascus Gate to hide, to get away from the burning church. He'd found himself pressed inside the Old City when the crowd had broken through the soldiers' cordon. Swept along in the hot, chanting press of the crowd, he'd seen in the darkened, sweating faces of the throng that one in every five or six people was an ugly *djinn* in disguise, urging the people on to violence, swishing their lustrous gray-black tails in excitement. The *djinn*, he'd discovered, could make their tails appear and disappear, retracting them at will when anyone trying to inspect them at close quarters, like himself, came too near.

Katie, where are you? I need you. Katie. Kelly. Mary. Sharon.

He was bewildered. Swept along like a cork on a river, he didn't know what he was doing in this violent crowd. He remembered going into the church armed with petrol but couldn't recall what had happened there. He remembered running to Damascus Gate. He knew he should get out. Go to Sharon's apartment. Sharon would help.

A phalanx of people was being herded along the street before him, squeezed out of the *souk* by the soldiers. Suddenly the crowd broke into a run. To dodge them he found himself diving for cover in a narrow recess off the main thoroughfare.

The place was familiar. He'd been there before. A sudden chill gripped him. There it was, the scent of balsam, the residual perfume, a blend of opal, musk and jasmine. This was the place where he'd originally encountered Mary Magdalene, on his first day in Jerusalem. The place he'd found the scorched map. He sensed her behind him, waiting for him to turn. He was afraid that, if he did, it would not be the beautiful Mary he would see, not the young, erotic Magdalene, but one who was leprous, weighted with time and with a face as lifeless as the Dead Sea.

But when he turned, there was nothing. No one, no woman, no *djinn*, nothing. She was gone. Somehow he knew she'd been exorcised and that, along with Katie, she was gone forever.

His surprise was interrupted by the breathless appearance of two Arab youths. Palestinian scarves were tied over their faces. They ran into his hiding place, and stopped dead on seeing him, eyes wide with alarm. Recovering, they climbed the wall at the back of the alley. The first swung his legs over the wall and dropped down the other side. The second followed, but as he scrambled across the capstone of the wall, something heavy clattered to the stones at Tom's

feet. The boy looked back in anguish. Whatever it was, he decided
to abandon it.

Tom looked down. It was a short-barreled lightweight rifle. He
picked it up.

Ahmed and Tobie followed Sharon away from the soldiers and
crowd pressed into the mouth of the gate and along a street loud
with the cries of excited, uncoordinated youths still looking for a
focus for their anger. The main crowd had been diverted up the
channel of the *souk* and was being forced back from there down a
side street. The cries and chants were inching closer.

It seemed they'd lost Tom. Ahmed thought the search was hopeless. He had let go of Tobie's hand as the older woman was determined to stay with Sharon; then reluctantly the Arab followed behind them. He wanted to get out of this. He wanted to go home.
He sensed danger everywhere. Too often in his younger days he had
witnessed, and even helped incite, this kind of disturbance; he had
developed a nose for when something bad was going to happen. He
knew how the *djinn* could provoke a crowd to claim their victim.
And he knew how the *djinn* loved the night.

He hurried behind Sharon and Tobie, who'd made twenty yards
on him. Then he saw two masked youths break from the area of the
souk to hurl themselves down a narrow alley. He stepped off the
street into the alley, watching them run, and was astonished to see
them pull up short. It was the Englishman! Tom was there at the
bottom of the alley, his back to the wall, looking dazed and frightened. The boys ignored Tom and scrambled over the wall, one of
them losing something on the way over. Shouts and a disturbance
behind him made Ahmed look up to see two Israeli soldiers breaking from the throng in the *souk* to chase the boys. As he looked
back, he saw Tom pick up the rifle that had clattered to his feet.

"No, Tom! No!" He stormed down the length of the alleyway,
snatching the rifle from the bewildered Englishman. "Get rid of it,
you fool!" He raised his arm to throw the rifle over the wall.

He didn't make it. A barked command from one of the soldiers arriving at the mouth of the alley was followed instantly by a shot. The bullet struck Ahmed in the midriff. Two further rounds from the second soldier, firing from a kneeling position, ripped through his chest and his throat. Ahmed's body slapped against the back wall of the alley.

Tobie and Sharon had been brought to the mouth of the alley by Ahmed's warning shout. Tobie screamed in Hebrew at one of the soldiers, pummeling at his arms. Sharon shrugged off the second soldier to run toward Ahmed's shattered body. A black lake of blood was beginning to soak into his clothes. She lifted up his head. He was already dead, but she was too stunned to know it. His head fell back limply, blood and saliva trickling from the corner of his mouth. Sharon kissed Ahmed's bloody mouth full on the lips. She cradled his head on her lap, looking up at Tom for the help or explanation that was beyond him.

Tom, pressed against the wall, could only gaze on in dumbfounded horror. He looked from Sharon's questioning eyes to the blood on the Arab's lips. As he stared, he distinctly saw a fat bee crawl from the inside of Ahmed's mouth, conjured from the trickle of blood. The bee was still for a moment on his lips, before lifting itself into the air, laboring upwards in tortured spiral flight, up into the spice-laden night sky over Jerusalem.

Tom watched it go.

55

The sky over Jerusalem was a spiritual blue. Ian Redhead, agent for the Anglicans, took off his sunglasses and got to his feet as Tom approached the café table. He shot out a nervous hand, too quickly it seemed, because he had to hold it in the air for a long time before Tom was close enough to shake it. Tom sat down and Redhead called a waiter.

Redhead had responded to Tom's phone call, and they'd arranged to meet at the Café Akrai in the pedestrianized area of the New City. Tom ordered coffee.

"I'm glad you contacted me," said Redhead, replacing his dark glasses. He looked hot in his black suit. He inserted two fingers between his white collar and his neck and leaned forward confidentially. "Did you know this is primarily a café for gays?"

"Is it?" Tom said innocently. "Imagine!"

This had been Sharon's suggestion. She said if Tom was going to give the Anglicans anything, it should be done at the Café Akrai. It was two weeks since Ahmed had been killed. She was trying hard to recover her sense of humor.

"I'm leaving Jerusalem this afternoon," said Tom. "I couldn't go without giving you this." He placed a large manilla envelope on the table. "Don't get too excited. It's only a copy. I don't want anything for it."

Redhead looked at the envelope without touching it. "The Magdalene Scroll? What happened to the original?"

"It's like the keys to the Holy Sepulcher. They have to be kept by a Muslim family. I can't trust the Christians with the scroll, or even the Jews, for that matter. So I've given it to an Arab scholar. A friend of the man who was looking at it for me."

"Is it true he was the man who was shot?"

"Yes." Tom's coffee arrived. "The scholar who has it now has promised to publish it. I decided it was only fair to give your lot a copy. I've also given a copy to the Hebrew Museum. I'm sure you'll all find a different way of interpreting the thing."

"I suppose we should be grateful. Though we would have liked the original."

"As I say, you're not to be trusted with history."

Redhead looked at him thoughtfully from behind his dark glasses. Sunlight starbursted on the black lenses. "Don't be too hard on us. This city has a way of affecting people. Sometimes you read a holy book, then you go back to it the next day and you swear someone has changed the words. It's that kind of city."

"I have an idea of what you mean."

Redhead took out his wallet and parked a banknote under his coffee saucer. Then he stood up, offering another handshake. "I have to go. I must thank you for the copy at least. Have a safe journey home."

"Thanks."

"I almost forgot. I have something here for you." Redhead swung his leather briefcase on to the table, flicked open its locks and withdrew something from inside. He handed it to Tom. It was a large stamp with a gilded and perforated edge, the kind children collect for attendance at Sunday School. It contained a scene, macabre and ridiculous, of numerous skeletons rising from the earth and from sundered coffins, their bones animated in an ecstatic jig.

"Hey," said Tom. "The Day of Resurrection. How about that? Now I have the set."

Redhead smiled briefly, grabbed his case and turned to walk back in the direction of the Old City. Tom watched him go: a hot man in an inappropriate black English suit, walking under a baking Middle Eastern sun.

Tom dropped the stamp into the dregs of his coffee cup.

After a while he left the café and took a slow walk toward the Old City. Sharon had arranged to meet him outside the walls, to drive him to the airport. After the shooting Tom had started to feel something like sane again; he stopped seeing *djinn*, he stopped seeing demons. But he had continued to see Tobie once a day at the center because he felt responsible, all over again, for someone's death. Neither Sharon nor Tobie blamed him, and, knowing how he staggered under his own crosses, the two women went to tender lengths to take the burden from him.

But he wanted to go home, back to England. He had asked Sharon to return with him. He had even asked her to marry him, but she was too wise, and she declined on both counts. "You spent too long feeling you couldn't love Katie. I can't make you do that all over again.'" She promised, at least, to come to visit him in England before Christmas.

He made his way down the Shekhem, down the hill from which he'd caught his first view of Jerusalem from a speeding taxi. At the bottom of the road he could see Sharon's parked car. She was waiting for him, leaning against the bonnet with her arms folded. When she saw him at the top of the hill, she waved. Before going down to her, he stopped to take a last look across the Old City.

The Golden Dome bulged from amid the bustle of white-pepper buildings, all lifted like a clamor of voices to the immaculate sky. The scent of warm, spiced dust was in his nostrils, and for a moment he felt a surge of holy terror at the thought of what he was leaving behind. It wasn't a city; it was a living creature, made of blood and clay and dust and dreams.

He was momentarily paralyzed by its insane beauty. Jerusalem, waking dream, nightmare, city of *djinn*, truth inside a lie, plug on the waters of the deep, threshing floor, crucible, *axis mundi*, fantasy and hologram, locus of slaughter and redemption, promise of peace. The city was an emblem of the source of all trouble, the human heart, with its limitless capacity for self-deception and fantasy, which one day may also be its salvation.

The sound of Sharon leaning on her car horn brought him out of his reverie. His eyes lifted to the Mount of Olives and the skyline beyond the city. Then he went down to where Sharon was waiting.

LaVergne, TN USA
24 September 2010
198354LV00002B/81/A

9 780312 864521